> "Woman, if I st[art]
> with you, s[omething's]
> gonna happen[...]"

The words erupted from him.

His words sank in and her mouth formed an *O*. Her cheeks pinkened, but she didn't run.

She plucked nervously at the top button of her bodice and he said tightly, "Go on back to the house."

She didn't. Looking uncertain, she drew in a deep breath, then said in a rush, "I wish I'd kissed you when I had the chance."

He nearly swallowed his teeth. "You can't say things like that to a man, Catherine. To me."

'It's true."

"I don't think so." Want thrummed inside him. He gripped his crutch so tightly that his knuckles burned.

Her skirts whispered around his legs, between them, and her pulse fluttered wildly in the hollow of her throat.

"Dammit, woman! Back up. I may be injured, but I'm not dead…!"

Praise for new Harlequin Historical author Debra Cowan's previous titles

"Penning great emotional depth in her characters, Debra Cowan will warm the coldest of winter nights."
—*Romantic Times* on *Still the One*

"Debra Cowan skillfully brings to vivid life all the complicated feelings of love and guilt when a moment of consolation turns into unexpected passion."
—*Romantic Times* on *One Silent Night*

"The recurrent humor and vivid depiction of small-town Western life make Debra Cowan's story thoroughly pleasurable."
—*Romantic Times* on *The Matchmaker*

Whirlwind Wedding

DEBRA COWAN

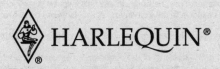

HARLEQUIN®

TORONTO • NEW YORK • LONDON
AMSTERDAM • PARIS • SYDNEY • HAMBURG
STOCKHOLM • ATHENS • TOKYO • MILAN • MADRID
PRAGUE • WARSAW • BUDAPEST • AUCKLAND

ISBN 0-373-29322-4

WHIRLWIND WEDDING

This edition published by arrangement with Harlequin Books S.A.

® and TM are trademarks of the publisher. Trademarks indicated with
® are registered in the United States Patent and Trademark Office, the
Canadian Trade Marks Office and in other countries.

www.eHarlequin.com

Printed in U.S.A.

Please address questions and book requests to:
Harlequin Reader Service
U.S.: 3010 Walden Ave., P.O. Box 1325, Buffalo, NY 14269
Canadian: P.O. Box 609, Fort Erie, Ont. L2A 5X3

In memory of my cousin, Billye Su Watson
For our shared love of words

Chapter One

West Texas, 1884

Catherine Donnelly had never been adept at handling men, and now she had to admit she was no better with boys. After more than a day spent searching in and around dusty Whirlwind, Texas, until well past dark, she'd finally located her oft-missing younger brother, Andrew, and marched him home.

Now Catherine sat alone at the small dining table in the front room of what had been her mother's house. A loud knock sounded on the door. After the harrowing span of time she had spent worrying over her twelve-year-old brother, she wasn't inclined to be charitable to whoever was calling so late.

Picking up the kerosene lamp from the small kitchen table, she opened her door to one of the tallest men she'd ever seen. The mild May night seemed to swirl around him. He wore a dark hat pulled low, and was dressed all in black except for his blue shirt, which looked nearly white in the filmy amber glow from the lamp. Moonlight sliced a sharp cheekbone and a whiskered jaw, making him quite possibly also the most intimidating man she'd ever seen.

Eyes that might be either blue or silver stared flatly at her. He braced a shoulder on her doorjamb, regarding her as if she were the one invading *his* territory. His dark, ragged hair and a tangible determination gave him the look of a man unused to niceties.

"Name's Lieutenant Jericho Blue." He held up an official-looking piece of paper. "I'm a Ranger and this is my Warrant of Authority issued by the Adjutant General's Department under authority from the government."

Apprehension skittered through her and her grip tightened on the lamp. The Sisters of Mercy had taught her too well for her to dismiss anyone out of hand. Still, she would dispense with him quickly. She smiled and asked as kindly as she could, "May I help you?"

He seemed to have trouble getting the paper back into his trouser pocket.

"Sir?" Out beyond him, at the edge of the lamplight, she saw a riderless horse, and another one beside it with a dark shape slung across its back. A body? The warnings about nearby outlaws she had heard only hours ago, as she had looked for Andrew, rushed back.

According to Sheriff Holt, the McDougal gang had ambushed a pair of lawmen yesterday. Catherine had been nearly ill with worry over the possibility that her brother might run into the outlaws. The sheriff had offered to look for the twelve-year-old with the posse he'd formed to track the gang. She'd accepted, but continued her own search, frantic that her brother might have gotten in the way of the brutal men and suffered a fate far worse than her denying him any more of her apple pie until he stopped sneaking out of their house at night.

The Ranger said huskily, "I'm on the trail of the McDougal gang."

"Our sheriff said they were nearby."

"Very near."

She had to lean closer to hear. His voice was grainy and flat, and his skin had a waxy sheen. He didn't look well. "Are you all right?"

Catherine had worked with enough patients at Bellevue Hospital in New York City to know when someone was ill. Something was definitely wrong with the man.

He stared over her shoulder into the house, as if searching for something. "Do you mind if I look around?"

"In the house?"

He gave a sharp nod.

She didn't want to advertise that she and Andrew lived alone. If one or more of the McDougal gang were hiding around her house, she certainly didn't want to be the one to find them. But neither did she want to let this strange man into her home.

"So, you don't mind then?" He straightened sluggishly and made to move inside.

A bit surprised, Catherine stepped back. A shotgun was out of sight behind the door, but she felt more confident about using a skillet if necessary. "All right."

He mumbled something and swayed, his eyes glazing. As if being pushed from behind, he toppled to the floor with a crash.

The wood shook beneath her and for a moment Catherine stared disbelieving at the long length of man stretched out at her feet. He had fallen over the threshold, half of him still outside.

In a flash, Andrew, his dark hair rumpled and his blue eyes drowsy, appeared beside her. He wore only the droopy cotton drawers she had seen when she'd checked on him an hour ago after marching him home. "What happened?"

"I'm not sure." Shaking off her shock, she knelt, holding the lamp high. He'd said his name was Jericho. "Help me turn him over."

Andrew was stocky and strong. With his help, she got the Ranger on his back. Blood smeared the weathered wood floor.

Her brother drew in a sharp breath and Catherine glanced up. He was pale, his eyes huge. "What's he doin' here?"

"Looking for the outlaws that Sheriff Holt told us about."

"Is he dead?"

"No. Not yet."

"He's mean-lookin'." Andrew stood frozen, staring warily at the stranger.

Catherine turned her attention back to Jericho. The man's black vest fell open to reveal the waistband of his trousers and a lean torso, but her gaze was drawn to the dark bandanna tied below his elbow. His shirt was torn and she could see a nickel-size hole in his forearm. Gunshot. "He's bleeding."

She reached for the chambray cloth, intending to roll back his sleeve.

"He's bleedin' there, too." Andrew's finger shook as he pointed to the man's leg. "Is he gonna die?"

"I don't know." She tempered her impatience. Her brother's sharp unease was undoubtedly due to witnessing the recent death of their mother.

Summoned by Mother's urgent letter, Catherine had spent two weeks traveling by train and stage from New York City to Whirlwind. By the time she arrived, Evelyn Donnelly was dead from consumption, and the brother Catherine had never known was fending for himself.

She shifted the lamp to get a good look at the Ranger's leg. A blood-soaked length of rope was tied high on his right thigh. Catherine had thought it was the leg strap for a gun belt, but he wasn't wearing one. An egg-size hole tore his denims. She spread open the fabric with gentle fingers. A low groan escaped the man.

"It's okay," she said, automatically soothing him while she

continued to examine his leg. His blood-caked flesh gaped. Raw, ragged and still oozing, the wound was deep.

She glanced up at Andrew. "We need to get him all the way inside."

"*Our* house?"

"Yes. There's no one else to help him."

Her brother swallowed hard.

"Andrew," she said sharply.

"He's big!"

"You pull one arm and I'll pull the other."

With considerable effort, they dragged him across the wood floor, angling around the table to position him a few feet from the stove. Catherine knelt, checking the injury to his arm again. It would keep, but his leg needed immediate attention. His pants were torn on his outer thigh several inches above his knee, and she discovered two small holes in his leg there, where the bullets had entered. Blood still seeped from the open flesh where the slug had exited. Because his trousers were stuck to his skin, she couldn't tell if the wound was on the top part of his thigh or the inside.

She stood and retrieved a pair of scissors from the freestanding cupboard behind the table, and cut through the rope. Laying the rope and scissors aside, she pressed her hand firmly to his leg, finding the rock-hard muscle hot and feverish beneath her touch. She ignored the flutter in her stomach. She wasn't generally nervous around *unconscious* men.

"Andrew, get me a clean cloth and some water. Put one of the brick pieces from the stove in the water to warm it up."

It was something the Sisters had taught her, and Andrew followed her instructions as carefully as she had always followed the nuns'. She cleaned the Ranger's injury as best she could, applying pressure when fresh blood seeped out. His denims stuck to his leg and Catherine knew she might have to cut them off in order to see the damage. Despite working with the Sisters for four years at Bellevue Hospital and around New York City, she didn't have all the skills needed to tend such a severe injury.

"You've got to ride to Fort Greer for Dr. Butler," she told her brother. "This man has lost a lot of blood. We can't let him die, and I'm afraid if we don't get the doctor here soon, he will."

In the wash of lamplight, the furrow of pain between the stranger's brows seemed to be permanently carved. An old scar ran high on his left cheekbone.

"Don't dally, Andrew." She got to her feet and took him by the shoulders. That she was his only family had thus far meant nothing to the boy. Quietly belligerent, he came and went as he pleased no matter if Catherine cajoled, threatened or bribed. "Don't disobey me in this, I beg you. This man's life could depend on it."

He nodded solemnly. For the first time since she'd come to Whirlwind, there was no hint of defiance in his face. Just a sober understanding and a hint of fear.

She walked to the corner behind the door and picked up their father's old shotgun.

"What're you doing?" her brother breathed.

She turned, her hands trembling on the stock. "Do you know how to use this?"

He nodded.

"Take it and go for Dr. Butler."

"Okay. Moe's fast—"

"No." The Ranger had said the outlaws were near. Until she knew where the McDougals were, she had to be careful. She didn't want Andrew taking any chances by getting their horse from the barn, where any or all of the gang might be hiding. "Take the Ranger's horse and don't disappear. Come straight back."

The boy rushed to his room and returned wearing his brown homespun trousers and buttoning the placket of a brown-and-white checked shirt. He stomped his feet into his worn shoes. At the door, he took the gun. "I'll hurry."

"Good." She began to roll up the sleeves of her plain white bodice.

"What will you do?"

"See if I can stop the bleeding."

He grimaced and disappeared into the night. His shoes scudded across the porch, then silence fell. Unease at being alone with the man tightened her shoulders, but she calmed herself by observing that he was unconscious. He couldn't hurt her.

Catherine knelt again, dragged in a deep, steadying breath and unfastened his pants. Her hands trembled so badly it was difficult to tug the heavy material down his hips. She abandoned that, fearing he might die before the doctor arrived. Picking up the scissors, she cut at the denim just below the rip so she could press her hand fully against the wound on the inside of his thigh.

She dipped the rag in water again and gently cleaned away more dried blood. Fresh crimson seeped out and she applied firm pressure.

He was lean and hard and his body burned with fever. Even in the pale light she could see the angry red of infection around the wound before fresh blood covered it again.

Maybe it was the fact that her mother had been buried two days before she'd arrived, but Catherine was determined that no more death would happen in this house so soon.

She kept the cloth in place, pressing with her hands. She closed her eyes, praying Andrew would reach Fort Greer and the doctor in record time.

When a rough, callused hand grabbed hers, her eyes flew

open. Her stomach dipped to her knees as she stared into his
pain-filled silver eyes. Then they closed.

"Hurts," her patient croaked.

"Yes," she murmured soothingly, telling herself to stroke
his brow as she'd done to so many patients these last few
years. But she couldn't.

Something about this man's voice, or maybe his touch,
shook her inside, setting off a spark of fear mixed with an anticipation she didn't understand.

His hand went limp and she stared at his pale, whiskered
face. Relief eased out in a long breath. *Hurry, Doctor.*

Half an hour later, Dr. Butler helped get the man into her
bed. The Ranger was so tall his booted feet hung off the end,
so they laid him at an angle.

After examining the patient, the doctor turned to her, compassion in his tired brown eyes. "He's lucky he ended up on
your doorstep. Not everyone has your skill at nursing."

Thanks to the nuns who'd raised her. "It's bad, isn't it?"

"I don't expect him to make it. There's a lot of tissue damage, possibly nerve damage, as well. Infection has already
started and he may have gotten help too late. Looks like he
was shot twice in the leg, so I'm going to check and make sure
there are no bullets left inside. My poking around can't make
things any worse for him."

She nodded, hoping he was wrong about the stranger
dying. Maybe this Texas Ranger was as tough on the inside
as he looked on the outside. "I'll heat some water and get
some soap for you to wash your hands."

"I'll need your help."

"All right." She stepped out of the room and wrapped a
cloth around her hand, reaching into the stove for one of the
brick pieces she kept inside. She dropped it into a bowl, which

she pumped full of water, then scooped up a tin of lye soap and carried everything back into the bedroom.

In the two weeks she'd worked for Dr. Butler at the fort, her aid had been confined to helping deliver babies and stitching the toe of a little boy who'd cut himself with his daddy's ax. But during her work with the nuns, she had assisted in surgery a few times.

After the doctor washed his hands, he removed the blood-soaked pad Catherine had placed on the Ranger's thigh. Dr. Butler's fingers probed the gaping exit wound. Catherine looked away, took a quick steadying breath, then stepped up beside him. She wet a folded square of linen with the carbolic acid Dr. Butler sometimes used for sterilizing wounds.

He cleaned around and inside the wound, then Catherine handed him a pair of forceps. He located a bullet quickly, but it took several minutes to dig it out. Though still unconscious, the Ranger moaned. This time Catherine reached up to stroke his brow.

Finally, Dr. Butler dropped the bullet into the soap tin's lid. The ping sounded sharply in the quiet room. "There's just the one. Looks like the other one in his leg and the one in his arm went on out."

With one hand, Catherine held the lamp for the doctor and with her other she continued to stroke the Ranger's forehead. His skin was flushed and burned her palm.

She counted each of the twenty-seven stitches it took to close the wound. She knew the danger lay in how deep the injury had gone, the degree of infection and the risk of the man ripping open his stitches.

Dr. Butler cleaned the wound again. He washed his hands, then, as he stared down at the patient, dried them on the fresh cloth she'd laid on the bedside table. "I fully expect he'll go, Catherine."

"Maybe not." She could only think that her fervent desire for the man to live was due to the fact that her mother had died so recently. "He could pull through."

"Maybe." The doctor looked doubtful. "I'll leave some laudanum in case he wakes up at all." He placed a small brown bottle on the washstand next to the bed. "That will ease his suffering. Just try to make him comfortable. I'll check back tomorrow."

Catherine nodded, then glanced at her bed. Even unconscious, Jericho Blue made her leery. She didn't care to have the big man under her roof for a prolonged period, but whatever her intention when she'd answered the door, she wasn't getting rid of this man tonight.

Chapter Two

Darkness shifted into light. Day into night. Jericho was swept along on a vicious red tide of pain. He burned, then froze. Searing agony gripped his leg and throbbed in his arm. Images floated through his mind. The face of his partner, Hays. A dark-haired boy. A woman with a soft voice and gentle hands that soothed his blistered flesh. He rocked on the ebb and flow of hurt before sliding into sweet surrender.

Something woke him. Pain or the light spilling through the window?

He struggled to open his eyes against the glare of the sun, awareness trickling back. A sharp ache pierced his skull. His right leg felt as if it were on fire. And he was naked. He didn't recognize the soft bed that held the clean, comforting scent of a woman. His gaze tracked from the right, noting a tall, dark-wood wardrobe in the middle of the wall, an open door, a small dressing table, a stand to his left holding a pitcher and washbasin. None of it was familiar. The window stood open a few inches to let in fresh, warm air, and a lacy curtain fluttered there. He was in someone's house.

He sorted through the blur of memories in his head. The

ambush outside of Whirlwind, a young boy shooting with the
McDougal gang. Bullets tearing through his arm and leg. His
partner's scream of surprise. Hays Gentry had been dead by
the time Jericho dragged his own lead-riddled carcass over to
his side.

Using a length of rope from his saddlebag, he had fash-
ioned a tourniquet for his thigh. He had wrapped a bandanna
around his bleeding arm, then clumsily secured his lanky
partner onto Hays's dun mare, and trailed the McDougal gang
as far as he could while the tracks were fresh. Hours later,
he'd lost them and returned to the scene of the ambush, picking up a single set of hoofprints. Hoofprints that had led him
here.

His gaze shot to the open doorway and he tried to sit up.
Agony clawed through his lower body and he cursed. Easing
down, he panted with the effort not to cry out. A clean white
bandage wrapped his right wrist up to the middle of his forearm.

He recalled waking a couple of times and a woman holding a cup of cool water to his lips. Cool dampness on his forehead and chest. He'd been shot in his gun arm. And his right
leg. With his left hand, he weakly patted his way across the
sheet and felt the bulk of bandages beneath.

His thigh was wrapped tightly and throbbing as if a coyote had made two meals out of it.

"Sir?" The sweet, lilting voice was tentative. The speaker
sounded breathless, as if she'd hurried to him. "Oh, good. I
thought I heard you."

Jericho struggled to focus on the figure in the open doorway. Her voice. "You helped me."

"Yes." She moved toward him, concern drawing her finely
arched brows together.

Sweat stung his eyes and he blinked. She was pretty. More

than pretty. Was he conscious? Her long black hair was pulled back with a white kerchief and flowed over one shoulder like ebony silk. He registered strong features and porcelain skin before his vision hazed. She leaned over him, smelling of sunshine and soap. A low humming sounded in his ears. She was talking.

"Dr. Butler removed a bullet. There was one in your leg, but not in your arm. You were shot twice in the thigh."

"What's my leg look like?" The room spun and he felt himself sliding away. He'd seen men with the same injury lose their leg to rot. "Will it keep?"

"I think so. You seem to be fighting off the infection." She smiled and he could see her eyes were blue. Clear blue like that fancy bird made of colored glass his ma had.

"I made it to Whirlwind."

"Yes. You were tracking the McDougal gang." Her hand fluttered over the bandage on his arm. "Dr. Butler will check your leg when he comes."

Jericho's head swam and he felt himself slipping away. "I came to your door."

"Yes. You told me your name, then went unconscious."

"How long have I been here?" The pain pulled at him, dragging him into a black hole of helplessness.

"Three days."

He grunted. "Your name?"

"Catherine Donnelly."

"Cath—" Everything went black.

The next time Jericho awoke, the sun was setting. His mouth was as dry as wool, the pain deep and gouging. He felt someone in the room and turned his head to the right, staring into the prettiest blue eyes he'd ever seen.

"Hello," she said softly.

"Hello." His voice sounded rusty and dry. He remembered her. "Miz Donald?"

"Donnelly."

"Catherine."

"Your fever broke." Triumph underscored her words as she fussed with the blanket draped over his body.

Pain pushed the fog from his mind. He felt as weak as a newborn babe.

"Let me get you something to eat."

"Was I out a long time?"

"You woke earlier today. Do you remember?"

He nodded. Three days he'd spent in this bed. Useless. Helpless.

"Dr. Butler will be pleased when he comes by to check on you." She seemed to glide out of the room, her fluid movements economical and controlled.

The plain gray dress and white apron draped her body in long, sleek lines. Curved in all the right places, she had full breasts and a slim waist. If a man weren't careful, her blue eyes could draw him in, distract him enough to forget why he was here.

She returned with a thick crockery bowl and a spoon. Pulling a ladder-back chair close to the side of the bed, she set the bowl on the bedside table. A fragrant steam drifted to him and made his mouth water.

"Do you think you can sit up?"

He tried, bracing his weight on his left arm. The movement had his thigh jerking in agony, but he managed to get his shoulders against the wooden headboard at his back. Sweat broke across his face.

The woman carefully spooned soup into his mouth. He hadn't thought he was hungry, but the rich chicken broth made him ravenous. Still, being forced to let someone feed him made Jericho feel as useless as a teat on a boar hog. His good hand clenched into a fist. "I can feed myself."

Her face didn't change, but he felt her doubt. "I'll hold the bowl if you want to try."

He nodded, taking the spoon from her. His hand shook as if he had the palsy.

Regarding him steadily with a hint of wariness in her eyes, she held the bowl. He dipped the spoon into the broth and brought it to his mouth, dribbling half of it down his chest. "Damn."

"Here." She rose and leaned toward him, using her apron to blot up the liquid.

Her touch was brisk and impersonal, but as she swiped the cloth from his chest to his belly, Jericho felt a jolt of heat. His grip tightened on the spoon.

She sat down, her fresh scent teasing him. "You're very weak. Please let me help you."

He didn't have any choice if he wanted to eat his food rather than wear it. What little energy he did have had been used to sit up. Frustration rolled through him, but he relinquished the spoon. "All right."

He sounded grudging even to his own ears, but she didn't seem to mind. She took the spoon and fed him another bite.

"My partner?"

"Sheriff Holt took care of the man who was with you. The sheriff said you were his cousin."

"Davis Lee buried Hays?"

"Yes."

"Damn." Jericho's mouth tightened. If he and Hays hadn't already been single-mindedly pursuing the murderous McDougals on special commission from the governor, yesterday's ambush would've assured that Jericho would hunt them down and exact justice for all the people they'd killed. The gang had unleashed hell throughout all of Texas, parts of Kansas and Indian Territory. Jericho had no intention of letting them continue any longer than it took for him to heal.

"I want to pay you, ma'am."

"Your cousin has already taken care of it."

"And my horse?" He swallowed the last bite of broth.

"In my barn. The sheriff took your friend's to the livery."

"Thank you." What the McDougals had done to Jericho was the least of it. He itched to lift the sheet and peel back the bandages on his thigh to judge for himself the damage those murderous bastards had wrought. His entire lower body was a throbbing mass of pain.

Alarm pricked him. Just what all had gotten shot off down there? It felt as if his leg was still attached, but what about his manhood?

"Are you all right? Maybe you should rest again."

"I'm wonderin' about my injuries. When do you think the doctor will come?"

"He's been stopping by late in the afternoon, but it depends on his patients."

"Humph." Jericho wished Miz Donnelly would leave the room so he could just look at himself and get it over with.

"I can probably answer any questions you have."

With that virginal face? "I doubt it."

"I'm a trained nurse. Are you concerned about your leg?"

"I'll just wait until he gets here to ask my questions."

"I helped him remove the bullet. I'm more than capable of telling you what you need to know."

Her clear, guileless eyes hinted that she had no idea what he really wanted to ask. "Somehow I don't think so," he muttered.

She pursed her lips and looked affronted. "You had lost a lot of blood by the time you showed up here. Part of your wrist bone was chipped, but there was no bullet. The tissue inside is damaged."

"You say the doc will be by sometime this afternoon?"

She rose from the chair. "Yes, but there's no need for you to wonder and worry. I'm sure I can put your mind at ease."

She might be soft-looking, but she was as persistent as a hungry mule. He gritted his teeth and stared her right in the eye. "Was my manhood shot off?"

She nearly dropped the bowl in his lap. They both grabbed for it. Her hands fumbled over the top of his and she pulled away with the crockery.

Her face flushed bright red and she choked out, "You'll have to ask the doctor."

"That's what I figured," he growled.

She hurried out of the room. "I'll get you something to drink."

While she was gone, he patted his groin but all he could feel was bandages.

A few minutes later, she returned with a tin cup, which she held for him. Jericho sipped at the cool water as he studied her. Slight pink still tinged her lovely face and her eyes were bright. She kept her gaze averted. For some reason, her embarrassment caused him to smile.

He'd thought a trained nurse would be more pragmatic about the human body. Her obvious discomfort sparked a long-buried need in Jericho, a purely male urge to find out how much experience she'd had. Man-to-woman experience.

Where had that thought come from? His brain was muddled from the injuries, that's all. The questions he needed to ask had to do with the ambush that had left him laid up and Hays dead.

Jericho glanced around the room. "I think I remember seeing a boy in here a couple of times."

"My brother, Andrew."

"How old is he?"

"Twelve."

That could be about the age of the boy he'd spotted riding with the gang at the ambush. Was Andrew Donnelly the one who'd shot and killed Hays? Jericho needed to see that kid and examine the horses around here to check if any of their shoes matched the tracks he'd followed.

A knock sounded on the front door and Catherine placed the tin cup on the bedside table. "I'll be right back."

He closed his eyes as she left, as much to rest as to try and make out her words in the next room.

She reappeared with a thin, brown-haired man who appeared to be a few inches shorter than Jericho's six-foot-four.

"This is Dr. Butler," she said. "He couldn't believe it when I told him you were awake."

Jericho wasn't sure how much longer he'd stay that way. Reaching out with his good hand, he awkwardly clasped the other man's. "Thanks for what you did."

"Captain, you should be thanking Catherine."

"It's Lieutenant, Doc."

The doctor aimed a warm, affectionate smile at her. "Well, Lieutenant, you're lucky to be alive, and it's because of her. She saved your life."

A slight blush stained his nurse's cheeks as she moved to the left of Jericho's bed. He looked over and nodded. A brief smile touched her lips before her gaze skittered away.

The doctor eyed Jericho critically. "You surprise me, sir. I didn't expect you to survive."

"You can call me Jericho."

"Your color is much better and your fever seems to have gone down a bit. I'd like to take a look at your wrist and leg."

"All right." Jericho wasn't too keen on having anything looked at, but there wasn't much he could do about it.

The doctor moved around the foot of the bed and up beside him. He cut away the bandage wrapping Jericho's wrist and forearm. The flesh was raw and torn. His hand lay limply, curled inward on top of the clean white sheet.

"Can you move your fingers?"

He could, but couldn't straighten out his hand.

"Hmm. Can you bend your wrist?"

Jericho tried and jagged pain flashed through him. "Can't. There's no give in it."

"Don't force it."

"What does that mean, Doc?"

"Some tendons were torn by the bullet."

"But I'll still be able to use this hand again, won't I?"

"I'm not sure yet."

"I will. I have to." Jericho was a lousy left-handed shot. He had every intention of making the McDougal gang pay for what they'd done, and to do that he had to be able to use his gun hand.

"I need to see how it heals up," the doctor said.

"How long?"

The other man raised an eyebrow. "Longer than three days. You're getting stronger. I sure didn't hold out hope for that, not like Catherine did. Let's check your progress in another couple of days."

"I'm gonna be gone by then. The gang's trail is already cold. The longer I'm laid up, the harder they'll be to find."

"You listen to me, Lieutenant." The doctor's brown eyes turned stern. "You lost a lot of blood. By all rights, you shouldn't be drawing breath right now. If you get out of that bed before Catherine or I tell you, you could rip open your stitches and bleed like a stuck hog. I can't put any blood back in you. Understand?"

"Yes." Jericho didn't like the doctor's words, but he appreciated straight talk. He did need to get on his way, but just the little time he'd been awake this afternoon had left him weak and shaky. He probably couldn't even saddle his horse.

"I want you to give me your word you won't try to leave." Dr. Butler unbuttoned the cuff of his white shirt and rolled it back. "And that you'll follow my orders."

Jericho wasn't used to following anyone's orders, but he did owe Butler and Miz Donnelly something for saving his life. Besides, he wouldn't be worth spit if he saddled up and rode out of here, then passed out. "You have my word."

"Good." The doctor glanced at the woman who stood quietly on the other side of the bed. "Catherine, let's change the dressing on his leg."

"I'll get the bandages."

As soon as she stepped out of the room, Jericho said in a low voice, "Hey, Doc, just what all was shot off down there?"

The other man grinned. "You still have your private parts."

"Will they work?"

"I believe you'll be fine, but there is some tissue damage. I'm also concerned about damage to your nerves. That shouldn't affect your manhood, but it might be a while before everything is back to working order."

Just as Jericho exhaled a relieved breath, the Donnelly woman returned with a handful of white strips torn from a sheet. Her face betrayed no emotion, but her eyes had darkened to near purple and her hands trembled. Since his manhood was still intact, Jericho didn't care to tempt fate by letting this woman near him with a pair of scissors.

"Uh, Doc, since I'm awake now, I'd just as soon the lady not see me in the altogether."

"She's a nurse, Lieutenant. She's been trained to ignore embarrassments."

"Well, she ain't never seen my embarrassments and I don't aim for her to start. No offense, ma'am."

"None taken. I'll wait outside." She left, and he thought she looked relieved.

Just what kind of woman had taken him in? Her voice smiled, but she didn't. She obviously had nursing skills, but not the drawl of Texas. Where was she from? Jericho wondered if there was a Mr. Donnelly. Children? Was her brother the boy Jericho had seen with the McDougals at the ambush? And if so, was his pretty nurse involved with the gang, too?

As he nodded in response to the doctor's instruction to stay in bed tomorrow, it wasn't the boy who had ahold of Jericho's mind. It was the blue-eyed woman who made him feel as if he mattered.

Catherine didn't want to think about Jericho Blue's manhood. She *shouldn't* be thinking about it. But even the next day, as she drove the wagon back from Fort Greer, the memory of his blunt question brought heat to her face. She had been the one to insist she could quell his concerns. But she had nearly dropped the soup bowl in his lap.

Thinking about his—*him*—in that way opened up other thoughts, sharpened her unsettling awareness of the Ranger. Why couldn't she simply think of him as another patient? Saints knew, she'd tended plenty of those.

Dr. Butler had told her it would take some time for Jericho to regain his strength. As much as Catherine wished for the man in her bed to get better and move on, she had no desire to see him at full strength. Just the taut, ropy muscles in his arms and legs hinted at the power he must possess when in good health. He was a big man. The idea of him regaining his strength reminded her too much of men who used brute force to intimidate. She liked Jericho Blue much better when he was asleep.

He wasn't handsome, but she found his stern, chiseled face compelling. A sense of purpose and command surrounded him, as if he was a man who knew what he wanted and would stop at nothing to get it. She shuddered to think how he would be if he wanted a woman. No man had ever made her heart race from anticipation one second, intimidation the next. She didn't understand it.

Around him, she felt skittish and on guard. When he'd woken, those silver eyes had been soft, then gone as sharp as a honed blade when he talked about the gang who had murdered his friend. Catherine didn't want to be on the receiving end of that dangerous gaze.

She'd finally seen a smile, albeit at her expense. His blunt question and her catching the bowl that had nearly dropped in his lap had somehow amused him. If he ever turned a charming smile on a woman, Catherine suspected that woman might surrender her virtue and thank him for taking it.

Her own four years of nursing experience had brought her into contact with men in various stages of undress, some completely naked. Yet not one of them had ever put flutters in her stomach or made her dread the return of his strength. It had only been in the last year and a half that she had become so wary around men.

She didn't like thinking about Jericho, but couldn't seem to help herself. What she needed was to focus her thoughts toward helping him get better and out of her bed.

Softly clucking to Moe, she drove the wagon back from the fort. Catherine had talked to Dr. Butler about one of her patients in New York City who had injured his foot and ankle. The doctor had agreed to her plan of working with the Ranger's hand, massaging the tissue and muscles in an effort to see if he could improve and eventually bend his wrist again. She hoped the Ranger would be able to fully recover.

The spring day was warm enough to cause a light sheen of

moisture across her neck beneath the heavy mass of her hair. Still, she welcomed being outdoors.

She had left her patient in the very capable care of his cousins, Davis Lee and Riley Holt, along with Riley's wife, Susannah. Riley's petite wife had told Catherine they had an infant daughter whom they'd left with a friend named Cora. Catherine had thought Jericho and his family might appreciate the privacy to visit freely, and she could use a respite from his probing silver gaze. Just what did he contemplate so hard when his eyes narrowed on her?

Her gelding, Moe, plodded up the gentle swell of ground, his sorrel haunches glistening in the sunshine. They topped a rise that looked out over town. Fort Greer, where she worked with Dr. Butler, was about two miles northwest of Whirlwind and much farther than the distance Catherine had traveled in New York to reach the hospital, but she didn't mind. The fort was self-contained, and because of that, its residents rarely came into Whirlwind. The town had been a natural outgrowth of people who weren't with the Army, but wanted to settle on the prairie.

Catherine liked the distance between her house and the fort. She also liked the small, charming town where her parents, emigrating from Ireland, had come to join Catherine's widowed uncle. He and Catherine's father had pooled their money to buy the house, though her uncle had died in his sleep shortly afterward. Father had never gotten all the farmland he'd wanted so desperately, but at least his family had had a nice roof over their heads. Catherine's mother had still wanted her to stay in New York with the nuns who'd taken her in at the age of six, so she would know Catherine was being fed and clothed.

In the letters she'd written to Catherine over the years, Evelyn had hinted that Robbie Donnelly's drinking had become frequent and worse. Her father losing job after job had convinced Mother that Catherine needed to stay where she had a secure home and food. With money so tight, Evelyn could barely afford to feed and clothe Andrew. And so the family had remained separated. Catherine sometimes wondered if the hollowness at missing so much time with her family would ever be filled. She knew she would always regret that Mother had waited so long to send for her. They'd had neither hello nor goodbye after waiting fourteen years to reunite.

Whirlwind's general store and telegraph office might be simple by New York standards, but she felt more significant in this town than she had back East despite all her hospital work.

She liked the vast open spaces. In New York, the sidewalks were always crowded and the streets always loud. Out here, a soul-soothing quiet settled across the prairie at night, broken by the occasional howl of a coyote or the chirping of crickets, the coarse call of a raven or whistle of a whip-poorwill. The town was laid out in the shape of a T, with the church on the east end toward Abilene. Catherine had attended three of the four Sundays she'd been here, and Andrew had grudgingly shuffled along with her.

Thoughts of her brother made her sigh. He had no interest in reuniting with a sister he'd never known. He appeared only at suppertime, and as she had learned a few nights ago, he habitually slipped out of the house after she sent him to bed. Thank the saints, the May nights on this West Texas prairie weren't bitterly cold.

What was she going to do about Andrew? His sneaking out at night disturbed her, especially with the recent shootings by the McDougal gang. But since the night the Ranger had arrived, Andrew had been around more. She checked on him several times during the night, pleased and grateful to see him asleep in bed. He asked a lot of questions about Lieutenant

Blue, wondering if the man were improving, and what he'd been doing at their house in the first place.

She thought he probably admired the Ranger, which was fine if Jericho Blue was a good man. Except for the unsettled sensation he put in her stomach, Catherine couldn't point to any specific bad thing about him.

Her mother's pale yellow house sat at the northeast end of town, on the outskirts. The nearest neighbors were in Whirlwind. Beside the small house was a fenced herb and vegetable garden, a root cellar and a spring house. The barn stood about fifty yards behind.

Whirlwind was visible from her bedroom window and an easy walk. Catherine felt secure and independent at the same time. The sheriff's office was one of the closest buildings if she found it necessary to go for help. So far it hadn't been, but since the Ranger's arrival, she had found Sheriff Holt's nearness comforting.

She would do well to keep her thoughts on Whirlwind's handsome sheriff rather than the ragged stranger in her bed, but too many questions about Jericho Blue chased through her mind. The pain and regret in his silver eyes when she'd told him about burying his partner conveyed that Jericho had been close to the man. Who else did he care about? Was there a woman somewhere wondering what had happened to him?

The possibility caused a strange twinge that Catherine defined as nerves. The man unsettled her, though logic told her he was too weak to be a real threat. Yet.

Still, something inside her tensed up when he was awake. Even when he wasn't looking at her, she felt his attention as if he were waiting for something. Something from her.

She was being fanciful. She'd been cooped up too long without fresh air. As she approached the frame house her father had built for her mother, Catherine noted the buckboard and black mare out in front. The Holts were still here.

Good. Catherine didn't relish the idea of being alone with the Ranger. The quick introduction she'd had to the sheriff's brother and sister-in-law told her she would like Riley and Susannah Holt. The powerfully built rancher and his petite wife were newly married. Susannah had told Catherine that she had taught Andrew in one of her charm school classes. Catherine had been thrilled to hear that her brother didn't run away from everyone the way he did from her.

She unhitched Moe from the wagon, then unharnessed and quickly brushed him down, leaving him with some fresh hay before going to the back stoop of the house.

The sound of laughter met her at the door, bringing a smile to her face. She walked up the narrow hallway to the front room. As she stepped around the corner, Susannah Holt peeked around the doorframe of Catherine's bedroom. Her blue eyes were kind and warm. "Hello! Was your trip all right?"

"Yes, fine. Thank you."

The woman's silvery-blond hair was piled on top of her head, stray curls teasing her neck. She wore a smart red-and-white gingham dress, making Catherine self-consciously aware of her plain chambray dress and apron, sprinkled with rusty Texas dust.

"How's the patient doing?" She walked into the room behind the other woman and stopped in front of her dressing table.

Jericho sat up in bed just as she had left him, wearing the clean white shirt she'd found in his saddlebag. A dark beard covered his chiseled jaw, testifying to the fact that he was still too weak to shave. So far, he'd waved off Catherine's offers to do the chore for him.

Secretly she was relieved. Just being in the same room with

him put that strange heat in her belly. She didn't want to be within inches of him. His dark, ragged hair was brushed back, drawing her eye to the scar on his left cheekbone. Though he still looked gaunt, there was a bit of color in his face.

Davis Lee Holt, the sheriff, smiled broadly at Catherine. His blue eyes sparkled. "I think Jericho's on the mend, Nurse."

"I'm glad to hear it." She glanced at her patient, but couldn't hold his gaze, which had turned hot and measuring.

"We sure appreciate you taking him in." Riley Holt, a handsome, broad-shouldered man, flashed her a dimpled smile that made her wonder how his cousin would look if he smiled that way. "We're gonna owe you a lot for this. We know he can be difficult."

"Humph," Jericho grumbled.

"If you have any problems at all, you send for me." Davis Lee's eyes twinkled.

"And you'll lock him up?" she teased.

"If I need to."

"Is this the kind of nursing you were taught?" Jericho's tone was light, but Catherine felt his intense regard like a touch.

She smiled as the others chuckled.

Susannah touched Catherine's arm. "I brought a few things. Flour, eggs and milk."

The Holts had already done too much by paying for her mother's burial before Catherine had arrived. "That wasn't necessary, but thank you."

"I also brought some biscuits. I thought Jericho might like them."

"Do you like honey with them?" she asked her patient. "Haskell's General Store had some fresh yesterday."

"He'd eat honey on everything if you gave him a chance," Riley said with a grin.

"Yeah, even tree bark," Davis Lee added.

"Biscuits and honey sound good," Jericho said to Catherine. Pain drew his features taut, but he didn't appear in any hurry for his family to leave.

She saw him glance at his injured arm for the third time since she'd arrived. "I talked to the doctor about your hand."

That blade-sharp gaze shifted to her. "What about it?"

"I had a patient in New York with a similar injury to his foot and ankle. He eventually recovered the use of both."

"Surgery?" Jericho asked tightly.

"No. I massaged his muscles every day and he worked on trying to bend his ankle."

Interest sparked in his eyes. "And it worked?"

"Yes. He was finally able to walk. He did limp, but he was pleased with his progress."

"It's worth a try," Davis Lee said.

Jericho's gaze measured her. "And you'd be willing to do that for me?"

"Of course."

For a long moment, he was silent.

Catherine added, "If you want."

He gave a curt nod. "Thank you. When do we start?"

"Dr. Butler wants to check you again tomorrow. He can tell us then when to start and how often it needs to be worked."

"Good." Jericho's gaze went past her to the door. "Hello."

She turned to find Andrew standing there. By the saints, the boy moved as silently as a ghost. No wonder she hadn't known about his nightly disappearances.

"Hi." She smiled warmly and stepped toward him. "How was school today?"

"All right." His blue gaze locked on Jericho.

"Hello, Andrew," Susannah said.

The boy's gaze jerked to the blonde and he smiled, one of

the few Catherine had seen. "Hi, Miz Holt." His gaze moved to Riley and Davis Lee. "Mr. Holt. Sheriff."

The two men greeted him warmly.

Catherine put an arm lightly around her brother's shoulders, pleased and a little surprised when he didn't pull away. "This is Lieutenant Jericho Blue. I don't think the two of you have been formally introduced."

"Hello, Andrew." Jericho's voice was nearly hoarse.

Beneath her touch, her brother stiffened slightly. "Hello."

"So you've been to school today?"

He nodded, staring in rapt fascination at the big man.

"How old are you?"

"Twelve."

Catherine thought Andrew's voice shook slightly. Maybe he was as intimidated by Jericho Blue as she was. Well, the man was imposing, even laid up in bed.

As Jericho thanked Riley and Susannah for coming, Catherine noticed how her brother studied the Ranger. Perhaps his interest was due to the fact that Jericho was a lawman. Or the way he dwarfed the bed with his door-wide shoulders and long legs.

Jericho didn't seem to notice her brother's unrelenting study, but Catherine gave his shoulder a warning squeeze. She walked Riley and Susannah to the door, biting off the silly urge to ask them not to leave her alone with the big man in her room.

She wouldn't be alone with him. The sheriff was still here. And so was Andrew, though she instinctively knew it would take more than those two to discourage Jericho Blue if he decided to cause trouble.

Surprisingly, Andrew followed her to the door.

Riley helped his wife into the buckboard. "Please let us know if you need anything," Susannah said.

"Or if Jericho gets restless." Riley walked back to where she stood on the porch, tapping his gray hat lightly against his thigh. "We really appreciate all you're doing. He said the doctor advised against moving him because of all the blood he lost."

She nodded.

"He also said you saved his life." The big man extended a hand. "We're much obliged."

"I'm glad I have some nursing skills."

"Thank goodness," Susannah interjected.

"Davis Lee or I will check in every day," Riley said. "Don't want him wearing you out."

"Visitors will be nice. That will help him along." Their presence would also keep her from being alone with him.

The younger Holt leaned toward her and said in a low voice, "Don't feel obliged to eat those biscuits. My wife hasn't quite mastered the recipe."

"I'm sure they're fine."

He chuckled. "If you break a tooth, don't say I didn't warn you."

"Riley Holt, I can hear you."

Catherine smiled at the saucy grin on the blonde's face as she shook a finger at her husband. The affection between the two glowed on both their faces.

"Good day." Riley levered himself into the buckboard and picked up the reins. "We'll see you tomorrow."

"All right." She waved as they drove away, then turned to see her brother standing uncertainly with his hands jammed in the pockets of his trousers. "What is it, Andrew?"

"Nothing." He shook his head and moved with her into the house. "I thought maybe they would take him."

"Shh." She glanced toward her bedroom. "You know Dr. Butler said he's too weak." Why did her brother's young face look so solemn? "Would you take the milk Miss Susannah brought and put it in the spring house?"

He hesitated. "Will the sheriff be here for a while?"

"I'm not sure. Did you want to ask him something?"

"No. Just curious." He picked up the crockery jug and started out the door. "I'll be right back."

Bemused, she nodded. What was going on in that head of his? She stepped into her bedroom doorway and saw that Davis Lee had pulled a chair over to the bed.

Sweat glistened on Jericho's face, giving witness to the effort it cost him to sit up for so long. She walked across the room. "You should probably lie back down."

He nodded, grimacing as he braced his weight on his left arm.

She dipped a damp rag into the bowl of clean water she'd left on the bedside table. "Sheriff, would you like to stay for supper?"

"I can't, Miz Donnelly, but thank you. Maybe another time?"

"Of course." She reached over to gently wipe Jericho's face with the damp rag.

He grabbed her wrist with his left hand. "I can do it."

Her gaze jerked to his and she released the rag. "Of course." Her voice sounded shaky and she curled her fingers into the pleats of her apron. "I'll go start supper."

"I won't stay long, Nurse," the sheriff said.

She walked out, her skin burning from Jericho's touch, her nerves as raw as if he'd hooked an arm around her throat. It took a minute to steady herself, and as she stoked up the fire in the stove for cornbread, she tried to dismiss the stamp of his touch on her skin. Had that jolt to her bloodstream been fear? Or something else?

The sheriff could stay all night as far as she was concerned. She was in no hurry to be alone with Jericho Blue.

Chapter Three

Davis Lee raised an eyebrow and gave him a steely-eyed look. "What was that about?"

"What?" Jericho said. He shouldn't have touched her. Her skin was every bit as silky soft as it looked. She smelled like spring rain with a hint of lemon verbena, while he probably smelled like he hadn't bathed in months. At least his drawers were clean.

"You were harsh. All she did was try to cool you down."

"I can still do some things by myself," he muttered, unsettled by the quick surge of blood he'd felt when she reached for him.

"So it was just pride?" The doubt in his cousin's eyes echoed inside Jericho.

"Yes." The plain fact was that every instinct he had honed over the last thirteen years as a Ranger screamed at him to keep as far away from Catherine Donnelly as he could. But even if he'd been able to move, he wasn't going anywhere.

Andrew Donnelly was the boy he'd seen at the ambush. Maybe the one who'd shot and killed Hays. And Jericho had known by the flare of wariness in his eyes, clear blue like his sister's, that the lad had recognized him, too.

Did his pretty nurse know that baby brother was riding with the McDougals? Was she protecting him? Was she involved, too?

Davis Lee leaned forward, bracing his elbows on his thighs. "I suppose you're watching that door like a hawk because you don't want her coming back in here to tend you some more?"

"Actually, I *don't* want her coming back in here." Jericho jerked his gaze to his cousin, relying on his ears to keep him apprised of her movements. "What do you know about her?"

"Not that much." His cousin grinned. "She's pretty."

Jericho's thigh throbbed and he grimaced. "How long has she been here?"

"Not quite a month. Her mother suffered from consumption, and toward the end, she sent for Catherine to come to Whirlwind and care for the boy."

"Sent where for her? Where was she?"

Davis Lee frowned. "What's got you all het up?"

"Where?"

"New York City. With some nuns."

"Nuns?" His leg burned like blue fire and he felt more than half-spent. Still, he forced himself to concentrate. Besides their age, he and Davis Lee shared an interest in the law. And justice. His cousin's instincts, except for one unfortunate incident, had never failed him. "Do you believe that?"

"I suppose." Davis Lee paused thoughtfully. "Evelyn, her mother, talked about her a lot. Said she and her husband left Catherine with the nuns when they came to America from Ireland."

"Why wouldn't they bring their daughter to Texas with them?"

"Evelyn said she didn't believe they'd survive here. At least with the nuns, Catherine would be fed, clothed and educated."

"What about later?" Jericho was intrigued in spite of himself. "When the family had become established here?"

"I'm not sure. Evelyn never said." He flashed another grin. "If you're not interested, then where's all this goin'?"

"Her brother was at the ambush."

"What?" Davis Lee's dark brows snapped together and he threw a quick look toward the kitchen.

Jericho heard the squeak of the stove door, the hollow tap of Catherine's shoes on the wooden floor.

"Are you sure?" The other man lowered his voice.

"I'm not likely to mistake it."

"You didn't see the boy afterward? Here maybe? You weren't very alert."

"He was there. And when he came in a while ago, he recognized me, too."

Davis Lee shook his head. "My posse has chased the McDougal gang several times and I've never seen the kid. Why would he be involved with those bastards?"

"I mean to find out."

"You're positive he was there? That he didn't ride up on the scene afterward?"

Jericho kept his voice low, as well. "He had a shotgun. It was long for him, but he had control of it. He may have been the one who killed Hays."

Davis Lee frowned. "Did you track him here?"

"After I lost the gang, I followed a set of tracks from the ambush. They led here, and Catherine—Miz Donnelly—answered the door."

"Did you tell her? What did she say?"

"I keeled over before I could say anything about the boy. She'd probably protect him, anyway."

"If he was with them—"

"He was."

"She may have no idea." Davis Lee shook his head. "Andrew went missing the day before and she was out looking for him. I'd say she was near panic."

"Maybe because she knew exactly where he was."

Davis Lee still looked doubtful.

Jericho shifted in the bed, trying to relieve the sharp pressure in his thigh. Weakness washed through him, but he fought it. "You believe her story about the nuns and New York City?"

"Yeah. Her mother was a good woman." Davis Lee dragged a hand down his face. "And Catherine seems like a good woman, too."

"Why? Because you think she's pretty?"

"Don't you?"

"I hadn't noticed."

"You were shot in the leg, not the eye," the other man pointed out wryly. "What do you want to do about Andrew? Want me to get him in here?"

Jericho felt himself sinking beneath a wave of pain. "Any news about the McDougals?"

"No. Nothing since the ambush. They're holed up somewhere."

"That's my guess, too. And that kid probably knows where. I want to watch him for a while. His sister, too."

"Are you telling me everything?" his cousin demanded. "Has she given you a reason to be suspicious?"

"If the boy's involved with the McDougals, she may be, too. Does she have a beau?"

"No." Davis Lee thought for a minute. "In fact, I haven't seen her show interest in any man around here. She's always polite, but that's about it. The Baldwin brothers usually have some luck with the ladies, but I don't think she's accepted one of their invitations."

"I can see why a man would be interested in her. Have you

had any luck?" The thought of Davis Lee setting his sights on Catherine Donnelly struck an uneasy chord inside Jericho, but he didn't know why.

"What makes you think I've tried?"

"You *always* try."

Davis Lee grinned. "No luck. Yet."

"And if she's not interested in you, she must not be interested at all," Jericho said dryly.

"Well, it does make a man wonder."

"It makes me wonder if she already has a man."

"Like a McDougal," Davis Lee concluded. "For what it's worth, I don't think so. Wouldn't we have heard if one of them had a sweetheart?"

"Probably, unless they found a woman who can keep her mouth shut. And maybe they did."

"I guess if your commission from the governor is still active, you're gonna see this through to the end."

"I'm assuming it's still active." Because of the gang's rampage throughout the state, the governor had issued a special commission for Jericho and Hays to work strictly on catching the outlaws. "But even if it isn't, I'm going after them."

"Because of Hays?"

"And the others they've murdered."

Davis Lee stared hard at him. "Are you sure? You've wanted nothing but to be a Ranger your whole life, ever since your pa died and left you that old badge he had made out of a Mexican coin."

"It was criminals like the McDougals who killed him," Jericho reminded him with some effort. "He wouldn't have stood by and let some politician tell him he couldn't pursue outlaws just because of a piece of paper."

"True enough."

"So you'll help me?"

"You can count on it."

Jericho shook his cousin's hand to seal the deal. "Before I forget, would you send a wire back East for me, to those nuns?"

"All right."

"Could you do one other thing for me?" Jericho told him about the tracks he'd followed to the Donnelly house, made by a horse carrying a lightweight rider, and sporting a chipped shoe.

"You want me to check the barn for this horse?" Davis Lee asked.

"Yeah."

"All right." He rose from his chair and scooted it against the wall. "I'll let you know what I find out, and I'll be back tomorrow to check on you."

"Could you hand me my gun and gun belt?"

Davis Lee did so and Jericho tucked them under the sheet next to his uninjured leg. "Thanks for coming."

"You sure you don't want me to wire your ma and sisters?"

"No. I'll do it when I'm stronger. No need to worry them." Jericho didn't want Jessamine Blue making a trip from Houston to Whirlwind, a journey that would surely aggravate her rheumatism. His ma had already spent herself, single-handedly raising him and his four sisters.

"I'll check the barn real quick," Davis Lee said. "Then I've got to get over to Haskell's. Someone broke in there last night."

"Was anything taken?"

"Some food and maybe bullets. I'm sure Charlie, the owner, will know down to the last nail by the time I get there."

Jericho's energy flagged and he felt a quick flare of frustration at his weakness. Just the effort of thinking, trying to determine what Catherine Donnelly knew about her brother's activities, sapped the little energy he'd had when his cousins had arrived.

"Take it easy, Jericho." Davis Lee settled his fawn-colored

cowboy hat on his head. "I don't want to see you chasin' that pretty nurse around."

"Don't worry. Wouldn't be even if I *could* walk."

The other man grinned and sauntered out.

A wave of fatigue and pain rolled over Jericho. He closed his eyes, hearing Catherine bid his cousin goodbye. He wished she would come in and wipe his face with a cool rag. Or bring him something to eat. Or plump up his pillow.

He wasn't asking for her help, dammit. He had all he could handle when she did come in here. For all his denial to his cousin, Davis Lee was right. Jericho was more than aware of the beautiful woman who'd taken him in and cared for him. More aware than he liked.

Her clear blue eyes seemed to see to the depths of his black soul. And as much as he tried, he couldn't dismiss her soft, lingering scent.

It didn't matter what she looked like or that his body surged to life when she touched him. What mattered was her involvement with the McDougals.

"Hey." Davis Lee's low voice drifted through the window just behind his head.

Jericho craned his neck to see his cousin framed in the open space.

Concern darkened the other man's eyes. "You were right. Their sorrel wears a chipped shoe on its right back hoof."

The triumph Jericho had expected didn't come. Instead, a weary resignation sighed through him. "Thanks."

"What are you going to do now?"

"Wait to see what you find out from New York City. Watch and listen until I can carry my own weight again."

Davis Lee nodded soberly. "I'll be back tomorrow and bring news if I have it."

"All right."

As the chirp of birds and the sawing of the wind carried into the room, Jericho felt himself giving out. Would Catherine Donnelly really be helping him if she were in cahoots with the McDougal gang?

His left hand curled around the butt of his revolver and he tried to make a fist with his right hand. He couldn't even touch his palm with his fingers. Until he could protect himself, he'd better hope Catherine Donnelly was as innocent as she appeared.

A noise woke him. Night air flowed through the window as Jericho opened his eyes and listened hard. He'd heard the creak of a plank. It had to be from the front porch. The bedrooms were built off the side of the house and set back several feet from the porch.

A soft grunt sounded in the room next to his, then the sigh of a rope bed. It was Andrew coming home from somewhere. Did his sister know? Perhaps she'd been with him. But if she had, why would he come in through his bedroom window?

Jericho strained to hear more, but there was no further sound. Where had the kid gone, and why? Had he returned alone?

Jericho pushed himself up with his good hand and slowly swung his legs to the floor. Pain arrowed up his right thigh, but he steadied himself by holding on to the bedside table to help him stand. Biting the inside of his cheek to keep from groaning, he gripped the wooden edge until the room stopped rocking.

This was the first time he'd been up, and his leg burned in agony. Nauseous and trembling from weakness, he limped to the wall and flattened his hand against the pine, feeling his way to the door. It opened silently and he leaned against the jamb, breathing hard from his short trip. Sweat trickled down his bare chest and beneath the waistband of his light cotton drawers.

A full, fat moon sent light slanting into the front room that also comprised the kitchen. His gaze searched the shadows to his left until he saw Catherine. She lay on a pallet beneath the front window, her hair a curtain of midnight black flowing over her shoulder. The windows in his and Andrew's rooms had been left open, but not in here. Stuffy air clogged Jericho's lungs and he wondered how she could even breathe.

Her white, sleeveless nightdress shone in the darkness. Pale moonlight fell across one cheek; gilded her straight nose and smooth skin. One slender hand pillowed her cheek; the other lay across her waist, almost as if she were protecting herself.

As his eyes further adjusted to the dim light, he saw a sheet draped low over her hips. Her breasts were in shadow, but Jericho had a good imagination. He looked away, blinking to focus in the darkness and search the corners of the room. Everything was quiet and calm.

He shuffled closer. If Catherine had been out with the boy, she showed no signs of it. Her breathing was slow and steady. There were no hastily discarded clothes. Her dress and apron hung neatly on a wall peg next to the fireplace opposite Jericho's side of the room. Beside them, a tin bathtub stood against the wall. Her wrapper was draped over the back of a rocking chair in the corner.

Pain snaked through him and ate away his strength. He could make out the cupboard against the wall to his right, the dining table in front of him. He gripped the edge. A moment of silence passed, then another. Andrew seemed to be in for the night, and Catherine appeared to have slept through her brother's absence and return.

Trying to gather what little strength he had, Jericho turned to go back to bed. And hit his thigh on the table's edge. Sharp, keening pain nearly drove him to the floor. His vision hazed and he cursed.

"Who's there? What do you want?" Catherine cried out, startling him.

"Shh." His fingers dug into the wood as he fought to drag in a breath. "It's me."

"What's happened?" She rose, a hazy figure pulling on her wrapper and coming toward him.

"Didn't mean to frighten you." Pain was a vicious band around his thigh, and Jericho braced himself against the table. "I'm sorry."

She stopped about a foot from him, her clean, fresh scent reaching through the thick night air. He wanted her to stay away, but it took all his energy to stay upright.

"What are you doing?"

At her accusing tone, he growled, "I'm on my way back to bed."

"You shouldn't be up. If you needed something, you could've just called out to me."

Her voice was cool and guarded; he could feel her wary gaze. What did she think he was doing—coming out here to have his way with her?

"I heard a noise," he snapped.

"What was it?" She looked around, alarm plain in her voice.

His lips twisted. "I'm not sure. Whatever it was, it's gone now."

Had Catherine really not heard her brother return? Or did she know he'd been out and was now protecting him? Jericho couldn't stand here much longer. The floor seemed to shift beneath his feet, and the heat in his thigh made him wonder if it were bleeding.

"Let me help you." She was once again the calm nurse who'd taken him in.

He wanted to refuse her assistance, but if he did he might fall at her feet again. Surely one time was enough for any man. "Thank you," he said gruffly.

The agony in his leg had subsided to a dull, bone-pinching throb. Catherine moved to his uninjured side and braced her shoulder under his arm, then put an arm firmly around his bare waist.

For just a moment, he balanced there and let her cool beauty soak into him. He hadn't allowed himself to be this close to a good woman in a long time. His arm rested on her shoulders and she gripped his wrist with her other hand. Her touch unleashed a longing he could scarcely admit. A long-denied part of himself greedily took in her clean scent, the brush of her unbound breast against his side.

"Ready?" Her body tensed to move.

He fought to keep his hand from drifting down her arm. "Yes. Ready."

He took slow, halting steps, fresh pain tearing at his leg. She served as a crutch and let him set the pace. But the press of her body against his sparked a savage heat inside him. He tried to move faster, get back to bed so he could stop feeling it. Stop wanting to feel more.

He inched forward awkwardly, ignoring her teasing scent and the satin of her hair tickling his arm. An almost giddy relief washed through him when they shuffled through the doorway and he saw the bed. He stepped toward it, releasing her at the same time.

"Wait—"

His leg gave out. She clutched at him as he grabbed for the wall behind her. Agony wrenched his leg, rattling his teeth.

"Damn," he muttered raggedly. Nausea rolled through him and sweat broke out across his forehead.

After long seconds, his breathing still uneven, he leaned against the wall.

Not the wall. *Catherine Donnelly.*

Bracing his weight on his good arm, Jericho eased back enough to look at her. She stood motionless, her gaze trained on his bare chest. Beyond the pain of his leg, a different kind of throbbing moved into his groin. Well, he could rest easy about the question of his manhood.

He felt every inch of her, and those inches felt damn good. The reason for his being here jumbled with the quicksilver reaction of his body to hers. Hard man to soft woman. Through the light fabric of her wrapper, her breasts teased his chest, while her hips and thighs pressed to his. Her breath fluttered against his throat, making his blood pound. He wanted to kiss her, peel down the straps of her nightdress and see the breasts shadowed beneath the fine lawn fabric. He wanted to run his hands through her hair, over her body.

"You are so sweet." It took a second for him to realize he'd whispered the words. In that instant, he registered something else, too.

Though she stood rigid against him, she trembled—not fighting him, but warning him off all the same.

He shifted so that moonlight fell over his shoulder. She stared straight ahead, her face ghostly pale, her lips compressed.

"Catherine?" His whisper sounded harsh in the silence.

Her gaze lifted slowly to his and Jericho drew back. Terror swam in her eyes. He recognized that fear, and it had nothing to do with what he knew about her brother and the McDougals. She didn't fear him as a Ranger. She feared him as a man.

Chapter Four

Catherine wasn't going to scream; she wouldn't panic. She needed to breathe.

At first Jericho had sagged against her in pain, but that had changed. Even with her limited experience she recognized the awareness that thickened the air between them. She tensed. His body was no longer rigid with agony. Now his hard lines molded to her curves; his thighs caged hers.

She had to be smart. She could get away if she were smart.

She didn't think Jericho would hurt her, but she hadn't believed that man in New York City would, either. Until it was almost too late.

Panic exploded inside her. "Get off," she said dully, dragging in air. "Get off."

The Ranger eased back until he was no longer touching her. His arms still kept her against the wall. "Catherine?"

She thought she might be sick. Not from the way his body had felt against hers—it hadn't been entirely unpleasant—but from the way her stomach rolled over. "Get off. Please."

"You better do it, mister."

Both Catherine and Jericho jumped at the sound of Andrew's voice in the doorway. The sharp cock of a shotgun ripped through the room like the crack of a whip. She jerked toward her brother and saw pale light skimming the barrel of their father's shotgun. "Andrew!"

"Put that gun down, boy." Jericho lifted his injured arm. "There's no call—"

"Back away from her or I'll shoot."

He slowly pushed away from the wall and Catherine saw pain slash across his face. Sweat gleamed at his temple. She realized he had truly needed her support. "Andrew, everything is all right. Lieutenant Blue hurt his leg again and I was helping him back to bed."

"That ain't what it looked like. It looked like he was trying to take advantage of you."

"I wasn't." Jericho hobbled back a step, his hands raised to shoulder level. "Son, you shouldn't be pointing that gun. See, I'm moving away."

"Not far enough." Andrew gestured with the weapon, indicating Jericho should go farther.

"Andrew, please." Catherine went to him, shaken as much by what she had felt with Jericho as she was that her brother held a gun on her patient. "Lieutenant Blue is in no shape to harm me. Certainly the gun isn't called for."

Andrew glared up at her.

Jericho reached the bed and sagged down upon it with a grunt.

Catherine turned toward him, concerned at the paleness of his face.

Agony carved his features. "Your sister's right, Andrew."

"Then what were you doing to her?"

"I fell. She was between me and the wall. That's all."

"He heard a noise and got up to check," Catherine said. "Please put that gun down."

Andrew kept the weapon leveled at the Ranger.

Though Jericho sat and Andrew stood, neither broke eye contact. She stood between them, trying to decipher their silent communication. "The lieutenant hit his injured leg on the table in the kitchen and I was helping him back to bed."

Her brother's gaze narrowed suspiciously on the big man behind her.

"I wouldn't hurt your sister." Jericho's voice was gritty with pain, his silver gaze locked on the boy. "Not after all she's done for me."

Finally Andrew lowered the weapon, and Catherine let out a deep sigh. She felt Jericho's relief as keenly as her own. Her heart thundered in her chest as she considered whether to hug Andrew or shake him until his teeth rattled.

She had never seen her brother be protective of her. Since her arrival three weeks ago, he hadn't appeared to care about her. Why now? Did Andrew feel Jericho was a threat because he had witnessed her own panic?

"Let me have that thing." She took the gun from him and gingerly carried it to its place behind the front door. "You scared me to death."

"Sorry," he mumbled.

She returned to find him still eyeing Jericho with distrust.

"I think you should apologize to Lieutenant Blue."

Andrew's chin came up.

"No," the Ranger said. "He was protecting you, and there's nothing wrong with that."

Her brother's eyes widened and Catherine searched the Ranger's face. Compassion was something she hadn't expected from the rough-looking man. But perhaps she shouldn't be surprised. The death of his friend, Hays, the Ranger who had arrived with him, had visibly affected Jericho.

"Very well. You don't need to apologize, Andrew." The

Ranger's pallor was too marked for further argument. She would have words with Andrew alone, though she wouldn't be harsh. He *had* been protecting her, and she wondered if perhaps they might develop a closeness, after all.

She slid an arm around his shoulders, surprised when he allowed her touch. "I think we've had enough excitement for tonight," she murmured. "Let's get back to bed."

"All right." Her brother gave Jericho one last warning look before letting Catherine nudge him toward his room.

Even though her pulse slowed, she still felt the imprint of the Ranger's body against hers. Chills rose on her arms. They had nothing to do with fear, a fact that unsettled her to no end.

In Andrew's room, she straightened his sheet and patted the husk-filled mattress. "I appreciate what you did, Andrew—"

"But you're mad at me."

She paused. "I'm concerned. You held a gun on a man."

He frowned as if he couldn't understand why she worried.

"What if that weapon had gone off?"

"I know how to use it."

"Would you have?"

He shrugged. "If I had to."

"Oh, my." She paced around his bed. "Are you saying that you could kill if necessary?"

"If that Ranger had hurt you, I would have," he said fiercely.

"But he didn't."

"You acted like he did."

"I was taken aback when he fell against me." She didn't want to recall the pleasant warmth that had spread through her after the initial jolt of panic. His entire body had hardened against her. As he was clad only in his lightweight drawers, Catherine had been keenly aware of his body's reaction. Every rigid inch of it.

"While I appreciate that you would protect me, I think bringing in the gun was ill-advised."

"Don't fret," Andrew grumbled. "I didn't shoot him. Yet."

She cut him a sharp look. "What does that mean?"

"I don't like him being here."

"I don't believe he's a threat to us. And his injuries are too severe for him to leave, so we'll just have to make the best of it." She didn't know how to handle Andrew or his apparent willingness to take a human life. "You could've hurt someone. It seemed so easy for you to threaten the man."

"He was threatening *you.* Wasn't he?"

"No." Her denial sounded weak. "I don't think so." With some distance between her and the Ranger now, she didn't believe he would have assaulted her. But he did dissolve her peace of mind. She was not going to explain to a twelve-year-old boy about the violent episode she'd experienced all those months ago.

"I know how to use the gun, Catherine. I can help you if I ever need to."

"I know. Thank you." She turned down the sheet and motioned him into bed.

She wanted to kiss him good-night, but the scowl on his moonlit face told her it wouldn't be welcome. "Good night. I'll see you in the morning."

"Good night," he muttered.

When she reached his door, she turned. "I do thank you, Andrew. I'm glad to know we can depend on each other."

"Yeah."

She closed his door, still jarred over the appalling sight of her brother holding a gun on someone. A Texas Ranger. Her patient. A guest in their home.

What had roused Andrew's protective instincts? Since the lieutenant's arrival, her brother had kept closer to home, but she hadn't realized it until now.

"Is he all right?"

Catherine started at the sound of Jericho's voice coming from her bedroom. She didn't want to go back in there. The giddy flutter in her stomach told her that would be asking for trouble.

But she couldn't ignore him, either. She walked the few steps to the doorway. The lamp on the bedside table had been lit, and filmy light washed over his bare chest. He sat on the edge of her bed. "Yes, I think so. I do apologize for him."

"There's no need. He did the right thing."

The sight of Jericho's muscles brought home to Catherine how he really could have hurt her. She wrapped her arms around her waist to ward off the resulting chill. "I'm not certain I agree."

"Out here he may have cause to protect himself or you. It's good he knows how," Jericho said quietly. "Where did Andrew learn to handle that gun, anyway?"

"I'm not sure."

"Have you ever seen him use one before?"

"No."

"Who do you think taught him to use it?"

"My mother, maybe? I don't know. Why are you asking so many questions?"

"He did have a gun trained on me," Jericho said lightly.

Catherine studied him, not sure if her lingering unease was due to seeing Andrew with the gun or the strange warmth that had moved through her when Jericho Blue's body had pressed against hers. That warmth stirred her even now. "I think he would've shot you!"

"I do, too, if I'd been a real threat." In the soft light, his gaze held hers. "Which I wasn't."

Perhaps he didn't think so, but for those long seconds she had.

"I would never hurt you, Catherine. Certainly not after you saved my life."

She believed him. Or wanted to. "It's forgotten now."

"Is it? You're pale and you were afraid of me."

"It's over. Why don't you rest—"

"C'mon, Catherine. I know something was going on in that head of yours. What did I do to make you tense up like I was going to take a whip to you?"

"Nothing. You startled me. And I certainly didn't expect Andrew to come charging in that way."

"Something happened in here, Miz Donnelly." The Ranger's voice turned soft and coaxing. "I'd like to know if it was because of me."

"And if it was?" She didn't like being pressed on this issue. She had no intention of allowing herself to get so close to him again. "As I said, I was startled. There was no harm done."

"Someone hurt you. A man you knew? Or didn't know?"

She wasn't stirring up those memories again. "I was raised by nuns, Lieutenant. There were no men there."

His narrow gaze said he didn't believe her, but Catherine didn't care. She wasn't about to tell him he was the first man to excite her more than frighten her.

Fear was the least of what washed through her right now. The sight of him sitting on the side of her bed turned her insides soft and warm. Hazy lamplight sculpted the hard muscles of the wide shoulders and chest that had been pressed against her only moments ago.

His gaze bored into hers, then dropped to her lips, sparking that unfamiliar warmth low in her belly.

She couldn't seem to stop remembering the undeniable press of his arousal. Her gaze went there involuntarily and a curious heat swept through her. Even now, he strained against the cotton of his drawers.

"Your leg," she gasped, stepping reflexively into the room. "It's bleeding again."

Blood glued the fabric to the corded muscles of his thigh and molded the part of him that had frightened and excited her only minutes ago. "I'd better change your dressing."

"I'll do it," he growled, grabbing the pillow and putting it in his lap.

"But what if you've torn the stitches?"

"I'm fine."

"I think I should—"

"I can't imagine you're that eager to get so close to me again, Miz Donnelly. I can change the bandage myself."

His words stung, but they were true. "Very well. I'll bring you some fresh dressings with some soap and water."

He nodded curtly.

Knowing that he wanted her should've scared her sense-less, but her apprehension was outweighed by the curiosity that had nagged since he had arrived at her front door. Curiosity she had no intention of indulging.

Turning, she walked out to get the things Jericho would need to change his bandage. The nurse in her insisted on tending him; the woman in her couldn't get close.

He slept poorly. Blood soaked through his fresh bandage and his drawers stuck to him. The pain didn't do much to keep his mind off the fact that he'd been powerfully aroused last night and Catherine had borne witness to it.

Jericho couldn't recall the last time he had taken his ease with a woman. Now, thanks to the brush of Catherine's breasts against him, that was about all he wanted.

Since he'd started chasing the McDougals, his focus had been solely on the outlaws. He'd spent more time contemplating a woman in the last week than he had in nearly two years. Not just any woman, but one who had kindly taken him in and tended his wounds. One whose brother had most likely given Jericho those wounds. The terror in Catherine's eyes was as much to blame for his sleeplessness as the discomfort of his freshly opened wound. But it was her words that pricked at him.

"Get off," she'd said.

He hadn't been *on* her, hadn't been touching her at all right then. Jericho found it strange that she hadn't asked him to "step back" or "back away," as Andrew had. The Donnelly boy wasn't the only one hiding secrets. So was his sister.

Jericho wanted to know who had hurt her. Was it someone she'd loved? She was sweet and, judging from her skittishness last night, most likely untouched. Her innocence drew him even though he knew his concern should be about what it hid.

Was she involved with one of the McDougals? Had one of them hurt her?

The thought of a McDougal putting his hands on Catherine had Jericho's fist balling. A savage protectiveness sprang loose inside him.

He didn't understand the ferocity of the emotion. What difference did it make what had happened to her? Losing so much blood had tangled up his reason. He was here to find the McDougal gang, not muse over the arousal triggered by his nurse. Something Jericho wouldn't act on because of her link to the outlaws.

Even though the image of her in bed with him came too easily, he needed to stay away from her. But for now all he could do was lie in her bed and hope his leg didn't rot off. He levered himself to a sitting position and leaned against the headboard.

Through the door he caught the sounds of her and Andrew moving around, the low murmur of their voices. His window was open and he heard the pair step onto the porch.

"Have a good day, Andrew."

The boy grunted, then darted past. After a few seconds, the front door shut and Catherine's light footsteps sounded on the wooden floor.

After seeing Andrew with that gun last night, Jericho was certain he'd spotted the boy at the ambush that had killed his friend and fellow Ranger, Hays Gentry. Andrew had been right up front with Angus McDougal. Either Catherine was a mighty good liar or she really didn't suspect her brother of being involved with the gang.

She walked in, interrupting his thoughts. She was a sight today. His gaze hungrily took in the silky fall of black hair over her shoulder. Her pale blue dress with its white apron made the blue of her eyes startlingly bright. She smelled clean, with a hint of verbena; he was so sick of his own smell.

"Good morning." Her voice was subdued and she didn't meet his eyes. "How did you sleep?"

Like hell. "Fine."

Moving to the right side of the bed, she aimed a smile in his direction but still didn't look at him. Beneath her cool competence, she was embarrassed, he realized. And his damn body responded to her even now.

"I trust you changed your bandage?"

"Yes." He wanted to set her mind at ease, but keeping his distance was probably best.

She frowned at the sight of the bloodied sheet. She drew it away from his hips and made a strangled sound in her throat. "Lieutenant!"

His leg muscle went into spasm and he winced, cursing.

"How long has this been bleeding?"

"Not sure."

Her gaze cut sharply to him as she carefully peeled the blood-soaked sheet from his drawers.

She looked so alarmed that he felt a jolt of concern himself. "It probably just needs a new bandage. I'm not too good at that kind of stuff."

"It's been bleeding all night, hasn't it?" She didn't wait for an answer, just breezed out of the room and returned in a few minutes with a bowl of water, a rag and a tin of soap.

"I knew these stitches were torn. I should've tended to you last night," she muttered under her breath.

Jericho didn't like to see her blaming herself. They both knew why she hadn't gotten close enough to him to see the damage. "It's not your fault. If it weren't for you, I wouldn't have made it this far."

"You're not going to die now, either." Determination firmed her lips. "I was afraid of this. I had Andrew go to the fort early this morning, but Dr. Butler was off tending a man who was crushed by a horse on his ranch. I'll have to restitch you, but it should be bearable, since I have laudanum for the pain."

"No laudanum." Jericho didn't fancy being knocked out when he had so many suspicions about her and her brother.

"I don't have anything else. I'm so sorry."

"You do what you have to and I'll be grateful. Got any whiskey?" he asked hopefully.

"No, but I can get some in town."

"I've got some in my saddlebag."

By pressing a warm cloth to his leg she eventually loosened his stiff, bloodied drawers. She stared uncertainly down at his leg, her neck growing pink.

"What?" Jericho's gaze shifted there, too, as he tried to figure out why she was blushing. His manhood was behaving, so he wasn't sure why Catherine seemed so embarrassed all of a sudden.

"I'll get that whiskey." She wiped her hands down the front

of her clean white apron. "Do you think you can get out of your drawers by yourself?"

So that was it. She didn't want to undress him. Why did he find that amusing? "Yeah."

His blood started humming and he could feel himself grow hard. Thanks to the pain that would come when she started to restitch his wound, that wouldn't last long. Still, he didn't want to scare the lady off again.

She walked to the corner and bent to rummage through his saddlebags, looking for the whiskey. Using his left hand, he pushed his drawers to his knees, then managed to tug them off with his foot. He was naked by the time she returned to the bed.

She passed the bottle to him without meeting his eyes.

"If you want to wait for the doctor, you can," he offered.

Distress drew her features tight. "No, I don't think we should wait. I'll do this as quickly as I can."

He nodded, uncorking the whiskey and swallowing a hefty amount. Maybe if he got drunk he wouldn't *rise* to the occasion the way he seemed to every time she got within a foot of him.

She crossed herself, then pulled a chair up to the bed. Gingerly she folded the sheet away from his injury, careful to keep his manhood and vital parts covered.

The first cool touch of her scissors between his skin and the bandage caused him to twitch.

Her gaze flew to his and she grimaced. "Sorry."

"It's okay. I'm okay. Just do it." He took another gulp of whiskey.

She quickly cut the bandage; it took her a few minutes to pry it away from his skin. Her touch was firm and capable as her fingers moved over his flesh.

His arousal grew, mounding the sheet. And there wasn't a damn thing he could do about it.

A flush rose on her neck, up her cheeks, and still she worked. That same flush heated his body. His jaw working, he closed his eyes until she removed the bandage.

He noticed her hands were shaking, and he set the whiskey bottle inside the vee of his thighs so she couldn't go poking that needle into any vital areas if she slipped.

She cleaned the wound carefully, frowning as she leaned over him.

"What do you think?"

She looked up, her gaze sober and earnest. "I'll do the best I can, Lieutenant."

He wanted to relax her a tad. It wouldn't help either of them if she stabbed too deep with that needle. Or too far to the north. "Maybe now would be a good time for you to call me Jericho, seeing as how we're getting pretty familiar here."

"All right." Her hands trembled.

"You're steady, aren't you?" he asked. "I won't have to worry about you sewing that sheet to my leg?"

"I—I'm fine."

He was nearing the end of the whiskey and still feeling more than he liked, pain and otherwise.

She picked up a bottle marked Carbolic Acid and poured a small amount of the liquid on the needle. "Ready?"

"Ready." He gritted his teeth, hoping he would pass out once she got started.

It didn't reassure him that she flinched before she even began.

He looked away, guzzled down another burning swallow of liquor. He felt a sharp prick, then a red-hot sting slicing through his flesh. "Damn!" he roared.

She bit her lip as she pressed his flesh together to take her first stitch.

Sweat trickled down his temple and his vision hazed. With

a shaking hand, he lifted the bottle and downed the rest of the liquor. Pain throbbed through his body, razor sharp.

"Try to breathe. It will help." Catherine didn't look up from her task. Even though her voice shook, she was reassuring.

She took another stitch and another. The hurt layered upon itself until Jericho grabbed the edge of the bed with his good hand. His knuckles burned. His arm quivered.

Her skirts brushed his hand, her warmth reaching out to him. He tried to focus on the fresh clean scent of her, and wished again he could pass out.

"Last night, I noticed you walked without your hip dipping. That's a good sign there's no nerve damage."

He grunted.

"Where are you from, Jericho?"

Her voice seemed thick and heavy, as if coming through a wall. "Southeast Texas. Outside of Houston."

"How far is it from here?"

"Far." A lifetime away.

"How long have you been a Ranger?"

How the hell was he supposed to remember? "Since I was nineteen. Thirteen years now."

"And before that?"

"I apprenticed with a gunsmith in Uvalde. Took me two years to get a commission."

"What made you want to be a Ranger?"

He appreciated that she was trying to distract him, and he struggled to force his mind on to something other than the pain. "My pa was one."

"Is he tracking the McDougals, too?"

Jericho watched her through slitted eyes. "He's dead."

"I'm sorry."

She kept stitching with a single-mindedness he envied. "He died when I was twelve. My ma raised me and my sisters."

"You have sisters?" She didn't glance up. "How many?"

"Four."

"Bless the saints!" She kept stitching. When would she finish? "Older or younger than you?"

"All younger." Agony made his voice crack. "How's it coming down there?"

"Just a few more stitches. Luckily, you didn't tear the wound all the way down."

He didn't feel so lucky right now, but if he lived through this, he probably would.

"What are your sisters' names?"

"Deborah, Jordan, Michal and Marah."

"All Bible names?"

"Yes, like mine. My pa was Noah, and he wanted us to all have a name from the Bible like he did."

"I know Jericho is a city and Jordan is a river, but Michal was a person, wasn't she? King David's daughter?"

"Yeah." He squeezed his eyes shut, using his flagging energy to focus on Catherine's voice.

"What about Marah? I'm not familiar with that name."

"My ma says it's the first camp of the Israelites after they crossed the Red Sea."

"And your other sister?"

"Deborah was named after a judge in the Old Testament. She's the oldest of my sisters."

"Do they all live outside of Houston?"

"Yes." He struggled to focus past the pain. "They're all still in school except for Deborah. She's a teacher."

Catherine tied a knot in the thread and snipped it with her scissors. "Do you miss them?"

Jericho's leg throbbed like blue blazes. He did miss his ma and Deborah. The other girls had been small when he'd left, and half afraid of him. "Yeah."

If his ma were here she would make him a pecan pie and spoil him lazy.

"I grew up wanting a sister or a brother," Catherine said.

"You've got Andrew."

"I heard about him after he was born, but didn't meet him until about a month ago. My mother talked about him in her letters."

The whiskey finally took hold, just enough to blunt the fierce discomfort in Jericho's leg. "Why weren't you with your family?"

"My parents came to America from Ireland. They were to meet my uncle in Texas, but not knowing what was in store down here, they left me with the Sisters of Mercy in New York City."

"How long?"

"Fourteen years."

Jericho frowned, resting his head against the wooden headboard as he struggled to draw in deep breaths. "That's a long time."

"My mother lost her parents in the potato famine in Ireland in the late forties, and she nearly starved to death when they did. She didn't want to bring me to Texas until she knew if she and my father could survive here."

Jericho certainly understood a mother's concern over raising her children. His own mother had grown old years before her time because of it. "And did they survive?"

"Until recently. They're both gone now."

"So there's only you and Andrew?"

"Yes."

"Did you leave someone special behind in New York?"

"Special?"

"A beau."

Horror chased across her delicate features. "No."

Did that mean she didn't have a beau? Or just not one who was back East?

"There, I think I'm finished."

He wanted to know more. Told himself he needed to learn as much as he could because of her possible connection to the McDougal gang. But in truth he was curious about *her.* He gingerly poked at his leg. "What do you think?"

"I did the best I could."

"I'm grateful for that." He touched her hand, which rested near his knee. "I meant do you think I'll keep my leg?"

"Yes." She smiled into his eyes for the first time since coming into the room. "I didn't see any signs of infection."

He found himself smiling back. Her hands were small, but there was nothing weak about them as she rebandaged the wound. The throbbing ache in his leg was fierce, but she had most likely saved his limb. "Thank you."

"You're welcome. I hope I didn't scar you."

"It's fine if you did." He touched the scar on his cheek. "You can see it won't be the first."

"How did you come by that?"

"Bullet creased me."

"While you were chasing the McDougals?"

"No." He smiled weakly. "I was in a shoot-out about five years ago with another gang, down in Round Rock."

"I have a feeling they ended up worse off than you."

She smiled, and he thought this much pain might be worth it if she would do that more often. "I appreciate you putting me back together."

She deftly folded a bandage and tied it around his thigh, somehow managing not to touch anything but his leg. "I should've tended you last night. I'm sorry."

There were other ways Jericho would like her to tend him, but he knew there was no future in that. He was glad to see the sheet now lay flat in his lap.

"Do you think you can eat?"

He nodded.

"I'll get you some biscuits and ham." She picked up the bowl of water. "And some coffee. Unless you'd rather sleep for a while?"

"I'd like to eat." He felt drowsy and weak; maybe some food would help. She was a good woman. He didn't see how she could be mixed up with the McDougal gang, but he couldn't let himself be distracted by her sweet curves and compassion.

"Later I'll wash those sheets and your unmentionables."

He grinned. "If anyone can mention them, I'd say it's you, Miz Catherine."

She smiled shyly, turning away to pick up his saddlebags and carry them over to the chair beside the bed. "Maybe you'd like a clean pair."

"Thank you."

Jericho waited until she left before he pulled out another pair of drawers, along with a folded piece of paper. The page contained the McDougals' names, as well as Andrew's, along with physical descriptions, height, speech peculiarities, eye colors. He had copied everything down from the "Crime Book" or "Bible Two" as his captain called it.

The gray paperback booklet was made up of information sent by sheriffs to the adjutant general, then furnished to each Ranger camp. Jericho studied his notes, but he saw Catherine's sweet face in his mind.

He shouldn't tease and try to coax her pretty smile out of hiding. She could make him forget why he was here, forget that he needed to heal as fast as possible and get back on the trail of those murderers. The McDougals and Andrew were the ones Jericho needed to worry about. Not the woman whose touch played havoc with his body. That was reason enough to leave her be.

Chapter Five

After Catherine left, Jericho dozed off for a few minutes. He woke with his mind rolling over the events of last night. He knew sure as shootin' that Andrew Donnelly was connected to the McDougal gang. Whatever secrets the boy was hiding were likely related to the outlaws, but Jericho didn't know a blasted thing about Catherine's secrets. Was she sweet on a McDougal? Protecting one or all of them?

He might be able to figure it out if his mind would stop drifting to what she looked like beneath the starched day dress and apron she wore today. The gown he'd seen her wearing last night before she pulled on her wrapper had covered, but not hidden her full breasts. And he could still smell the sweet, subtle scent of her skin, which rose around him when they touched. Things he would do well to forget.

The sound of light footsteps on the front porch had him looking over his shoulder and out the window. Catherine walked out into the yard carrying a basketful of clothes. She stopped in front of a huge kettle about five yards from the house and deposited the basket on the ground. A fire had already been laid and she poked it with a stick, then tested the water in the kettle by dipping in a finger.

No doubt Jericho's blood-soaked drawers were already soaking in cold water. He didn't really want to think about her hands on those, or how much he wanted her hands on *him*.

She dunked several pieces of clothing into the water, then scooped up a handful of soap and slanted the washboard into the pot.

The morning sun glinting on her black hair made it look like hot silk. She wore it up today, the simple chignon exposing her elegant neck as she bent over the washboard. Her pale blue bodice pulled taut across her back, outlining slender shoulders and a slim waist. He'd felt the delicate lines of both last night through the light cotton of her wrapper and gown. Jericho's body hardened.

What was it about this woman? While it had been excruciating to lie still as she stitched him, he had been in his right mind enough to admire the fine texture of her creamy skin, the rose-pink lips she worried too often with her teeth. More than once he'd imagined loosening her hair and burying his hands in the silky thickness, feeling it slide over his chest and belly. No other woman had ever gotten to him like this.

His fascination wasn't just because he wanted her. She intrigued him. She was shy about his body and yet she doctored him as well as any medicine man he'd known. Her stitches were more even and smaller than Dr. Butler's. Jericho's scar would be big but maybe not hideous.

And he had observed that she managed to keep him talking, while revealing little about her own past. Being raised in New York City explained her Eastern accent. Maybe it also explained the shadows he sometimes glimpsed in her eyes. Fourteen years was a long time to be separated from one's family, but Jericho could easily imagine his mother leaving him behind the same way, to make sure he was clothed and fed. The regret and sorrow in Catherine's voice when she'd explained about being raised by nuns had changed to hope when she spoke about Andrew.

Was her desire for a family strong enough that she would protect her brother if he were involved with the McDougals? Probably so. As she had stitched up Jericho's leg, and the pain carved away the arousal he felt at her touch, he'd found himself letting his guard down, trying to reassure her that he wouldn't hurt her. The truth was he would if necessary. Not physically, perhaps, but apprehending her brother when the time came would surely wound her.

For her sake, he hoped none of the outlaws held her heart. She would hate Jericho even more if that were true. But why should he care? he demanded as he pushed away the bite of regret. He was here to do a job, and her brother was the starting point.

Catherine might be unaware of Andrew's midnight trip, but Jericho planned to find out where the boy had been, what he'd been doing out so late and with whom.

The clop of hooves drew his attention, and Davis Lee rode into view. Good. Jericho needed someone to take his attention off Catherine and put it back where it belonged. Maybe his cousin had some news from those nuns in New York.

Davis Lee dismounted and walked over to Catherine, taking off his hat. "Morning, Miz Donnelly."

"Hello, Sheriff."

"Please call me Davis Lee."

"All right. Please call me Catherine."

Jericho heard a smile in her voice.

Davis Lee grinned like a possum eating a yellow jacket. "How's my ornery cousin this morning?"

She shaded her eyes, moving closer to him. "He tore his stitches last night but I think he's okay today."

"If you're tending him, I'm sure he's right as rain."

Jericho rolled his eyes.

She shook her head, wringing out a shirt that looked about Andrew's size. "I'm no doctor, Davis Lee. I just know a few things."

"Things that probably saved Jericho's life. Is there anything I can bring you or help you with?" He slid his hat back on and circled the kettle. "Let me stoke up this fire."

He knelt and poked a stick into the burning wood, just as she'd done moments ago.

It didn't surprise Jericho that his cousin was paying so much attention to Catherine. The woman was pretty; even Jericho would admit that. What he didn't like was the burning in his gut every time Catherine smiled at Davis Lee.

"Thank you." She hesitated, then asked, "I wonder if you might help me with your cousin?"

"You're not wanting me to take him off your hands, are you?"

She laughed and Jericho's lip curled. Ha ha.

"I need to wash the sheets on his bed, but I don't think I can get him up by myself."

"I'm more than happy to oblige."

The two of them started for the house. Jericho thought it would serve Catherine right if he threw the sheets off and greeted her in the altogether. She probably wouldn't be so friendly to Davis Lee then.

A second later his cousin stepped into the room, with Catherine close behind him. She moved to Jericho's right, laying a cool hand on his brow. She smelled of lye soap and fresh air.

"Good. No fever."

Except in his blood, Jericho thought wryly. Good thing she couldn't gauge that.

"How does your leg feel, Lieutenant? Do the stitches seem to be holding?"

So she was back to calling him by his rank, while she addressed his cousin familiarly. "Yes."

"I thought I'd wash your sheets," she said.

He kept his surliness to himself. She had undoubtedly saved his life. "Okay." He sat up, biting back a grunt of pain. "Where would you like me?"

Her gaze flew to his and for a brief instant he read desire there. Pure, naked desire. He was completely flummoxed. Then it was gone, her blue eyes cool and clear. He had misread the emotion. Hadn't he?

"If you have the strength, you can sit in this chair by the window. If not, we can move you to Andrew's bed."

"The chair will be fine."

He thought it odd that she'd asked for Davis Lee's help to get him up. She had managed fine last night, and Jericho was a little stronger today. In fact, he probably could've managed on his own, balancing on his good leg while making his way to the chair she pushed against the wall next to the window. He braced his uninjured hand on the bed and levered himself to his feet. The sheet fell away, and out of the corner of his eye he saw Catherine look elsewhere.

At least his drawers and bandages were clean.

Davis Lee moved to his left and braced a shoulder under Jericho's good arm. "You steady?"

"I think so."

His cousin helped him to the chair, while Catherine stripped the sheets from the bed. The large spot of dried blood on the cloth in her hand reminded Jericho of all that had passed between them. She kept her gaze carefully averted from his bare chest, his near nakedness. And that's when he understood why she had asked for Davis Lee's help.

She didn't want to be alone with Jericho. After this morning, when she'd seen that he was aroused again, she probably didn't want to touch him, either.

She spread clean sheets on the bed, then folded a light quilt at its foot. "That should feel much better."

"Thank you, ma'am."

She looked at him then, her blue eyes cool and impersonal once more, reestablishing a distance Jericho should've maintained all along. An emotion he couldn't name flashed across her face, then disappeared.

She tore her gaze away, smiling at his cousin. "Davis Lee, could you help—"

"I can do it," Jericho said through clenched teeth. Planting his good leg solidly on the floor, he used the chair to help himself stand.

Davis Lee watched expectantly and Catherine's hands automatically went out as if to catch him.

Jericho hobbled the few steps to the bed, his thigh screaming with the effort. Lowering himself onto the clean linens, he let out a deep breath.

"Wonderful, Lieutenant!" Catherine sounded pleased. "But don't overdo it."

He figured he might overdo just about anything if she asked him to. "No danger of that," he said hoarsely.

"Can I get you anything? A drink of water maybe?"

He wanted more whiskey, to blot her blue eyes right out of his mind. "No thanks."

Davis Lee scooped up the soiled sheets from the floor. "I'll carry these out for you."

She followed him to the door, glancing back at Jericho. He gave her a flat stare. There was nothing between them and there wouldn't be. He'd gone soft in the head because of his injury, but he had hold of his senses now.

She searched his face, opening her mouth as if she wanted to say something. Then she shook her head and walked out. "I appreciate all your help, Davis Lee."

Jericho heard them step outside, saw them walk past the porch toward the kettle. A warm breeze moved over his chest and legs, calling to mind the soft caress of her hands on him earlier today.

His cousin dumped the linens in her basket next to the kettle and held her gaze much longer than necessary. "It's already warming up today, isn't it?"

"Yes," she murmured, reaching into the basket for one of her shirtwaists.

"How are you settling in?"

"Fine, thank you."

"Do you like Whirlwind?"

"Yes, very much." Her fingers pleated and unpleated the bodice in her hands. She kept some distance between herself and Davis Lee, but she didn't run away.

"I'm glad to hear it, though you haven't seen much of our entertainments yet. We always have a big to-do on the Fourth of July."

"I look forward to it."

"Likewise." Davis Lee smiled, hooking a thumb toward the house. "If it's all right, I'll go back in and visit with Jericho for a bit."

"Of course." As he returned to the house, she called in a lilting voice, "Don't you tire out my patient."

His cousin made some stupid retort and Jericho's good hand curled against his thigh.

The front door opened and closed; Davis Lee stepped into the room as he rapped on the jamb with his knuckles. "You awake?"

Jericho stared flatly at him, lowering his voice so Catherine couldn't hear through the open window. "Why are you sniffing around her?"

Davis Lee scrutinized him for a moment, then leaned

against the door, crossing his arms. "Maybe I'm trying to find out if she has a man."

"Is that what you're doing?"

"No." Davis Lee grinned.

The brief spate of relief Jericho had felt, over the possibility that Davis Lee wasn't interested in Catherine, vanished. An unfamiliar heat tightened his chest.

His cousin moved into the room, sobering. "Do you really think she knows where the McDougals are?"

"I'd say the odds are even."

Davis Lee shrugged. "She seems too sweet to be tangled up with those bastards."

"I'm sure I don't need to remind you what happened the last time you were blinded by a girl's sweetness."

Davis Lee's eyes turned hard. "Catherine has nothing in common with Betsy."

"That we know about."

The sheriff stared out the window as Catherine hung clothes on a line she'd strung from the house to a tall post near the kettle. "Yeah, that we know about. I'm not blind. I like her, that's all."

Jericho regretted throwing the past in Davis Lee's face. His cousin had learned his lesson after falling for a con artist, a woman who'd stolen money from half the citizens of Rock River, where Davis Lee had been sheriff before.

The other man eased down on the windowsill, his back to the woman outside. "I don't think she knows anything about those outlaws."

Jericho looked past Davis Lee's shoulder, to where Catherine industriously scrubbed clothes. "She might."

"Until we know for sure, I don't see why I can't enjoy her company."

Because I can't, Jericho thought savagely, before remind-

ing himself that he had no claim on Catherine and didn't plan
to stake one.

"I didn't come here to give an account of my social life,
anyway." His cousin moved from the window to the chair in
the corner. "I came to tell you that the McDougals may be hiding real close."

"What happened?" He braced his left hand on his good
knee, cursing his useless right arm.

"Remember that Haskell's General Store was burglarized
yesterday?"

At Jericho's nod, Davis Lee said, "The only things taken
were food. Tins of sardines, cans of peaches and cherries.
Some salt pork and a basket of eggs."

"Enough for a gang of four?"

"Yep." Davis Lee nodded. "I've already searched high and
low in town in case they were holed up somewhere unbe-
knownst to anyone. Or in case someone decided to shelter
them. I even checked under the schoolhouse. Kids hide there
sometimes. All I found was evidence that a skunk or a possum has been digging around."

"Good idea to search Whirlwind. Hays and I weren't that
far from here when we were ambushed. Maybe the gang circled back this way for food and supplies."

"They probably think we wouldn't look for them in a place
they'd just left," Davis Lee said.

Jericho nodded. "Have you heard any news from those
nuns in New York City?"

"Not yet."

The sound of galloping hooves had both men turning toward the open window. A stocky, red-haired man reined up
his spotted mare in front of Catherine and slid out of the
saddle.

"It's Jed Doyle," Davis Lee murmured.

The man jerked off his hat and gave her a half bow. "Miz, I'm the gunsmith in Whirlwind. I heard Sheriff Holt was out here."

"Yes. He's inside."

"Jed, what's happened?" Davis Lee called out the window.

Catherine glanced at Davis Lee, then back at the man fingering the brim of his hat. He stared uncertainly at her.

"Go on inside," she urged, her questioning gaze flicking to Jericho.

He wondered if the McDougals had struck again. Did she suspect the same thing? As her gaze followed the man to the house, worry furrowed her brow. Jericho wondered if it was because he had another visitor who might tire him out. Or something else entirely.

The man hovered in the bedroom doorway. "Pardon me, Sheriff. I wouldn't have come except it's important."

"That's all right. Jed Doyle, this is my cousin, Jericho Blue."

"How'do." Jed bobbed his head, his fingers crimping the edge of his hat. "I rode over from Abilene this morning, so I was late opening up my shop, but when I did I noticed some rifle and shotgun cartridges were missing."

Davis Lee stiffened. "How many?"

"Two hundred. I had them in some old military cartridge boxes."

"Was the store broken into or did someone perhaps steal the ammunition while you were open yesterday?"

"The glass in the door was broken."

"Okay." Davis Lee clapped the man on the shoulder. "I want to come over and look at your place."

Jed nodded, his gaze shifting to Jericho. "You're one of the Rangers who was shot in that ambush, aren't you?"

"Yes."

"I hope you're healing up. I was sorry to hear about your friend."

"Thank you."

The gunsmith paused. "It's occurred to me that someone from the McDougal gang might've stolen those cartridges."

"Could be, but let's not speculate." Davis Lee patted Jed on the back. "I'll be along directly. Just need to finish up here."

"Very good then." The man bobbed his head at Jericho again and left.

Jericho wondered once again if Catherine knew anything about the outlaws' latest movements. "Looks like you're right about the McDougals picking up a few things for their hideout."

"I think I'll give the town another once-over after I've had a look at Jed's place."

"Good idea. I wish I could go with you."

"I'll let you know what I find out."

Jericho nodded, frustrated that he had no more energy than a baby bird.

Catherine appeared in the doorway. "Is everything all right? Mr. Doyle seemed upset."

"Someone broke into his shop last night and took some things," Davis Lee said.

Jericho watched her face carefully to see if suspicion or fear that her brother might be the culprit crossed it, but she only looked concerned. "I hope Mr. Doyle's things can be recovered."

They probably would be—from someone's back, Jericho thought darkly.

"I brought you something to read." She handed him a book worn on the spine and edges. "I thought you might want some diversion."

He certainly needed to focus his mind somewhere besides her sweet self. He nodded, glancing at the book, entitled *Twenty Thousand Leagues Under the Sea.* "Thank you."

His cousin said goodbye, giving Jericho a silent glance to let him know he'd be back with information when he had some.

Catherine started out, as well, then paused in the doorway. "I'll be outside awhile longer, then I'll bring you some lunch. Please let me know if you need anything."

"Okay."

She smiled and left.

She was taking real good care of him. Too good. Maybe she didn't know about Haskell's store being burglarized, and so didn't suspect her brother. But did she wonder if Andrew had anything to do with the break-in at the gunsmith's? Jericho sure as hell did. The kid's absence last night was too much of a coincidence, and Jericho didn't believe in coincidences.

He'd seen nothing on Catherine's face to indicate that she feared the thief might be her brother. In fact, she'd given no indication today that she even suspected he had sneaked out of the house last night. Was it possible she really didn't know?

She walked out with Davis Lee to his horse, her hands clasped behind her back as she looked up at him.

"Be careful until we know where those McDougals are," he said, mounting and tipping his hat to her. "Let me know if you need anything at all. My office is just a holler away."

"Thank you." She stepped back when he turned his buckskin toward town.

As Davis Lee rode off, she went back to her washing. Jericho watched her, fighting the hot rush of blood in his veins. He didn't like Davis Lee showing an interest in her, but it was none of his concern. No other woman had ever distracted him from his job. Catherine wasn't going to be the first.

After a lunch of beans and bread, Jericho slept off and on for the next couple of hours, waking midafternoon feeling sore and out of sorts. He knew it was because of the interest Davis Lee had shown in Catherine. Or rather, because she hadn't acted one bit skittish with his cousin.

Jericho rubbed a hand over his face, pushing away thoughts of her.

A movement caught his eye and he looked up in time to see Andrew pad softly past the bedroom's half-open door on the way to his own room.

Still feeling weak, Jericho pushed himself up with his elbow and clutched the bedside table for balance. He stood, sweat breaking out across his back as pain jabbed into him. His injured hand hung uselessly at his side. He limped to the door and braced one shoulder against the frame, hoping he looked more in control than he felt.

Andrew's door opened and he stepped out, rolling up the sleeves of a dingy white work shirt. He saw Jericho and froze. "Are you supposed to be out of bed?"

"Gotta do it sometime."

The kid chewed the inside of his cheek, then started past Jericho.

"You were right to protect your sister last night."

The boy paused at the kitchen table, glancing over his shoulder. Jericho kept his tone casual and easy, talking to Andrew as he had dozens of suspects before. "I guess you're the only protector she has. Unless she's got a beau."

"She doesn't." Andrew took a step toward him. "Well, the sheriff is kinda sweet on her."

Jericho clenched his fist. "You sure did handle that gun well. Who taught you to do that?"

Wariness darkened the kid's blue eyes and drew his stocky body tight. "I just practice."

"I don't imagine that's what you were doing last night, when you were out after midnight."

The boy's gaze shot past Jericho to the front door. "Did you say something to my sister?"

"What were you doing last night, anyway?"

Andrew angled his chin stubbornly, but Jericho saw fear in his face. "I don't have to tell you."

"Nope." He deliberately lowered his voice, hoping to intimidate the boy into revealing something. "You don't."

Andrew shifted from one foot to the other, his gaze fixed somewhere behind Jericho's head. "I was with Creed Carter and Miguel Santos."

"Friends of yours?"

"Yes. From school. We were out behind Creed's pa's saloon."

"Doing what?"

Again defiance blazed in his eyes, and also distrust. "Smoking," he said grudgingly.

Jericho didn't believe him for a minute. "Funny, I didn't smell any smoke on you last night. And if your sister had, she probably would've said something."

Andrew glowered at him. "You're not gonna tell her, are you? About me being out?"

"That's up to you." Jericho sank against the doorframe, cursing the sweat that trickled down his spine. His legs were ready to fold; he hoped the kid couldn't tell.

"Really?"

Jericho shrugged. "You're old enough to know what's right, what you oughta do."

Andrew stared hard at him. "Thanks for not saying anything."

Jericho gave a curt nod.

Andrew went outside, his voice carrying as he told Catherine he was going to clean the stalls and pump some fresh water for their horse and Jericho's. Jericho pushed away from the door and hobbled back to bed, easing himself onto the mattress with a groan.

The apprehension on the kid's face said he figured Jericho was on to him, but he didn't know how much he knew. Jericho intended to keep the kid guessing. And find out whatever he could while he was laid up.

A couple of hours later, as the sun began to set, Catherine asked Jericho if he thought he could eat dinner with them at the table. He accepted. Surely he could manage to sit in a chair for half an hour without keeling over.

As they ate, Andrew kept his gaze fixed on his plate or on Catherine. Jericho could tell by the sideways looks the boy gave his sister that he hadn't confessed his absence yet.

The stew and fresh bread were delicious, but Jericho felt a palpable tension in the room. Catherine talked to her brother about his schoolwork, in particular his sums. But she spoke to Jericho only to ask if he wanted more food.

The fact was the lady had probably had all of him she wanted. Which was just as well. He ripped a piece of bread savagely in half, trying to cool the ire in his blood, and narrowed his attention on the Donnellys. They didn't exchange looks that hinted at secrets. No silent messages passed between them. Jericho could tell by the way Andrew grew quieter and quieter that the boy was nervous.

At his sister's request, he went out to the spring house to get more buttermilk. Silence enveloped the room, so deep that Jericho thought he could hear Catherine's heart racing. Their utensils scraped the last of the stew from their bowls. Outside, a quail called.

"The meal was delicious." Even though he told himself not to care, he wanted her to be at ease with him. "Thank you."

"You're welcome." She was polite but didn't meet his eyes or relax her stiff posture.

"That pie sure smells good."

"It's cherry."

Andrew returned, putting a jar of buttermilk in the center of the table before taking his seat. He reached for another helping of stew, ladeling up twice as much as even Jericho would eat.

"Slow down, Andrew," Catherine said. "There's plenty to go around."

He returned half the stew, then sat down and began to spoon it into his mouth.

Having eaten his fill, Jericho picked up his cup of coffee. "The sheriff was out today."

"What did he want?" Andrew fired the question at him so fast that even Catherine gave him an odd look.

"Why would you think he wanted something?" Jericho drawled.

Catherine frowned at Jericho as if she thought he might have a fever. Then she turned to her brother. "Sheriff Holt came to check on Lieutenant Blue."

Andrew met his gaze, trying for defiance, but looking apprehensive.

"He thinks the McDougal gang may be nearby," Catherine said. "We all need to be careful, try not to go anywhere by ourselves."

The boy swallowed, putting his spoon down as if he couldn't eat one more bite.

She glanced at Jericho, holding his gaze for the first time since that morning. "Is it safe for Andrew to go to school?"

"I'm sure the sheriff would've said if he didn't think so. He checked all over town today and didn't find any sign of them. Even looked at the school, I believe."

Andrew was wound so tight Jericho thought he might bounce right out of his chair.

"Did you see the sheriff today, Andrew?" Catherine asked.

"Oh. Yeah." He seemed mighty interested in the table.

Jericho leveled a look at the kid. "Haskell's store was bur- glarized night before last. And last night someone broke into the gunsmith's shop."

Andrew paled considerably.

"Does Davis Lee thinks the gang did both things?" Cather- ine crossed herself. "Why would those horrid men come back here?"

Worry chased across Andrew's freckled features and sat- isfaction curled through Jericho. The boy was hiding some- thing about those outlaws, maybe even the outlaws themselves. Every instinct Jericho had honed over the last thir- teen years told him Andrew knew where they were. "Maybe they have some unfinished business."

"With you, you mean?" she asked.

He shrugged. "Maybe me. Maybe someone else."

"We must be extremely careful then." She gave Andrew a warning look, and Jericho wondered if it meant she knew the boy had been gone last night, or if she were simply trying to make him understand there was a threat.

The kid was now a deathly shade of gray, and he scratched nervously at the table beside his bowl. "Catherine?" he said quietly.

She looked over at him.

"I snuck out last night. That sound the Ranger heard was me."

A sigh of disappointment broke from her. "Why? Where did you go?"

"I was with Creed and Miguel."

His pause told Jericho he'd been right about the boy lying the first time he'd used the alibi. It wouldn't be hard to check his story.

Catherine frowned. "I don't know them."

"Creed's pa owns the saloon and Miguel's uncle runs the telegraph."

She clasped her hands in her lap, visibly searching for control as she asked tightly, "And what were you doing?"

Andrew's gaze shot to Jericho before he said, "We were smoking."

"By the saints!" She stood, her chair scraping across the floor. "I won't have it! I know you don't want to obey me, but in this you will. No more smoking and no more sneaking out. I'll catch you if I have to set a trap outside your window."

His eyes grew large and Jericho chewed on the inside of his cheek.

"You can't keep doing this. Those outlaws could be close and you could be in danger." Frustration edged her voice for the first time since Jericho had met her. "It does no good to ask you or bribe you or threaten you—go on to bed."

"But—"

"Now. There will be no pie for you tonight."

Andrew shoved his chair back and rose, his chin quivering. "I did the right thing by telling you."

"Yes, you did, but you are still being punished. What if you were to come across those awful men?"

"I don't think they'd hurt me," he mumbled.

"I think they would," she retorted, before Jericho could ask why not.

Her face stern, she pointed to his room. "Go on now."

He stayed put, defiance flashing in his eyes. For a long moment Jericho wondered if the boy would obey her.

"Now, Andrew."

He finally stomped around her and went to his bedroom, slamming the door.

"I'll be checking on you every ten minutes, young man," she called after him, then added under her breath, "And I think I'll nail your window shut."

She walked to the cupboard and knelt to open a lower door, pulling out a hammer and a tin can of nails.

"Maybe you oughta hold up on that," Jericho suggested gently.

She threw him a look that clearly told him to mind his own business.

He raised a hand in mock surrender. "I'm just sayin' you should give the boy a chance to do right on his own. Don't cage him in the room unless you have to."

"I don't want him to get hurt. He won't do what I ask or even what's prudent."

"It's his age. And you did say the pair of you haven't known each other that long."

She considered her brother's closed door. "I suppose he did confess on his own."

Jericho nodded, keeping to himself that he figured Andrew had only done so to keep Jericho from squealing.

She shook her head. "Very well. I can give him another chance."

After returning the hammer and nails to the cupboard she moved to the table to clear Jericho's dishes. "That was considerate of you. Do you know much about children?"

"Not really."

She tucked a stray lock of hair behind her ear, then bent over the pie, knife in hand. "I can't believe I didn't know he was gone. I've been checking on him every night since I learned he was sneaking out. How could you hear him and I couldn't?"

"In all fairness, you were probably exhausted from nursing me."

"If I'm so easy to get past, he'll never obey me."

"Maybe he will in time."

"I think you're being kind." She set a piece of pie down in front of him and stepped over to get the coffeepot from the stove.

He took a bite of the warm cherries and flaky crust, then groaned in pleasure. "That is damn good."

She looked startled. "Thank you."

"Honey, if you threatened to make *me* go without this pie, I'd do whatever you wanted, wherever you wanted."

She was only inches from him and froze in the act of pouring his coffee. Fragrant steam curled between them as she stared at him. Her deep blue eyes were filled with uncertainty.

His gaze traced the delicate line of her jaw, the wisps of raven hair that tickled her neck. Lingered on her soft lower lip. His body grew tight as desire clawed through him. Did she feel even one bit of what he felt?

Her gaze stayed fixed on his face. He wanted to reach up and touch her petal-smooth skin, release her hair from the chignon she'd worn all day. Kiss her.

She was the one who broke the invisible link between them, barely managing to right the coffeepot before the hot liquid spilled over the top of his cup. The same fear he'd seen last night in her eyes skittered across her face.

Now she would cut and run. He cursed his stupid mouth.

"I guess I've found your weakness then, Lieutenant. Now I just have to find Andrew's." She laughed lightly, but he saw her swallow hard, as if the words were choked out of her.

A deep blush stained her neck as she moved back to the stove. He finished his pie slowly, wishing he hadn't brought that wariness back into her eyes. The sight ripped something deep inside him.

He pushed the feeling away, reminding himself that he didn't want her fear; he wanted her secrets. And he would do whatever was necessary, use whoever he had to, in order to get them.

Chapter Six

For the next five days, Catherine told herself she was going to forget what had passed between her and Jericho in the kitchen. He had complimented her, that was all. It wasn't his words about her pie that had her replaying the incident over in her mind. It was how he'd said them, his voice low and raspy the way it had been when he'd first awoke. And the way he had looked at her—as if he wanted to gobble her up.

Heat streaked through her. Before, just the thought of a man's touch would knot her up for days, and sometimes set off a bad dream. But not with him. She didn't understand it.

Jericho had gained strength during the last week and was now able to sit for longer periods of time. He ate at the table with her and Andrew. When Riley and Davis Lee stopped by, they all sat on the porch. Dr. Butler had been out three times, pleased with the healing of his patient's thigh and wrist. He ordered plenty of rest and food, and cautioned that the wound in Jericho's thigh was not completely closed up.

Though Jericho moved slowly and leaned heavily on the crutch Davis Lee had brought a few days ago, his visits to the outhouse were accomplished alone. He had waved off Catherine's attempts to help him dress, even though it took him ten minutes just to get into his trousers. And half that time to get into his tall boots, extravagant compared to the ready-made work boots she'd seen on most men here.

She was skittish around him when she brought his meals or his basin of water each morning, and especially when she changed his dressing, but he didn't touch her. He didn't speak about what had happened—or not happened—but he didn't need to. In the heat of his silver gaze, she could still feel the wash of his breath on her lips, see the savage desire he'd felt.

She wondered what might have happened that night if she hadn't frozen like a, well, a virgin. Which she was. That moment, the space of a few heartbeats, had started something unspooling inside her. She was restless, curious. All about him.

He had asked about her having a beau, and the memory brought a wry smile. If he only knew how she avoided men. When she could, anyway.

The question had churned up memories of another patient. One who had become infatuated with her, obsessed after he left the hospital. Ty Banding had followed her from the hospital one night and attacked her in an alley. She hadn't run at first because she knew the man and thought he'd just happened upon her. But she'd been wrong.

Jericho didn't frighten her in exactly that way. She sensed he wouldn't hurt her and yet he breached defenses no man ever had. She didn't know what to make of him half the time. He put distance between them, then looked at her with the hunger of a man who'd starved his whole life.

That unsettled her, but it also sent excitement curling through her.

She tried to ignore the sensation, but when he met her on the porch on Thursday afternoon, she felt unsteady and a trifle breathless, much to her dismay.

Despite the heat, Jericho had asked if they could work on his wrist outside, and Catherine agreed. As he carefully made his way from the house to the porch and the chair she had braced against the wall, she resisted the urge to support him. Touch him.

Instead, she checked to make sure the kerchief holding back her hair was secure. "Even though Dr. Butler said it was all right to begin on your wrist, we could wait another day."

"No, I'm ready." Impatience scored his words.

The occasional breeze and the shade provided by the porch would keep them from getting overheated. Despite the crutch and the cautious way Jericho lowered himself into the chair, he seemed dangerous to her, powerfully compelling in a way that made her nervously finger the buttons at the throat of her bodice. With Andrew in school each day, Catherine had become increasingly aware of being alone with Jericho. She had chosen now as their time to work because her brother would soon be home.

The whiskers that had shadowed Jericho's jaw when he first arrived were now grown into a dark beard, and he scrubbed his face. "I hope this treatment works on my hand, because I'm definitely going to want to shave pretty soon and I can't do it with my left."

She had shaved dozens of men in the hospital. He would be no different, she told herself, managing to keep her voice level as she offered, "I can shave you if you want."

His clear gray gaze measured her, drawing her nerves tight. He looked as if he wanted to say yes. "Maybe. Sometime."

"Whenever you like." She breathed a sigh of relief, dragging a small table from the far edge of the porch.

Thinking of him as only a patient was hard enough. She didn't want to know the feel of his solid jaw or the high slant of his cheekbones.

Pulling another straight-back chair from the kitchen, she turned it to face his and sat, her skirts brushing his leg. A black shirt molded his deep chest and broad shoulders. He'd left the four buttons undone, and Catherine swallowed at the sight of crisp black hair in the deep V there, the supple bronze of his chest. His long, denim-clad legs barely fit beneath the table. His boots were absent and she smiled at the sight of his bare feet.

Her gaze wandered to his lap. She remembered very well what had happened when she'd stitched his leg, and her stomach curled a little.

Jericho pointed to the set of checkers she had removed from the table and placed against the wall. "Do you play?"

"I haven't in a while." She gently lifted his injured arm and laid it on the table. "You know not to expect this treatment to work immediately?"

"Yeah, I know." His voice was gruff as he pushed his sleeve up to his elbow. "When do you think I might see some progress?"

"Let me look at it first." She unwrapped the bandage that covered his forearm, and checked the bullet wound. The nickel-size hole in his wrist was healing nicely. "It looks good. I don't think you'll need a bandage here anymore. Can you make a fist?"

He tried but could only curl his fingers halfway toward his palm.

"It's all right," she said. "We have to start somewhere."

She smiled, hoping to encourage him, but his silver eyes just stared at her darkly.

"How long?" he asked.

"Everyone is different."

"But you do think I'll be able to use it?"

"I can't say for sure, but yes, I do think so. Can you bend your wrist at all?"

He tried. "No."

She slid her fingers gently down the inside of his arm to the wound. "Does that hurt?"

"It's tender right on my wrist bone, but nowhere else."

"Good." Curling her fist into his palm, she moved her thumb around the pad of his hand. "How about that?"

"Kinda tickles." The way his voice dropped sent excitement shimmering across her nerves.

She glanced up at him. "But it's not sore?"

"Not when *you* touch it."

She owed him the best care she could give, but when he said things like that, she had no idea how to respond. She felt giddy, which she had never felt with a man. But also wary. Always wary, she thought with a sigh.

She reached into her apron pocket for the bottle of liniment she had gotten from Dr. Butler. "I'm going to rub this into your wound, then into your arm and hand. Another patient told me this made him feel relaxed. I want you to tell me how it feels. If I hurt you, tell me right away."

He nodded, his jaw tight, his eyes cool and distant.

"Promise?"

His gaze flicked to hers. "Promise."

His silver eyes held hers in a way that sent warmth streaming through her. She'd never noticed that black rim around the outer part of his silver irises. Or how thick and black his eyelashes were. Or—

"You gonna put that stuff on me?"

"Yes." Mercy, what had she been thinking? She poured a generous amount of ointment into her palm, then rubbed her hands together. Gently she took his forearm between her slick hands and started at his elbow, using her thumbs to gently massage her way to his wrist.

His last two fingers jerked in reflex and she paused. "Are you all right? I'm not hurting you?"

"Yes. No."

She lifted her hands immediately.

He gave her a crooked grin. "One question at a time. Yes, I'm fine. No, you're not hurting me."

"Okay." She smiled and resumed her task.

She reached his wrist and lightened her touch, not pressing on the flesh or the muscle, just rubbing liniment lightly over the wound. She did the same to the heel of his palm, then increased the pressure when she reached the middle of his hand. She massaged the base of each finger, then started back up his arm.

He sniffed the air. "What's in that stuff?"

"Eucalyptus, cloves, camphor, wintergreen. The cloves help cut the sharpness of the eucalyptus and camphor. Is it too sweet smelling?"

"No." He gave a small laugh. "But by the time we're done, I'll be as soft as you."

That caused a little hitch in her breathing, but she kept working. She couldn't look at him. If she did, she might melt right in her chair. This time when she touched his wrist bone he drew in a sharp breath.

She stopped. "Sorry."

"It's all right." He nodded for her to continue.

She moved her thumbs farther up his arm. "How about here? Does this hurt?"

"No."

She stroked up to his elbow, then back down again. Cupping his fist, she tried to use her thumb to massage the base of his fingers and heel of his palm, but his hand was too broad.

She grasped it in her left hand and used her right one to massage. "Is this hurting you?"

"No," he said hoarsely.

"Are you sure? You'd tell me? There's no shame in it."

"I'd tell you," he said tightly.

She rubbed a few seconds more, until his hand was warm and relaxed in hers. "Now I'm going to try and fold your fingers into your palm. Don't be discouraged if we're not able to go farther than you did before, all right?"

His lips flattened and he nodded.

"We won't try to bend your wrist today. I don't want to do too much." The tiny hairs on the back of his hand tickled her palm. She folded his fingers inward, but didn't try to push them as far as he had a while ago.

"I can do more," he said.

"Not yet. It's tempting to want to rush, but you'll only hurt yourself if you do."

His gaze slid over her entire body, lingered at her breasts before shifting toward town.

Bless the saints! "We must go slow."

"All right."

She focused on his hand. He tensed up and she feared she may have ruined the progress they had made. She massaged until he relaxed again, then she curled his fingers inward once more and straightened them.

"I've been wondering about something, Lieutenant." She looked up to see his gaze move from her lips to her eyes.

"Uh-huh."

She wished he wouldn't look at her like that. "Did you convince Andrew to confess the other night? When he sneaked out?"

"Why do you ask?"

"Because even though he's slipped out before, he's never told me about it."

"It's good he had a change of heart then."

She searched Jericho's face, but could read nothing on his craggy features. *Had* he spoken to her brother, gotten Andrew to tell her where he'd been? Since that night, her brother hadn't slipped out again. Yet.

"He made the noise you heard that night, didn't he? The night we—I mean you—"

"I think so." Jericho cleared his throat. "I'm glad the boy has stayed around here. Davis Lee said there was another break-in at Haskell's two nights ago."

"Yes, he told me yesterday when he stopped by." Catherine felt tension fill the air between them.

"You sweet on him?"

She blinked, wondering at the dark flush on his neck. "I—I don't know."

Was she sweet on Davis Lee? Catherine liked the sheriff very much, but he didn't tease some deep secret inside her, didn't cause her palms to dampen with just a glance the way Jericho did.

That was due to fear, she told herself. What she felt for Davis Lee was calm and safe. That was better. Wasn't it? "I invited your cousins to dinner tomorrow night."

"That was kind," Jericho murmured, his voice curling around her.

She continued to work his hand a few more minutes, then poured more liniment. She massaged his fingers once more, then in between each one. Her hands slid over his hot flesh. Calluses roughened the skin of his index finger and the inside of his thumb. His hand was huge against hers, bronzed and weathered against the paleness of her skin.

He sat motionless, but Catherine felt a rigidity in his body, a leashed control.

He said in a raspy voice, "I'm wondering if we should try this on my leg."

Shocked, she darted a glance at him and saw laughter in

his eyes. He was teasing her. "I'm sure Dr. Butler would be happy to oblige you," she said smartly.

He chuckled.

Smiling, she slipped her fingers down to the heel of his hand once more, then over the wound, gently touching but not pressing. She had to lean forward as she moved up his forearm, her thumbs making small circles on the hard sinew.

She reached his elbow and her hands lingered. Situated as she was, her breasts rested perilously close to his hand. His heat pulsed around her, teasing her with the scents of liniment and male and soap. She was finished; she should release him.

Her hair caught on something and she reached up to gather it behind her shoulder.

"No. Wait."

His voice rasped and her gaze froze on his face. She had never heard that tone before, certainly not from a man.

His rapt attention had her heart skipping a beat, and she realized his hand was in her hair. The words would barely pass through her tight throat as she asked. "Your fingers aren't caught, are they?"

He shook his head, his gaze locked on her hair. His injured hand delved into the dark mass. With his other hand, he gently trailed strands between his fingers and over his palm. Her breath lodged painfully beneath her ribs.

"So black and silky. Like a soft dark night."

She couldn't look away.

He tried to close his fingers on her hair.

Automatically she covered his hand with hers, concerned that he might damage his wrist. "Don't—"

He released her hair, lifting his injured hand to brush her cheek with one knuckle.

"—hurt yourself," she whispered, completely aflutter. Her

hand fell from his. She thought about jumping up, but couldn't move.

He dragged his knuckle lightly down her jaw, coming close to her lips, making them tingle in anticipation. An unfamiliar warmth stole through her. She wanted what?

She wanted to kiss him.

The shock of that held her immobile for a moment. She searched his eyes, looking for the mean lust she'd seen in another man. It wasn't there.

All she had to do was slightly turn her head and she could brush her lips against Jericho's knuckle. It would be easy. He nudged her chin, so gently she thought she might have moved it herself. His hand smelled of eucalyptus underlined with the faint sweetness of cloves. She needed only to lean forward to feel his lips on hers. Desire flared in his eyes, fierce and frankly sensual. Realization jolted her. If she kissed him, he would take control and it would not be a gentle kiss. It would rock her, consume her.

She couldn't do it.

In that instant he recognized her decision. A muscle flexed in his jaw and he lowered his hand.

Abruptly she rose, barely catching the bottle of liniment as it tumbled from the table. She grabbed for it and pushed in the cork with a trembling hand.

He levered himself out of the chair, towering over her, his shadow merging with hers. "Are we going to do this again?"

Her gaze flew to his mouth.

"I meant work on my hand," he said through gritted teeth.

"Yes, of course." Heat rose in her cheeks. She cleared her throat, shoving away the languorous sensation flowing through her.

"If you'd rather I do it myself—"

"Absolutely not." She was his nurse, for goodness' sake. She would do what she had been trained to do.

"I think it's going to help." Using his crutch, he limped to the steps and felt his way down the first one.

"Where are you going?" Alarm sharpened her voice.

"For some air. The walls are starting to close in on me."

He meant her. He didn't want to be around *her.* "Be careful of your leg."

"I can't very well run now, can I?"

Despite his light tone, she felt a coolness pass between them. Catherine nodded and watched him struggle down the last step. Once at the bottom, he reset the crutch under his arm and hobbled toward the corner of the house. Disappointment stabbed through her at his aloofness. *At her hesitation.*

She had nearly kissed him. She thought from the flare in his eyes he had wanted her to. He had waited, anticipation arcing between them, yet when she'd backed away, he hadn't tried to hurt her with words or his fist, as Ty Banding had. Hadn't tried to change her mind at all.

Jericho's consideration reached a place deep inside her, and she touched her lips in regret when he'd disappeared. A strange sense of loss filled her. She'd made a mistake. One she would never forget.

That just beat all to hell. She had nearly kissed him.

Jericho couldn't have been more stunned if she'd up and shucked off her dress. He was painfully hard and twice as touchy as a trigger. There was no way he could go back in that house right now, to be surrounded by her scent, her softness, the reminder of what had nearly happened. The barn was the place for him. Desire clawed deep. He had only so much restraint. And energy, he reminded himself wryly. Still weak, he tired easily, but that didn't stop his brain from working double-time.

His mind should be working on how to get fit enough to re-sume his chase of the McDougals, not his pretty nurse. Though eager to get away, he tempered his pace as he limped behind the house to the barn. The dry grass, showing red dirt in spots, felt prickly between his toes. He couldn't have pulled on his boots to save his life, so he'd gone barefoot. A pebble gouged the sole of his foot and he winced. Pausing, he took note of the house, which he'd mostly seen from the inside until now.

Built of planked pine with real windows, it was small, but someone had obviously put some quality into it. There was a stoop off the back, and Jericho vaguely recalled a narrow hallway leading to the front room. Herbs and vegetables sprouted in a small garden, fenced on the opposite side of the house. The spring house sat several yards away.

The woman had him spinning like a wild bronc. His thigh ached, but not as much as his groin. It had been all he could do not to close the distance between them. A fraction of an inch and he would've tasted her. Sitting motionless while she contemplated his mouth, he'd been wound tighter than an eight-day clock.

A curse hissed out. He wanted to shuck her out of her clothes and put his hands on her, in her. Touch her. Taste her. What he needed to do was remember that she was possibly involved with the McDougal gang.

He resisted the urge to go right back and finish what she'd started. No way in hell would he make a move that might put the fear back in her eyes. He didn't want her scared of him the way she—

What was he thinking? He wasn't making a move, period.

He stepped into the dim cool shadows of the barn, trying to shrug off the memory of that dreaminess he'd seen in her eyes just before she'd bolted. Trying to forget the smooth glide of her hands on his arm was like spitting into a high wind. As soon as he got what he wanted from Andrew he would leave with the boy in custody. She wouldn't be thinking about kissing him then.

The soft nicker of a horse drew Jericho's attention, and he glanced at the two stalls in the rear of the small barn. Catherine's sorrel gelding watched him with dark, wary eyes. In the next stall was Cinco, his Appaloosa mare.

Catherine Donnelly was a trail he didn't want to go down. Which would be easy to remember if he could get his mind off how she had nearly set him off with just a touch of her lips.

His gaze resting on her horse, Jericho decided to have a look at the gelding. Even though Davis Lee had confirmed that Moe had a chipped shoe on his right back hoof, Jericho needed to see for himself.

He lifted the mare's foot. Sure enough, Moe's shoe made the exact print Jericho had tracked to this house. His gaze swept the hay-strewn dirt floor and two fresh hay bales in the front corner. Something in his gut told him he should take a better look around the barn.

Moe's saddle and blanket were draped over the slatted wall of his stall. Jericho's own saddle and blanket rested on the wall of Cinco's stall. Low feed troughs were built into the front corners of each enclosure. Two bridles hung on nails on the barn's back wall. The curry comb and brush sat neatly on top of one of the corner posts. There was nothing here to indicate outlaws or secrets.

In the middle of the barn a tall, heavy-runged ladder reached into the loft. Jericho knew he wouldn't be able to climb up there yet. Near the door, a pitchfork, hoe and shovel clustered together in the corner behind the hay bales and a bucket.

His horse nickered in recognition. "Hey, Cinco." Jericho

limped over and gave her a good rub on the neck. The horse had been named when he bought her from a rancher outside Round Rock. That had been five years ago, when he rode with the men who had chased Sam Bass and his gang.

His right hand, still warm and oiled from Catherine's touch, wasn't much use out here, but he had use of the other. He could at least feed and water the horses. Reaching into the stall, Jericho slapped Cinco on the rump. "C'mon. Move out."

His mare stepped out of the doorless space and Moe did the same. Jericho slapped both horses to prod them on outside. The animals would most likely graze in the grassy area beside the barn.

With the sun already in the west, the building was cool and shaded. Jericho limped over to get the bucket he'd seen earlier. His gaze scanned the corners, looking for something out of place—dirt or straw that may have been disturbed, something that didn't fit. The dusty canvas bag in the corner was empty, as was the bucket he retrieved. He saw no freshly dug holes in the earthen floor, nothing unusual.

Gripping the bucket handle in his good hand, then wrapping it around the crutch, Jericho started out the door. The crutch hit a bump and he wobbled, struggling to keep his balance. Then he glanced downward.

It wasn't a stone or bump in the earth. Whatever he had felt under his crutch was oblong, about an inch and a half long. He squinted in the dim light. What was it? A piece of metal? It wasn't silver, but a dull brown. Using his crutch, he poked at the object until it rolled toward his feet. A rifle cartridge. Unspent.

Well, well. He didn't trust himself to bend over without falling, so he eased down on a bale of hay and picked up the bullet. Yep, definitely a rifle cartridge. The gun in the Donnellys' house was a shotgun, so why was there a rifle cartridge in the barn? Did it match the ones stolen from Jed Doyle's gunsmith shop?

Gritting his teeth against the pull of his wound, Jericho struggled to his feet. He slid the round into the front pocket of his denim trousers. His gut told him Jed would identify this as the same type of ammunition stolen during the burglary.

Jericho didn't know if Catherine was aware of it, but he'd bet money Andrew was. Through Davis Lee, Jericho had already checked the boy's story from a week ago, about sneaking out to be with two school friends. That dog didn't hunt.

Miguel Santos had been ill that day and two days after. It was unlikely Andrew had spent any time at the Santos house or he would've taken sick, too, just as Miguel's uncle had after caring for his nephew.

If this cartridge came from where Jericho suspected, it was another piece that tied the boy to the McDougals. He just had to keep pressure on the kid. And keep himself away from Catherine.

Realigning the crutch under his arm, he started out the door toward the pump just as Andrew came around the corner of the house.

Hitching up his brown homespun trousers, the boy stopped short at the sight of Jericho holding the bucket. "I'm supposed to feed and water the horses."

"Sorry." He handed the bucket to the boy. "I thought I'd try to help out. After everything y'all have done for me, it seemed the least I could do."

Andrew glanced over his shoulder.

Wanting to see the kid's reaction to the cartridge, Jericho casually slipped it out of his pocket. "Looking for your sister?"

"Does she know you're doing this?"

He grinned, fingering the shell. "You won't be taken to task for it."

"If you hurt yourself, she'll be mad." Andrew's gaze homed in on the bullet. His eyes widened in surprise, a reaction he quickly tried to hide.

Jericho rolled the cartridge between his thumb and forefinger. "I'll go easy."

The boy's gaze shifted to the barn. "Uh, if you want, you can get that water and I'll dish up some oats."

Jericho had noticed a feed bin along the wall. Was Andrew volunteering so he could make sure Jericho would find nothing else? "I don't mind doing both if you have some schoolwork to do."

"No. I—I was just going to go to town." The kid's gaze returned to Jericho's hand. "Me and Miguel and Creed were going to play checkers."

Jericho closed his fist on the shell. "Well, run along. I can take care of the horses. I don't mind."

"I'll help." Andrew thrust the bucket at him and practically ran past Jericho into the barn.

A tool—the hoe or shovel?—banged against the wall. Long seconds passed before he saw the boy walk back toward the stalls carrying another bucket, this one full of oats.

Jericho grinned.

The kid returned with an empty bucket and paused in the doorway. "Are you sure you can get the water?"

"Yeah." Jericho adjusted his hold on the bucket so he could slide the cartridge back into his pocket. "So you're meeting Creed and Miguel?"

"Yeah." Andrew dragged his gaze from Jericho's hip and wiped his hands down the front of his trousers. "I better get going."

"See ya later."

The boy muttered something and darted off toward town. Jericho leaned his crutch against the barn wall and started for the pump at the front of the house. Dragging his leg made for a slow trip, but he didn't want to become dependent on the crutch. He hoped the kid was starting to feel the pressure. As Jericho pumped water into the bucket, he glanced toward the front door, still open as Catherine had left it. There was no sign of her. Good. His body had only now cooled down.

Limping back to the horses, he set the bucket near where they grazed on short green grass. While Cinco slurped at the water, Jericho stroked a hand down the gray mare's dappled back. She swished her dark tail and shifted toward him, indicating she wanted more.

The sound of laughter drifted from the direction of the house, and Jericho looked up to see two boys about Andrew's age coming toward him. They were approximately the same height, but one was reed thin and pale, the other dark.

"Hello." The boy with black hair and eyes spoke first. "Are you the Ranger? My uncle Tony says Andrew's sister found you nearly dead."

"That's mostly right, I guess. She's been kind enough to doctor me."

"And you're really a Ranger?" the pale one breathed.

"Yes. And you two are…"

"I'm Creed Carter." The fair-haired boy hooked a thumb toward his friend. "This is Miguel Santos."

"Nice to meet you." Jericho shook their hands, hiding a smile at how serious they turned. "I'm Jericho Blue."

Miguel glanced past the horses and around the yard. "Is Andrew here? His sister said he was."

"Were y'all supposed to meet him here?"

"Nah. We found his lunch pail—"

"He forgot it at school," Miguel finished.

"We figured we'd bring it to him and see if he could go crawdad fishing with us," Creed said.

"He already left. He mentioned something about going to town."

"Okay, thanks," Miguel said, as the boys trotted off. "Nice to meet you, Ranger."

Jericho lifted a hand and waved goodbye. Well, well. If Andrew wasn't meeting his two friends as he'd said, was he meeting someone else? If so, where?

Jericho needed to follow the kid, but with his lame leg, he'd make more noise than a stampede. He cursed. Just a few more days and he'd be able to trail the boy if necessary. In the meantime, he'd take care not to spook him.

He suspected Andrew had gone to meet the McDougals, but it was gut instinct more than anything solid. Right now he couldn't prove it. All he could do was put a subtle pressure on the kid, and he intended to do just that.

Jericho had his chance a few hours later. He was sitting on Catherine's bed, trying to clean his gun left-handed, when she called him to supper. She barely looked at him and even then a deep pink suffused her cheeks. Her embarrassment fired an urge in him to try and erase the tension between them. But he wouldn't.

He hobbled to the table and glanced out to see Andrew at the pump. "I'll be back. Need to wash up first."

"All right." Catherine opened the stove door.

As Andrew dried his face, Jericho carefully made his way down the porch steps. Sweat dampened his neck by the time he stopped beside the kid.

Andrew looked up from the towel. "Hey! How'd you sneak up on me?"

"I wasn't trying to. Just came to wash up." He gave the

pump handle two strong yanks and cupped his hand under the water to splash it on his face.

When Andrew handed him the towel and turned to go, Jericho blotted his face. "Did you win today?"

"Huh?" The kid turned, squinting through the glare of the setting sun.

"At checkers."

"Oh. Yeah." He started into the house.

Jericho said easily, "Don't see how you could've since your friends were out here looking for you."

The boy froze and Jericho limped a step closer. "You weren't with them, were you?"

Guilt shone clearly on his face and then he stuttered, "Yes, I—I was."

"You may not answer to me," Jericho said lightly. "But you do answer to your sister. It will kill her if something happens to you."

"Nothing's gonna happen," Andrew said defiantly. "Are you gonna blab this to her?"

He noted all the color had leached out of the lad's freckled face. If Jericho told Catherine about Andrew's lie, she'd probably nail the boy's window shut as she'd threatened to do. That wouldn't suit Jericho's purposes. But he didn't want the kid to think there was no danger, either.

"Don't go searchin' for trouble, boy. There's no call for you to worry your sister like this."

He looked ashamed for a moment. "I'm fine. I keep trying to tell her I can take care of myself."

"She's concerned about the outlaws. They're around here somewhere."

Andrew stilled. "Has someone seen them?"

"There are signs. Using a little caution would be good. These men are murderers. They wouldn't hesitate to shoot you."

Andrew didn't speak, but Jericho could see his mind working.

The kid hesitated as if considering something, then he shrugged. "I'll be fine."

"Just watch yourself," Jericho warned. *Because I'll sure be watching you.*

He followed Andrew into the house, fingering the cartridge in his pocket. As they sat down to eat, Jericho fully expected Catherine to confront her brother about the lie he'd told today. She had to know about it. She'd been the one to speak first to Andrew's friends when they came to the house.

But she said nothing, not during dinner and not afterward. Why not? Was it because she knew exactly where Andrew had really been?

Chapter Seven

Catherine fretted all night. She had given up hope of ever finding a man whose touch didn't make her freeze up. She thought Jericho might be that man, but instead of finding out, she had run like a scared rabbit. She didn't know what to do about him. Or the exchange she had witnessed between him and Andrew at the pump. She hadn't been able to hear their conversation, but Jericho had looked stern. And it wasn't until Andrew turned for the house that she saw equal parts fear and anger on his face. Something had happened between them. What?

She knew her brother had lied yesterday about being with his friends. Did Jericho know, too? Maybe so, but Andrew wasn't Jericho's responsibility. He was hers. And it was Andrew Catherine was concerned with the next morning as he rushed out of his room, stomping into his shoes and finger-combing his hair.

The day was starting out with pale gray skies and the promise of rain. According to Jericho, it would pass. Whirlwind and these parts didn't get much rain going into summer.

He sat on the porch in the chair he'd used yesterday, only one shoulder and the white bandage on his arm visible.

Catherine had seen him lay his gun on the table, and she wondered what he was doing.

Andrew grabbed his books, bound together with a leather strap, and raced out without his lunch pail. She picked it up from the place next to the pantry where she'd hidden it. Stepping outside, she asked Jericho, "Will you be all right for a few minutes?"

Curving his hand around the revolver, he glanced at her, then at her brother. "Yeah. Sure."

"Andrew," she called.

Her brother turned around, saw the lunch pail she held and trotted back. She met him halfway.

When he tried to take it, she switched the pail to her other hand.

"What are you doing?"

"I want to talk to you." She started toward town, her skirts swishing against grass that was a bright spring green. The prairie spread around them, mostly flat and dotted with the occasional mesquite tree or scrub oak. Patches of wildflowers flung color across the pasture as if splashed there by a paintbrush.

The two of them followed the slope of the land, cutting across a road and continuing through a field.

"I'm gonna be late for school," Andrew stated.

"No, you won't."

"C'mon, Catherine." He jogged in front of her, walking backward as he reached again for the pail. His books thumped against his leg. "I can't be late today. We're having a spelling quiz."

"Can you spell *lie?*"

He stumbled, then righted himself. "What?"

"I know you lied to me yesterday, Andrew. Again."

His gaze flicked over her shoulder toward the house. To Jericho? She'd deal with that later. "Did you think I wouldn't notice that your friends came by asking for you *after* you were supposed to be with them?"

"I'm sorry, okay? It didn't hurt anything."

Frustration rose inside her. "The point is you lied. It's wrong, not to mention you could've gotten into trouble."

He rolled his eyes. "Can't you lecture me when I get home?"

She came to a stop. "You listen to me. I'm tired of your lying and your sneaking around. I won't abide it anymore. From now on, I'll walk you to school and walk you home."

He blinked as if he hadn't heard correctly. "Aw, what do you want to do that for? If you're worried about those outlaws, don't be—"

"I'm worried about *you*. If you can't be trusted to tell me the truth about something simple like playing with your friends, how can I trust that you're even going to school?"

"You can ask the teacher!"

He slung his book strap over his shoulder and picked up his pace. Catherine's own steps were brisk as she followed. The town was stirring to life as businesses opened. Greetings were called back and forth, doors opened, shades lifted. Horses clopped down Main Street, some stopping in front of the schoolhouse.

Andrew shot a desperate look toward the white clapboard school. In groups of two and three, children made their way toward the building, which also served as Whirlwind's church. The clang of ringing hammers sounded from the opposite end of town, where a new saloon was being built.

"I don't need anybody walking to school with me," her brother said hotly.

"Evidently you do."

"Everybody's gonna call me a sissy if you show up with me."

"I'm sorry if you'll be embarrassed, but I'm at my wit's end. I've tried reasoning with you, threatening you, bribing you. Maybe my walking you to and from school every day will work."

At the bottom of the slope, still yards away from the school, he stopped dead in his tracks. "I'm not going there with you holding my hand."

"I'm hardly doing that."

"It's just as bad."

"Maybe you'll think twice about lying from now on."

"You're not Ma." His chin jutted out and his eyes blazed brightly. "And I don't want you here."

"Do you think I like chasing you around? Never knowing where you are?" Her temper snapped. "Cooking and cleaning for a kid who hates me?"

He looked taken aback. "I don't hate you," he mumbled.

She rubbed her forehead, trying to breathe past her anger. "I know I'm not Mother. I'm sorry she's gone. Don't you think I miss her, too?"

They hadn't discussed their mother since Catherine had arrived.

"You weren't here when she got sick," he accused, his voice quivering. "Or when she died."

"No, I wasn't." Catherine swallowed the tears burning her throat. She wanted to reach out, but knew her touch wouldn't be welcome. "I had no way of knowing she was ill until it was too late, and I didn't want to go against her wishes that I stay in New York until she sent for me. Now I wish I had. I'll have to live with that regret for the rest of my life."

He eyed her uncertainly.

"But my being away doesn't mean that I didn't love her. Or you. She wrote me letters telling me everything about you. We have to help each other through this, Andrew."

"It won't help me for you to walk me to school like a baby."

She thought about giving in, but couldn't. "I don't like it, either. I have plenty of other things to keep me busy, but until we establish some trust, that's how it's going to be."

He threw another anxious look toward the school. Catherine saw two figures—boys—standing beside the building, waiting. Watching them. A slender man came out on the landing and rang the bell.

"I've only got five minutes, Catherine. How about if you leave me off right here? You can watch me go in." He grabbed at his lunch pail.

"No." She held it out of reach. "You won't get this until I see you to the front door. Every day."

"Well, I won't do it!" He dropped his books and bolted, heading behind the schoolhouse.

Purely on reflex, Catherine darted after him. She lunged and caught him by the back of his shirt. Clutching a handful of fabric, she yanked hard, slowing him enough that she was able to reach out and clasp his arm. "No, sir. You are going to school and you are going with me."

"You're gonna tear my shirt." He wiggled and twisted, trying to escape her grasp.

She grabbed him by the ear. "Then you can mend it."

"Ouch!" He glared up at her. "I don't know how to sew."

"If you try running again, I'll make you learn how."

He looked horrified. In the instant he took to absorb that, she started for the school, towing him behind. After letting him pick up his books, she marched him to the bottom of the steps and said, loudly enough that the young man waiting in the doorway could hear her, "I'll be back to get you this afternoon. I'll wait over by the hotel."

Andrew's face flushed with anger.

"But if you pull another stunt, I'll come inside with you from now on. And stay. I'm sure you don't want that."

"What if I'd gotten away?" he challenged. "What would you have done?"

"Taken your lunch home with me. And sent the sheriff to find you." She hoped he believed the bluff. In truth, she would've panicked. She still might.

He rubbed his ear, looking sullen. "You're really gonna make me go hungry unless you walk me to the school door?"

"That's right."

"That's about the meanest thing I've ever heard." He stomped up two steps and turned.

She handed him the pail. "Remember what I said. Go on now, before you really are late."

The teacher, a young man about Catherine's age, put a hand on Andrew's shoulder as he walked inside, then turned to her. "You must be Andrew's sister."

"Yes. I'm Catherine Donnelly." She climbed the steps to shake his hand.

"I'm John Tucker." He glanced over his shoulder. "Anything I should know?"

"I'm sorry if we caused a commotion. We're having a little trouble, er, coming to terms. If he doesn't behave, please let me know. We live in the house up the slope away from town."

John's hazel eyes were kind. "He's usually good as gold."

"I hope he is today."

She waited until Mr. Tucker closed the door before she left. Anger propelled her home with long angry strides. The little dickens. She wanted to tan him good, but knew she wouldn't be able to do it. That's why she had thought this might be a good idea. Now she wasn't sure.

What if he didn't come home tonight? What if he didn't come home tomorrow? What was to prevent him from taking off at the noon break or after school? What had she done?

As she neared the house, she saw Jericho sitting where

she'd left him. She tried to calm herself before she reached the porch. He held his gun in his left hand, aimed toward her.

Looking into the gun's barrel, Catherine found her steps faltering.

He quickly put down the weapon. "Everything all right?"

"Yes." No. But she wasn't about to bare all to him. Emotion seethed inside her, from anger to uncertainty to sympathy for what her brother had suffered alone. "I'll get the liniment if you're ready to work on your wrist."

"Okay."

Questions were plain in his eyes, but she walked on into the house and retrieved the bottle from the cupboard. If he thought it odd that she wanted to do his treatment this morning instead of in the afternoon, he said nothing about it.

Jericho had situated her chair facing his, and she sat. He pushed his sleeve up to his elbow, watching her closely. She briskly placed his arm on the table.

Then, irritated and flustered, she stood, her hands on her hips. "Did you know he lied about being with his friends yesterday?"

Jericho warily eased his chair away from her a bit. "I put that together, yeah."

"Why didn't you say anything to me?"

"Well, I didn't think I should be getting into your business."

She leveled a look at him. "You're already in it. I saw the two of you outside last night. Were you talking about his lie?"

Jericho's silver eyes hardened to hammered steel. "Yes."

"He looked scared to death. What did you say?"

"I warned him about the outlaws." He held her gaze, but she saw secrets in his eyes. She practically felt them. "And told him to stop worrying you so much."

Taken aback, she felt her anger ebb. "You did?"

"Yeah." He eyed her cautiously. "What did *you* say to him?"

She relayed that part of the conversation.

A smile touched Jericho's lips. "You walk him to school or he doesn't get lunch?"

"Yes." She paced to the edge of the porch, then back. "What if I did the wrong thing?"

"I think it's pretty smart, Catherine. It would sure have worked on me. A full belly is pretty important to a twelve-year-old boy."

She sank into her chair and uncorked the liniment bottle. "Where do you think he goes? What does he do?"

Jericho's gaze settled on her watchfully, but he didn't answer.

Pouring ointment into her hands, she began massaging his arm. The steady motion soothed her somewhat, calmed her ire enough for the fear to creep through. "I thought after a while he would accept me being here, but he hasn't. What if I go to get him this afternoon and he isn't there?"

Jericho took so long in answering that she looked up. "I'm sorry. I shouldn't burden you—"

"It's no burden. If he wanted to leave, I think he would've already done it."

"I hope you're right."

He put his good hand over both of hers. "Tell you what. If you want, I'll go to town and check on him."

"No! You're still recovering. In fact, you probably need to rest right now, and I'm prattling on."

"If I don't start using these legs, they're going to wither away."

"No. Thank you, but no."

"I can work on my hand if you want to go yourself."

"I don't know." Should she give her brother a chance? See if he was willing to fall in line with her? She had no one to ask for advice. All she could do was what felt right. "The next move is his. I'll wait until after school and see what it's going to be."

"I think that's wise."

She smiled at Jericho, only then realizing his hand still covered hers. His skin was calloused, his fingers long and elegant. She wanted to turn her arm over and press her palm to his.

As if he realized they were still touching, he removed his hand and reached down to scoot his chair closer to the table. She stifled her disappointment.

"Thank you." She smiled, and tried not to react when he gave her a lazy grin in return. "Could I ask you to please keep this just between us?"

"Of course." He narrowed his eyes at her. "You're not gonna cut off *my* food, are you?"

"Well, maybe that honey you like so much." She tried not to smile, but couldn't help it.

He grinned. "You've got me at your mercy, Catherine. Be kind. You could break me here."

She laughed. She was hardly a match for him, even with only half his strength. His eyes softened, crinkling at the corners, and she found herself recalling that near kiss yesterday.

She had lost her chance to find out how it would be to kiss a man. *Him.* She only cared about kissing *him,* she admitted. No one else.

Later, when she went to town, that thought plagued her as much as her worry over Andrew. As she stood next to the Whirlwind Hotel, she pushed everything out of her mind except her brother. A loud clatter sounded inside the schoolhouse as desks were shoved back and children raced out the door.

Her throat closed up tight. What if he wasn't here? What if she'd run him off— There! There he was, coming down the steps with Miguel and Creed. Her chest ached with relief.

He said goodbye to his friends and walked over to her. "I'm ready."

"Okay." She kept her voice cheery, but her heart sank. He looked belligerent, still angry. She had no idea what she was doing.

Her questions about his lessons were met with grunts or half answers, so she fell silent. They were almost to the house when he mumbled, "I'm sorry, Catherine. I'll do better."

Surprised, she stared at him. This was more than she'd ever hoped. "You know I'll still walk you to and from school for a while."

"I know." His stomach growled loudly and he gave a crooked grin. "Better that than no lunch pail."

She clasped her hands behind her back so she wouldn't reach over and hug him. Jericho had been right about her brother's penchant for food. Maybe she had done the right thing by following her instincts with Andrew. Maybe she should've followed them about kissing Jericho, too.

Jericho thought back over his and Catherine's conversation about Andrew. Her questions about her brother's whereabouts and what he did could've been an attempt to find out if Jericho knew anything, but they had seemed genuine. Enough so that he no longer suspected her of being involved with the outlaws.

He couldn't ignore the satisfaction he felt that she had talked to him, not Davis Lee, about Andrew. And that satisfaction led his thoughts to what had almost happened between them. The desire Catherine had teased to life with that near kiss drummed through him, low and insistent. Constant. Urging him to take more; triggering a level of hunger he'd never felt for a woman. Physical, yes, but also beyond that. Deep inside. One he knew would not be so easily satisfied or left behind.

Every time he tried to dodge yesterday's kiss-that-wasn't, the memory would plow through his mind. He tried to wait it out. Thought about his wounds, his guns, the outlaws. Anything to keep his attention off her.

The rest of the day dragged. He focused his mind and his energy on working with his six-shooter. Even though he had shot with his left hand before, he was by no means skilled. He practiced picking up the revolver and aiming, trying to smooth those motions into one. He might be able to hit the broad side of a barn, but not a running target. He would be without a holster. As a sign to himself that his right hand would heal, he had decided he wouldn't buy one for a left-handed person.

But he still needed to be able to use his left hand. His right one wasn't even flexible enough to push the cylinder in or out for loading, so he worked on popping it out and in with his left. After a while, he braced the revolver against the palm of his injured hand, then slid bullets into the chambers, emptied them and started again.

While the sun climbed higher, he did it over and over until his left hand curved easily around the handle and his finger went naturally to the trigger, though the gun's heaviness was still awkward and his aim was off. Jericho felt next to useless and looked to keep busy, needing to occupy his hands, as well as his mind. But he couldn't escape Catherine. Frustration over his injuries hammered at him just as much as the seething desire he felt for his nurse.

As they ate dinner, her warmth seemed to surround him. Afterward, he sorted herbs from her garden while she moved about the house, her soft scent trailing in her wake. The front room smelled of her—of sunshine and verbena. Her nightdress hung discreetly behind the door, and Jericho's gaze went there, stirring his imagination.

Since yesterday she had worn her hair in a braid, which only made him itch to release it and bury his face in the lush strands. She made it too easy to forget what had brought him here in the first place. He called up the memory of the ambush that had killed Hays and filled Jericho himself full of holes. Then he mentally cataloged the other people who had been killed or injured by the McDougals, such as Ollie Wilkes, the stage driver from Whirlwind. Catherine's brother was involved with the gang, and Catherine…well, Jericho believed she wasn't.

He had to get out of the house before he compromised his judgment. Or her.

The next morning, when she left to walk Andrew to school, Jericho limped to her wardrobe. His saddlebags rested in the corner where the big piece of furniture met the wall. By sitting in the chair, he managed to lift his bags and heft them over his right shoulder. He'd never thought them heavy before, but the effort now caused him to pause a minute before he pushed himself to his feet. He settled the crutch under his arm and moved slowly to the porch, the added weight on his right side making his balance precarious.

Once outside, he dumped the bags at the corner of the house closest to Catherine's room. All he'd done was move his things and he was breathing hard, feeling weak. If he had wondered about riding Cinco yet, there was his answer. After he caught his breath, he eased down the porch steps and started for the barn.

The sun was back in full force today and no rain had fallen. The day would only get hotter. He stopped just inside the barn, breathing in the slightly cooler air as his eyes adjusted to the dimmer light. He limped to the back where his saddle hung over Cinco's stall. Still tied under the lip of the cantle was his bedroll. Both Cinco and Moe blew softly. Jericho murmured to them as he loosened the thin leather straps holding his bedding. Sticking the roll under his right arm, he adjusted his balance for the return trip.

As he hobbled back, he found an awkward, dragging rhythm. More than his thigh screamed for relief; his entire body ached, and sweat broke across his neck. He paused next to the ladder that led to the loft, and rested.

The smells of earth and animals surrounded him. This was where he should be. Here where he couldn't smell the sweet scent of a woman.

He was becoming too soft, and too interested in a woman he shouldn't let himself care about. Sleeping on the porch would remind him why he'd come to her house in the first place.

If he could make it to the porch, he thought wryly. Hell, he didn't have the energy of an overfed pup. After a long moment, he wiped his forehead against his shoulder and braced the crutch under his arm again.

The soft swish of skirts caught his attention and he looked up as Catherine rushed inside.

She paused just inside the doorway, her face lighting with relief. "Oh, here you are. You weren't in your room and neither were your things. Is everything all right?"

"Yes." She looked spring fresh in her chambray dress and white bib. He leaned against the ladder, grateful for the support. "I'm getting my bedroll."

"Why?"

"It's time for you to have your bed back."

She moved forward, her skirts swaying gently, making his hands itch to span her waist, to feel her curves against him. "You're not well enough!"

"I can get around, Catherine. I'll sleep on the porch and you'll be in your own bed."

"That's where you should be."

It was exactly where he shouldn't.

"You can't be outside with the dirt and the bugs," she insisted. "It's filthy. What if you get an infection?"

"You'll only be a few feet away. I've imposed on your generosity long enough."

"Please don't do this." She stepped closer, concern shadowing her eyes. "At least until Dr. Butler thinks it's all right."

"I'm fine. Sleeping on the porch won't hurt me." He wished she'd back up a little bit, just enough so he wouldn't be tempted by the freshness of her skin. Or wouldn't count every breath, watching the rise and fall of her chest. "I'll have a roof over my head. I've slept with a lot less."

"You hadn't nearly just died, though." Frustration sharpened her voice. "I can't let you do this. It's irresponsible. It could even be dangerous."

Even standing here surrounded by the smells of dirt and horseflesh and leather, he picked up her subtle scent. "I have my gun."

She threw her hands up. "That won't do you any good against infection, will it? Or help you if you need something in the middle of the night."

"Look." He gritted his teeth against the slow tightening of his body. "I didn't mean to get you riled up. You'll still be close enough that I can call you if I need to."

Which he would not do.

"I think you should stay in the house, and I imagine Dr. Butler will agree with me."

"I don't need either of you to tell me if I feel well enough to move."

Hurt flashed across her features and he felt as if he'd knocked the wind out of her. "I'm only trying to care for you the best way I know how. Is that it? You're lacking something? You think *I'm* lacking?" She moved closer. Too close. Only inches separated them. "I can ask the doctor what more I should do."

"There's not one thing wrong with you or the care you've

given me." He tried to temper his words this time. She had started that humming in his blood and he couldn't stop it.

"Then I don't understand. Just tell me what you want—"

"Woman, if I stay in that house with you, something's gonna happen between us." The words erupted from him.

His meaning sank in and her mouth formed an O. Her cheeks pinkened, but she didn't run. She didn't back away at all the way she should.

She plucked nervously at the top button of her bodice, and he said tightly, "Go on back to the house."

He straightened, making it plain he wanted to move, expecting her to do the same.

She didn't. Looking uncertain, she drew in a deep breath, then said in a rush, "I wish I'd kissed you when I had the chance."

He nearly swallowed his teeth. "You can't say things like that to a man, Catherine. To me."

"It's true."

"I don't think so." Desire thrummed inside him. He gripped his crutch so tightly that his knuckles burned. "You're pale as chalk."

Her skirts whispered around his legs, between them, and her pulse fluttered wildly in the hollow of her throat.

"Dammit, woman! Back up. I may be injured, but I'm not dead and—"

She placed her hand on his chest and he released the crutch to grip her wrist. "You don't want this. It's in your every move, Catherine. In your eyes, the way you tense up when I'm around."

"I don't want to feel that way. Not with you."

What was he supposed to do with that? "That's not what you felt just yesterday."

"I made a mistake."

"So if I kissed you right now, you wouldn't bolt?" He made sure that scorn sounded in his voice, and he gave her time to run. "Go. Inside."

"No," she whispered. Her eyes were bright, but with determination, not fear. "I want this. I've never wanted it before."

His restraint faltered. He wanted to haul her against him, make her feel the way he hardened for her. But he couldn't forget the terror he'd seen in her eyes that night. Angry that he ached for her, that she wouldn't leave him be, he pulled her body flush against his and stared into her eyes. The bedroll slid out from under his right arm. His wrist twinged.

She trembled against him, but she didn't resist, didn't look away. Instead she brought her other hand to his chest. "Jericho?"

She breathed his name, and his hold on her tightened. His arm circled her waist completely, plastered her to him so she could feel what she did to him, what he wanted. Yet her blue eyes never left his.

He dipped his head, asking hoarsely, "Do you know what I'm about?"

"Yes." She lifted her face only a fraction, but it broke him.

With his eyes open, he kissed her. Just a gentle touch of his lips at first, though he shook with the effort not to take her mouth the way he wanted.

She stiffened, and disappointment carved deep in his belly. Just as he started to release her, she kissed him back—unpracticed but willing. Her breasts flattened against his chest and he found his good thigh between her legs.

Hell for breakfast. Her lips were soft on his, tentative and searching. Tightening his arm around her, he pressed into the ladder. Catherine pressed into him. His thigh ached, but not as deeply as the rest of him did.

He coaxed her mouth open so he could taste her, and her eyes fluttered shut. When his tongue dipped inside, she made

a small sound in the back of her throat. He nearly came undone right then. She tasted of heat and honey. Jericho cursed
his lame leg. He wanted to gather her up, lay her down on the
sweet-smelling straw and shuck off her clothes. But he
couldn't move without falling down.

She shyly touched her tongue to his. Sharp, blazing need
sliced through him as he drank her in, losing himself in the
sweetness of her tender mouth. His kiss wasn't rough, but it
was fierce, and he couldn't stem the fire raging through him.
His body throbbed, demanding to be buried inside hers. He
should stop, but somewhere in the back of his mind he knew
this sweet torture was all he'd ever have of her. When he was
gone and she hated him, he wanted to remember it.

She pulled away, causing him to blink, to make a grab for
his self-control. Like waking out of a stupor, he slowly came
to his senses. Her breathing was as ragged as his. Her lips were
swollen and red, her velvety skin marked by his beard.

"You are so damn sweet you make my teeth ache," he rasped.

She looked astonished. No one had ever looked astonished
after kissing him. The trust in her eyes was blinding, and
tugged hard at his conscience.

"*That's* why I can't stay in the house, Catherine. I'd compromise you and your reputation for sure."

She stared at him with such wonder, such naked desire, that
he felt his heart sink. If she only knew why he was really here.

The reminder cleared his head as fast as smelling salts. He
released her, trying to ignore the wounded look on her face.
"That shouldn't have happened. I beg your pardon."

"No!" Protest replaced the desire in her eyes. "I wanted
you to."

"I overstepped." Stunned by the force of his reaction to her,
he had to struggle to make his voice cold. Detached. "It won't
happen again."

Her eyes welled with tears. "Jericho, please."

He couldn't get involved with her. And he couldn't bear her tears. He glanced down, looking for his crutch through a haze of self-loathing. He stepped on the stick's end to tip it up so he could grab it.

Catherine bent and passed it to him with a visibly trembling hand.

He straightened, staring at her until she moved back.

"Are you leaving?" She wrapped her arms around her waist. "You're in no condition."

"I could go to Davis Lee's or Riley's, but until we know where the McDougals are, I don't want you and Andrew here by yourselves. If anyone tries to get in, they'll have to go through me."

She reached for him. "Jericho—"

"No." His voice cracked the still air. "Go on, Catherine. Go on, now."

Her eyes bright with hurt, she lifted her chin and walked out.

Cursing himself, he sagged against the ladder, the wood biting into his shoulders, his backside. In the wake of her touch, the surrender of her body against his, he had forgotten himself. But he couldn't do it again.

He closed his eyes. He had to stay away from her. Not only because of her brother, but because his time here could easily become about more than that. It could become all about her.

Chapter Eight

She was still fuming as she prepared supper that evening for Jericho's cousins.

"Overstepped," she muttered, lifting the lid of her Dutch oven and stabbing a fork into the roast. Finding the meat tender, she lifted the heavy pot and set it inside the fireplace to keep warm. "Begging my pardon."

She didn't want Lieutenant Jericho Blue to beg her pardon. She wanted him to kiss her again.

She hefted another pot, this one full of water, from its place on the hot brick and hung it over the fire to boil.

All day, she had wavered between utter humiliation and anger. And underneath, like a clear cool stream, had been wonder. She had responded to his kiss. Not with fear but with want. And she did want him, even now.

Completely surprising and welcome was her body's reawakening, as if her senses had broken free of steel tethers. Jericho's kiss, gentle at first, then demanding, had set off a tingle under her skin that she felt all these hours later. She had responded to him. Hope that her body would answer a man's in such a way had been relinquished in the last months.

She shouldn't set such store in a single kiss, but the joy, the *relief* that she hadn't frozen in fear, whirled through her, making her long for more of him. She had never felt that for a man, even before the attack. Jericho Blue had given her that.

But he didn't want her. Why? Because he was thinking of her reputation? Or was she too naive for him? Physically he had wanted her; she *knew* that. Did it matter why he had pushed her away? He'd been plain enough about it.

And she had been mortified. Still was. So she would keep a good distance, though it would help if she didn't have to work on his hand every day. She would do the best she could. Putting him—that kiss—out of her mind would be difficult, but she had to. It wouldn't do for him to see how he affected her.

She checked the potatoes on the stove and realized she had a little time before the water boiled.

Jericho had kept to himself all afternoon. She didn't know what he'd been doing, but when he limped into view and headed for the pump, his face looked drawn and exhausted. Her heart softened a bit. She turned away and eyed the table. Her mother had had a piece fitted for the middle to make it longer, and Catherine slid the sides apart to slip the wood into place. Along with their four chairs she would need the bench tucked away in the narrow hallway where she kept a small supply of coal.

Sister Clem and Sister Marguerite had packed a crate of china for Catherine's move to Texas. The plates and teacups had been donated to the convent, only to gather dust in a lower room there. Catherine had hoped to show her mother the dainty rosebud pattern before Evelyn died.

She pushed away a wisp of hair and added dried corn to the pot in the fireplace. Steam from the boiling water misted her face. She puffed out a breath, blotting her damp forehead with the back of her hand. Catherine missed having a woman to talk to. Sister Clem would know what to do about Jericho. Or if Mother were here, Catherine could ask her advice. The visit she'd made to her mother's grave after he had run her out of the barn was a poor substitute for talking to the woman in person.

Reeling from his sensual assault, Catherine had felt anew the overwhelming loss of her mother as she'd reached the cemetery behind town. So much had happened in the weeks since her arrival that she hadn't been able to spend the time she wanted there, but maybe that was good. Maybe if she didn't dwell on Evelyn's death, Andrew wouldn't, either.

The clatter of wagon wheels broke into her thoughts. Taking off her apron, she smoothed her hair and checked her chignon. Her cheeks were flushed from working over the fireplace and stove. Part of her wished she hadn't invited all of the Holts to dinner tonight, but it would save her from being alone with Jericho.

Andrew came out of his room with his hair combed down and wearing a clean shirt as she had asked. Catherine smiled as they walked out to the porch. Jericho stood next to the pump, running a cloth across the back of his neck. He wore his boots. A fawn-colored shirt molded his broad shoulders and flat belly, tucked into the waist of his dark blue trousers. His gaze flickered to hers briefly before settling on Riley and Susannah and their baby daughter.

Davis Lee rode up on horseback, calling a greeting as he dismounted. Riley braked the wagon and climbed down, taking the baby from his wife. Andrew jumped off the porch and walked out to them.

"Hi, Miz Holt." He smiled at Susannah, looking more at ease than Catherine had ever seen him. "Hi, Mr. Holt. Want me to take Lorelai?"

"Sure." Riley carefully placed the little girl in Andrew's arms.

Davis Lee reached into the back of the wagon and brought out a towel-covered basket. "Susannah, I'll get this for you."

Andrew held the baby carefully, starting toward the house. Catherine smiled as Lorelai's fat legs pumped the air.

"How old is she?" she asked as Riley and Susannah neared.

"Three months." Susannah let go of her husband's hand and stepped up on the porch. "Thanks so much for the invitation. May I help you with anything?"

"I think everything's ready." Catherine smiled at the petite blonde, not missing the way Riley's gaze lingered on her.

Leaning on his crutch, Jericho brought up the rear, greeting his cousins warmly. He and Davis Lee hung back to let the others go inside first.

Catherine's gaze caught Jericho's, then slid away. She leaned over the baby, touching her pale gold curls. "She's a darling."

"She takes after her uncle," Davis Lee said proudly.

"Yeah," Riley said. "When she's putting up a fuss."

Catherine smiled at their bantering, beckoning everyone inside. The men took off their hats and hung them on the wall hooks inside the door.

"Jericho, you're looking well." Susannah smiled up at him.

He ran a hand over his beard, looking self-conscious, but his lips curved. "I sure feel a lot better than I did the last time you were here."

Holding the baby, Andrew sat on the end of the bench Catherine had scooted to the table. Jericho eased up behind her brother, looking down at the pair with an inscrutable expression on his face.

Davis Lee stepped around the table to Catherine's side. He tapped the basket he'd brought in. "I think these are Susannah's biscuits," he whispered conspiratorially.

She smiled. "Put them on the table. I think there's some honey left."

Laughter lit his blue eyes. "Are you sure you want these?"

"Davis Lee Holt," Susannah said indignantly. "I'll have you know my biscuits turned out this time."

He lifted an eyebrow at Riley.

His brother laughed. "I think they did."

The sheriff grinned, leaning across Catherine to set the basket on the table.

She started at his nearness, but didn't move away. He smelled nice, like soap and water and sunshine. With his dark hair and blue eyes, he was quite handsome. He had broad shoulders and a lean waist. And even though his hands were large she'd seen his gentleness with his niece.

Catherine felt Jericho's gaze on her and turned away. "Everyone have a seat."

With much scuttling and laughing, they all gathered round the table. Catherine chose the chair nearest the stove. Davis Lee pulled it out for her, then sat beside her at the end of the table. Jericho chose the opposite end, his gaze resting on her so frequently that her nerves knotted.

All through the talk at dinner, he made quiet conversation. He seemed to enjoy having his family around, but Catherine sensed an impatience in him. Due to frustration over his injuries or to what had happened between the two of them in the barn? She slammed the door on any thoughts of that kiss. Even though she couldn't completely ignore him, she felt more at ease once the meal ended.

As she rose to help clear the table, Susannah shooed everyone out to the porch, sending the drowsy baby with Riley.

Catherine stacked dishes and carried them to the sink, glancing out at the men. Jericho had angled his chair toward the doorway so that he could see into the house. Davis Lee sat to his left with the same view.

But they weren't paying attention to her or Susannah. They

spoke in low tones, including Riley in the conversation when he joined them. Catherine saw Andrew hovering behind Davis Lee, but her brother made no attempt to join the men. All of them wore dark, serious expressions.

"It's so nice that you have a pump indoors for your sink."

Catherine pulled her attention from the men and smiled at Susannah. "Mother wrote to me how Father tried to give her a modern kitchen, but still I was surprised to see it."

While the other woman pumped water into the sink, Catherine picked up the pot of water she'd left warming on the stove. The men's quiet voices drew her gaze again.

Jericho now held the baby. She nestled in the crook of his injured arm, while Riley stood nearby. Light from the lamp on the windowsill played across Jericho's face and broad shoulders, painting the baby in gold light. She grabbed his finger with her tiny hands and he smiled with a tenderness that made Catherine blink. Her breath caught in her chest and she forced her gaze away. She poured hot water into the sink to mix with the cold.

Susannah scooped a handful of soap from an open crock. "How are you getting along?"

"Very well." She scraped the plates clean and passed them to be washed. "Thank you for asking."

"It seems you've hardly had a moment's peace since you arrived. First your mother's passing, then Jericho ending up here."

Catherine had no comment about her patient. "Sometimes I go to the cemetery to talk to my mother. Thank you again for seeing she had a proper burial. I'd still like to repay you for that."

"Please don't. We were honored to do it. She was a kind lady."

Catherine thought back to the last time she'd seen her mother. Evelyn's face had been unlined, her blue eyes brimming with tears as she left her daughter in the care of the nuns. "Andrew tells me he attended your charm school."

"Yes." Susannah smiled fondly. "I enjoyed getting to know him. He was quiet, but he attended every class."

Every class? "He never missed and said he forgot, or that he had to be somewhere else?"

"No." Sympathy shadowed Susannah's blue eyes. "Your mother was very ill. I think it weighed on him."

"Yes, I'm sure it did." Both she and Andrew had lost Evelyn, but in truth the loss was one Catherine had felt for years. Her brother had only now come to experience it.

Susannah glanced briefly at Andrew. "Are the two of you having trouble adjusting to each other?"

"I think we're both feeling our way," Catherine admitted. "I don't exactly know what to do with a twelve-year-old boy."

"If you want to talk, I'm happy to listen. I don't claim to know twelve-year-old boys, either, but I did check on him frequently during your mother's illness and just before you arrived."

"Thank you." Catherine took the last teacup from the other woman, wiping it dry with a cloth.

Susannah dunked a plate into the water. "You certainly seem to take everything in stride. I was completely out of my element when I came to Whirlwind."

"Really?" The blonde appeared as much a part of the rugged land as her husband did. "You seem so at ease."

Susannah laughed. "Riley did everything he could to run me off."

Catherine's eyes widened. "Why would he do that?"

"He was afraid for me to live here."

"But why?"

"He felt it was too dangerous for a woman from the city. Outlaws, snakes and all that." She waved a dismissive hand. "I told him St. Louis has its own share of dangers, but he was hard to sway. His first wife was killed during a dust storm."

Catherine couldn't imagine Riley being married to anyone other than Susannah. "And now what does he think?"

"He's getting better, but only because he was forced."

"Oh?"

She sighed softly, telling Catherine the story of how her brother had sent her to Whirlwind under the assumption that Riley wanted to marry her. "He didn't want anything of the sort."

"Then how…?"

Susannah smiled. "I don't know. It took him a while to realize that I meant to stay. When he finally got it through his thick skull, I was head over heels for him."

Warmed by her new friendship, Catherine said, "I like it here, too. I feel at home."

"I'm glad. You've certainly been a blessing to our family, though I imagine you're worn out from taking care of your brother and Jericho."

"He doesn't need constant care like he did at first." She took the last plate from the other woman and dried it carefully.

"I take it you're talking about Jericho."

"Oh, yes." Catherine laughed self-consciously. "Sorry."

Susannah glanced back at the men. "Is he well enough to move out? He's more than welcome at the ranch."

"He talked about that." Why did the thought of Jericho leaving put an ache in her heart? She would be glad to have her house back, she thought defiantly. "But he says he doesn't want to leave us by ourselves until the outlaws are located."

"That's a good idea."

"He's sleeping on the porch." She didn't think the other woman would gossip, but Catherine wanted to be sure the living arrangements were clear.

"Yes, I saw his bedroll." Susannah paused, searching Catherine's face. "It's none of my business, but things seem tense between you two."

Her cheeks heated even though there was no way the other woman could know about that kiss. "I think he's frustrated that he's not coming along faster."

"Men. They want it all right now, don't they?"

Catherine had no idea, but she murmured agreeably.

"What are you two ladies whispering about?" Riley walked up behind them, slipping his arms around his wife's waist.

"Never you mind." Susannah nestled into his chest, smiling at Catherine. "Nosy, isn't he?"

"Watch out, woman," he growled against her neck.

She looked up at him adoringly and he dropped a kiss on her nose. "We'd better go, sweetheart. Lorelai's ready for bed and so am I," he murmured.

Susannah blushed, but Catherine saw a silent message pass between the two of them. She felt a sharp stab of longing at how comfortable they were with each other, how easily they expressed their feelings with a touch or a kiss.

Susannah laid down the cloth she'd used to dry dishes, and squeezed Catherine's hand. "Thank you for dinner. It was lovely."

"I'm glad you enjoyed it. I hope you'll come again."

"Only if you promise to come out to the ranch," Riley said with a warm smile.

"I'd like that." She walked them to the door.

Jericho had moved his chair back against the wall. Davis Lee leaned against the porch column at the top of the steps. The two men stopped talking when Catherine and the others walked out, but they looked so serious she decided they must have been talking about the McDougals. All this time?

Riley took a sleeping Lorelai from Andrew. Then Susannah and he said their goodbyes, as Catherine walked to the wagon with them. Once Susannah was seated, Riley handed the baby up to her. After saying they'd see everyone at church on Sunday, the Holts drove away.

"Nice evening," Davis Lee said from the porch.

"Yes, very nice." Enjoying the cooler night air, Catherine admired the half-moon in a dark blue sky. She turned to find Andrew and Davis Lee standing in the doorway, examining something.

"Catherine, look!" Andrew waved her over. "Sheriff Holt can whittle. He made this birdcall and he's giving it to me."

The excitement in her brother's voice caused her to smile as she moved up the steps.

Andrew turned, showing the whistle to Jericho. "What do you think of that, Lieutenant?"

"It's a fine piece. You do beat all, cousin." Jericho shook his head. "I never did have your patience."

"Well, that's true." Davis Lee grinned.

Standing between him and Jericho, Catherine exclaimed over the sleek wooden whistle. Her skin prickled with the weight of Jericho's slow, steady gaze, but she refused to look at him.

"You outdid yourself on the meal, Catherine." His quiet voice sent a shiver down her spine.

She glanced over, wishing her stomach wouldn't jump every time he spoke to her. "Thank you. And Davis Lee, thank you for Andrew's gift."

"Oh, yeah, thanks." The whistle trilled with a low bleat as Andrew experimented.

She put a hand on his shoulder, pleased when he didn't shrug it off. "Time to get ready for bed."

"'Night, Sheriff. Lieutenant." Blowing short chirps on the bird call, he went inside.

"I'd better scoot, too." Davis Lee reached inside the door and plucked his hat from the hook, then walked down the steps. With a foot on the last one, he turned. "I wonder if you might like to go to church with me on Sunday, Catherine?"

She blinked. A sudden tension lashed the air and she felt a pointed gaze boring into her back—Jericho's.

"You and Andrew, I mean." The sheriff's eyes, clear blue in the flickering lamplight, were kind. "If it's not too hot, we can have a picnic afterward. What do you say?"

"Thank you for asking." Habit had her ready to refuse, but a tiny whisper stopped her. Davis Lee wouldn't hurt her. For the first time in almost two years, she wanted to say yes to an invitation. She wasn't unaware that Davis Lee liked her, but until now she had never given a thought to finding out if she liked him. "Yes, I'd enjoy that very much."

Behind her, heavy silence pressed like a weight against her shoulders.

Davis Lee grinned, slapping his hat against his thigh. "I look forward to it. I'll be by about a quarter till nine to pick y'all up."

"All right." She didn't know if she was nervous or excited to have taken a step out of the shadow that had dogged her for almost two years. Since the attack, her trust of anyone was hard-won, but having gotten to know the sheriff, she believed she would be safe with him.

"Bye, Jericho." Davis Lee settled his hat on his head and walked to where his horse nibbled grass a few feet away. He swung into the saddle. "You're gonna make my whole day, Catherine."

She laughed softly and waved goodbye, staring into the darkness until she couldn't see him any longer.

Turning, she found Jericho watching her, his gaze pinning her to the spot. She could read no emotion in his face, but his eyes burned with silver light. She felt almost guilty. Annoyed because there was no reason for her to feel she had slighted him, she walked past him and stepped inside. "Good night."

"I didn't mean to hurt your feelings, Catherine." The words sounded forced, but genuine. "What I said in the barn—it was for the best."

It was his kiss, not his words that flashed through her mind. She paused in the doorway, wanting to plead for something. A truce? "It's all right. Let's forget it."

"I was harsh. The words could've been said better."

She had wished he might say he regretted them altogether. "It's forgotten."

"I felt like I was taking advantage of your hospitality."

"I didn't feel that way at all." She half turned toward him, wrapping her arms around her waist.

In the shadows, his shoulders seemed even more broad, and his eyes glittered. Though the mouth that had done such wondrous things to hers was tight now, and his crutch lay across his lap, he was every bit the man who had kissed the sense out of her in the barn. She swallowed. "Maybe you *should* move to your cousin's."

"No. Not until we know where those outlaws are. You saved my life. I'm not leaving as long as the McDougals might be a threat to you."

His steel-threaded tone said there was no use trying to change his mind. He would stay on her porch with or without her permission. "Very well."

She stepped inside and paused with her hand on the door. "Won't you at least reconsider sleeping inside? I can make up a pallet in the front room, like I did for myself."

"It's better if I stay out here. We need to be careful—I do mean to consider your reputation."

"All right." She closed the door, opened it. "Do you have a blanket?"

"Don't think I'll need it. It's plenty warm out here."

"A pillow?"

"I have one." There was a smile in his voice.

"Good night, then."

"Good night." His voice tickled a place low in her belly.

After a long moment, she shut the door and waited, trying to settle her nerves. Her palms were damp and she gripped the folds of her skirt. Oh, bother! Plucking her nightdress from behind the door, she turned down the lamp and went to her bedroom.

The thought of sleeping in her bed again was appealing, but she couldn't help worrying about the man outside who needed it more than she did.

Without his compelling presence, the room seemed larger. She thought she could smell the soap he used each morning, and maybe the dark masculine scent she had breathed in so often.

Taking off her clothes, she slipped her nightgown over her head before easing down on the edge of the bed. Only then did she notice he'd changed the linens. When had he done that?

With a smile, she blew out the lamp and began to braid her hair. Moonlight dappled the floor. The lace curtain hung motionless in the still air. Her hands worked as she stared out the window, trying to keep her mind off Jericho. The house felt empty. She missed him being inside, missed knowing he was only a few steps away, though he was really no farther now.

Suddenly he stepped into view. He'd come off the porch without his crutch and now he limped past her room to Andrew's, then started back. Through the open window, she could hear his dragging gait. A faint cloud of dust circled his feet.

He was pushing himself, no doubt anxious to get back on the trail of the McDougal gang. And away from her?

She dismissed the stinging thought, telling herself she cared only that he didn't try too much too soon. She bit back the words of caution she wanted to call out. As long as he didn't break open his wounds, he probably needed to move as much as possible.

Something about his silhouette in the moonlit shadows tugged at her heart. He looked lonesome, but maybe she thought so because that was how she felt.

She lay down on her side, staring blankly at the weave of light and dark coming through the window. She tried to think about her invitation from Davis Lee, but the memory of Jericho's searing kiss crowded out every other thought. He had said he would stay away from her, and she knew he believed that was best. One minute she thought he was right. And the next minute she only wanted him to kiss her again. To touch her.

It was a long time before she fell asleep.

Jericho didn't like the idea of Catherine going to church with Davis Lee. Or anywhere else, for that matter. But he had no claim on her. He was *not* going to stake one, so he had no right to say anything. It still nagged him like a sore tooth the next morning as he sat naked on the right side of her bed, awaiting the doctor. A sheet covered his flanks, but dipped too far down his backside for his liking.

Butler wanted to check his thigh even though Jericho had told him it was fine.

What needed to be checked were the thoughts of that kiss. And his words afterward. He should've taken more care for her feelings, but even now he felt tension score his belly. Her innocent yet fervent response played havoc with his resolve to keep away from her, but keep away he would.

She stood quietly at the end of the bed, observing the doctor as he moved aside the sheet just enough to bare Jericho's injured thigh and examine the wound. The doctor's hands were capable and impersonal. Jericho wanted *her* hands on him.

"You did a fine job restitching the wound, Catherine." Dr.

Butler glanced at Jericho. "You'll scar, but not nearly as badly as if I'd sewn you up. My stitches are nowhere near as tidy as Catherine's."

He nodded, wishing he could put his pants back on.

The man turned his attention to Jericho's hand, studying it first, then carefully trying to bend his wrist. "I think Catherine's treatment is working. The fingers and the hand aren't nearly as stiff as they were last week."

"I still can't make a fist," Jericho pointed out.

"All in good time, son." The doctor clapped him on the shoulder and moved to the end of the bed, where his bag sat. "Any questions?"

"No. I'm glad for the good report."

"I have a question." Catherine folded her hands in front of her, lacing and unlacing her fingers. "He's taken to sleeping outside. I've tried to tell him it's too soon, that he's risking infection or illness, but he won't listen. Won't you tell him, Doctor?"

Butler's brown eyes turned speculative. "I think his wound has closed enough that he's safe from infection. Unless he injures it again, he should be fine."

Jericho's gaze went to her. *See?*

"But he was so weak." She didn't acknowledge him at all. "Can his health already be restored enough to fight off an illness if necessary?"

"He appears stronger each time I come."

"I am," Jericho said shortly. "The weakness doesn't overtake me as quickly. And I'm trying to walk and work my leg every day."

"That's good." The doctor fingered his chin. "Where are you sleeping? On the ground? In the barn?"

"On the porch. I have my bedroll."

"I've told him I don't mind giving up my bed a few more

nights." Catherine looked at the doctor hopefully. "Just to be safe."

"And I've told her I should move out so as not to compromise her reputation."

"He's right about that, Catherine." She didn't look pleased as the doctor continued, "I think sleeping on the porch is all right, Lieutenant, but if you do start to feel like you're coming down with something, you should take her advice and move back inside."

Jericho nodded, relieved the doctor had sided with him. "One more thing, Doc?"

"Yes?"

"I hope I'm not insulting you, but I wonder if you could give me a shave?" Jericho rubbed at his beard. "My face is getting lost under all these whiskers and I figure you can wield a blade pretty well."

"If you're worried about it, Catherine has ample—"

"No." Jericho didn't try to temper his harsh tone. He absolutely could not have her that close. "Maybe you could send the barber out? I could walk to town, but it'd take me some time."

"No need for that." The doctor cast a sideways glance at Catherine. "I'm happy to do it."

"Thank you." Jericho grabbed his drawers and pants. "I'll just put on my clothes, then get my straight-edge razor and my shaving soap."

"I'll get it." Before he could say anything, Catherine left the room.

Jericho took the opportunity to pull on his trousers, ignoring the doctor's look of speculation. He didn't like the flash of hurt in her eyes, but having her so near whittled away his self-control. Made him think dangerous, stupid thoughts about kissing her again.

She returned with Jericho's things and placed them on the

bedside table as the doctor moved the chair between the bed and the wall.

"I'll get some water," she said quietly.

"Thank you." As she left the room, Butler rolled up his sleeves. "Can you sit over here so I can reach you better?"

"Yeah." Jericho eased down into the chair.

The other man worked a pair of scissors, eyeing Jericho's beard. "I'll trim off as much as I can before I put the razor to you."

"I really appreciate this, Doc." He tilted his head to one side while Butler cut his whiskers. He might rather have Catherine touching him, teasing him with her scent and the brush of her skirts against his legs, but this was smarter.

"I suppose" *snip, snip* "that I shouldn't ask" *snip, snip* "why it is you don't want the prettiest nurse in Texas to do this for you?"

He angled Jericho's head the other way and started on his right side.

"No."

"Here's a wet cloth," Catherine said.

While the doctor turned away to pick up Jericho's shaving soap, she dropped a hot rag on his face.

"Ouch!" He snatched the square away, then gently touched it to his beard, narrowing his eyes at her.

She smiled sweetly, too sweetly, and he resisted the urge to turn her over his knee.

The doctor lathered up Jericho's shaving brush and dabbed soap on his beard. He tested his straight-edge against his thumb, then tilted Jericho's head to the side, starting under his sideburns with quick even strokes. "You want it all off?"

"Yes, please."

The doctor worked with steady hands, a few strokes taking him to the other side. "Catherine, when you're ready, I could use you back at the fort. Private Gormly has been help-ing me, but he doesn't have your way with the patients."

"Certainly." She sounded eager. "When would you want me to start?"

Jericho didn't like it. She didn't need to be back there until the McDougals were caught.

"How about Monday?" Butler finished Jericho's chin with a few short scrapes.

"How far is the fort, Doc?" Jericho used the damp towel to clean the remaining soap from his face. Ah, he felt almost human again.

"Less than two miles."

Catherine stared hard at his clean-shaven face, as if she didn't recognize him. "I've driven it many times."

"You can't drive it now." He spoke bluntly to combat the strange heat her gaze was generating.

"What? I guess I can—"

"Until we catch those bast—outlaws, it's not a good idea for you to go anywhere alone, especially a trip that takes thirty minutes one way. I'm sure the doctor would agree."

Butler's gaze swung from Jericho to Catherine. "I didn't think about the gang. Any word yet on their whereabouts, Lieutenant?"

"No. That's why I don't want her driving alone."

"I'll be fine," she said tightly. "I can take the shotgun."

"Do you even know how to use it?"

Her silence was answer enough.

Jericho balled the linen in his hand. "It's too risky."

"It is." Dr. Butler wiped his hands on the dry towel Cather-ine handed him. "I'll send a soldier for you, the best marks-man we have. He can drive you back and forth every day. That will surely satisfy the Ranger. Right, Lieutenant?"

It did not satisfy him. Jericho hadn't considered that the doctor might come up with the idea of *someone else* driving

Catherine. But how could he argue with that when his own objection had been based on her traveling alone rather than traveling at all?

"That's a wonderful idea." Sparks flashed in her blue eyes. "I'm sure that would be just fine. Wouldn't it, *Lieutenant?*"

Jericho gritted his teeth. She would have protection. That should be his main concern, not who provided it. "Thanks, Doc. Your offer is very generous."

"None of the men will mind a bit." He smiled at Catherine. "They've all been asking after you."

"How is Lieutenant Clark? His tooth was really bothering him the last time I saw him."

"I had to pull it, but he's fine."

Who was this Lieutenant Clark? Jericho wondered. How well did the man know Catherine? How well did she know him?

Annoyed that he even cared, he levered himself out of the chair and reached in his pocket for two bits.

The doctor waved him off. "Riley gave me enough beef to pay for a year's worth of trips."

"That was for doctoring me, not shaving me. You probably don't have much call to do that with your patients."

"I didn't mind doing it, but thanks for the offer." He rolled down his sleeves, then picked up his bag.

Catherine walked him to the door and Jericho stuffed the coins in his pocket, limping out behind them. He noted the stiffness in her shoulders, and anger vibrated in every line of her body.

As Butler drove away in his buggy, Catherine turned on him. "You didn't have to make me look incompetent. I do work for him, you know."

Jericho blinked. "That wasn't my intent at all." He could smell the tang of his shaving soap and her soft verbena on the towel she held. "He knows what a fine nurse you are."

"You made it sound as though I haven't properly cared for my patient."

"Just because you didn't shave me?"

"I did offer," she reminded him tartly.

She was talking to beat the band. Jericho was surprised. Since that kiss, she'd been quiet. Hurt, he knew. He hadn't meant to hurt her, but she'd be glad for the distance when she learned his real reason for being here. "I thought you might like some respite from taking care of me twenty-four hours a day."

"Is that really why?" Her gaze bored into his, clear and questioning.

She was asking if it was because of her, because he didn't want to be near her. Hell, he wanted more than that, but what he wanted could have nothing to do with his decisions regarding her. Still, he hadn't meant to offend her. He grinned, hoping to erase the sting of the clumsy way he'd handled things. "After yesterday I thought you might be tempted to use that razor across my throat."

Her gaze sharpened. "I might have."

Good. "The doctor knows you're a fine nurse, Catherine. I don't think he saw my request as any slight against you."

"You think, but you don't *know.*"

She snatched the towel he still held and brushed past him to go inside. She disappeared into the nook beside the fireplace, then reappeared with her laundry basket.

He stayed by the door, but turned so he could see her. "I think you should reconsider going back to the fort. At least right now."

"I'll have an escort, which you said was a good idea." Carrying the basket on her hip, she swept into Andrew's room. "And it won't be every day."

He couldn't argue, couldn't tell her that what he didn't

think was a good idea was her spending that much time with some soldier. His jaw tightened. "I don't like it."

She appeared in Andrew's doorway, looking at him coolly. "We all have to live with things we'd rather not."

"Like Rangers sleeping on your porch?"

She shrugged and disappeared into her room.

Now why did that have to hurt so much?

He stabbed a hand through his hair. Having a soldier drive her would afford the protection she needed. She was right. It should've given Jericho some peace of mind. In fact, all it did was make him want to hurt the nameless, faceless man who would come for her on Monday.

Chapter Nine

Catherine was looking forward to her time with Davis Lee. On Sunday morning, she buttoned up her black kid boots and smoothed the light cotton of her dress. The pale blue skirt, dotted with dark blue rosebuds, was one of her favorites; she paired it with a white shirt and blue vest.

Her hands shook and she wasn't sure if it was from anticipation or apprehension. But she had nothing to fear from Davis Lee. She had spent time around him for weeks now. He was a good man, a gentle man.

She took her parasol out of the wardrobe, then dug several hairpins from atop her dresser and moved into the front room to listen for his arrival. Sunlight slanted through the window and the door. She brushed her hair back, plaiting the dark strands, then twisting them into a low chignon. Holding the thick mass in place, she slid in the pins, fumbling the last one and dropping it.

Oh, bother. Keeping one hand on her hair, she knelt, searching the weathered pine. The pin glittered under the kitchen table. She scooped it up and secured her hair. Gathering her skirts in one hand, she stood, straightening them with a quick flick of her wrist. A shadow fell across the floor and she looked up.

Jericho stood with his left arm braced against the door-frame. Morning sunlight streamed into the room from behind him, lining his lean, rangy body in gold. His wide shoulders blocked the sun's glare and Catherine blinked at his clean-shaven face, still unused to it. She kept her gaze from his mouth.

She straightened. "Good morning."

"Morning." Hungry and hard, his eyes roamed from the top of her head to the tips of her boots peeking out from under her skirts.

She wanted to demand he stop looking at her, but she couldn't move, couldn't breathe. Her mind might have frozen, but her body hadn't. Heat sluiced through her, and as if he had put his hands there, her nipples hardened.

He saw. His face darkened. A muscle worked in his jaw and he turned away.

A breath rattled out of her. Her legs shaky, she sank down in a chair. She didn't understand how she could respond that way to a mere look, but she couldn't…couldn't…. Her numb mind searched for logic. She couldn't greet Davis Lee like this!

Closing her eyes, she began reciting a Hail Mary. Long minutes later, she heard the snort of a horse and the thunk of a brake being set. Davis Lee invited Jericho to church with them, but the Ranger refused. Thank goodness.

There. Her breathing was normal even though her skin prickled. She hustled Andrew out, told Jericho she had left him some lunch by the dry sink, and accepted Davis Lee's hand helping her up into the shiny buggy he'd rented from the livery.

Jericho spoke to his cousin, his gaze touching her briefly. Her scrambled brain didn't understand one word he said. As

Davis Lee drove them away, Jericho's silver gaze burned into her. Catherine refused to look at him, refused to give him another thought.

She enjoyed her time with Davis Lee though a faint unease nagged at her. After church, he drove them about a mile outside of town to a spot thick with wildflowers. Catherine had never seen such abundance—patches of purple, orange, yellow and blue flowers—scattered over the prairie as if dropped from the sky.

He spread a blanket and they ate a lunch of fried chicken, pickles, cheese and molasses cake, which he told her he'd gotten from the Pearl Restaurant. He picked a big bouquet for her, engaging both her and Andrew in conversation. She liked that.

Now she sat on the blanket, holding her parasol for protection from the sun. A few yards away, the man and the boy sat in the grass. Davis Lee was teaching Andrew how to attract a quail with his new birdcall.

"It's two short notes, then a third rounded at the end. *Bob-bob-white.*"

He demonstrated by whistling the pattern, and Andrew tried to replicate it on the call. He practiced and practiced for what seemed a long time, but Davis Lee never became irritated or impatient with him, praising him when he got it right.

Andrew whistled repeatedly until Davis Lee nudged his shoulder. "Look there."

Catherine followed the direction of their gaze and saw the grass move. A plump brown bird with tiny white speckles strutted through the grass. Then another.

"Did I draw them in?" Andrew breathed.

"You did." Davis Lee patted him on the back, the movement scattering the birds into hiding.

Andrew was relaxed with the sheriff, obviously liking the

older man. She felt a pang that her brother wasn't so comfortable around Jericho. All the way home, Andrew talked about calling up the quail, causing her to share a smile with Davis Lee.

As the buggy rolled up in front of the house, Jericho limped around the corner. The sleeves of his pale blue shirt were rolled to midarm, baring a dark dusting of hair over strong sinew and muscle. Unless one knew to look, even his injured hand appeared whole. His dark cowboy hat, molded by wear and weather, fit low on his head. She couldn't see his eyes, but she felt his attention. He lifted a hand in greeting.

"Lieutenant!" Andrew jumped down and rushed over to him. "Davis Lee taught me how to whistle for quail and we called some up. They almost came right over to us."

Jericho stayed at the corner of the porch, the afternoon sun slanting over his shoulder. His eyes were serious, studying Catherine intently. "Is that right?"

"Yes, listen." Her brother replicated the call exactly as Davis Lee had taught him.

The Ranger nodded in appreciation. "You've got a knack, boy. It took me a week to get it right."

"Really?" Andrew flushed with pleasure. He turned to Davis Lee, who was helping Catherine down from the buggy. "Do you think there are any quail around my house, Sheriff?"

"Wouldn't hurt to try your call and see."

Clutching her bouquet in one hand, Catherine gathered her skirts with the other. Jericho's gaze flicked over the flowers, and her stomach fluttered nervously.

"How was church and all?" he drawled.

"Very nice. It was a lovely day." She smiled at Davis Lee, though her mind stayed on Jericho. This was the first time she'd left him alone since his injury. "Did you do all right?"

"I was fine." He gave a thin smile.

She knew he wouldn't tell her even if he weren't. "I hope we weren't gone too long."

"You'll be gone longer than that when you go back to the fort."

"What's this, Catherine?" Davis Lee frowned.

"I'm going to resume helping Dr. Butler."

"Starting when?"

"Monday," she said.

"Tomorrow," Jericho said at the same time.

The sheriff's gaze flicked to his cousin, then her. "It's not a good idea for you to drive back and forth by yourself."

"That's what I told her."

Catherine refused to look at Jericho. "Dr. Butler has already seen to that. He's sending a soldier for me."

"His best rifleman," Jericho interjected.

"No need for that." Davis Lee smiled broadly. "I can take you."

"Oh, no. I couldn't ask you to do that."

"I'd enjoy doing it." Sincerity warmed his eyes.

"What about your jail, Sheriff?" Jericho hooked one thumb into the front pocket of his trousers. "You do have a job."

Catherine wished he would be quiet. "That's true, Davis Lee. You do have that to think about."

"I can leave Jake in charge. It won't be for long."

The thought of riding with him rather than a young man she didn't know as well, settled the nerves bunching across her shoulders. "Are you sure?"

He grinned. "Am I sure I'd rather be riding with a pretty woman than sittin' in a jail? Yes, ma'am."

She smiled, though she could feel Jericho's mood darken. "Since the doctor already has someone coming for me tomorrow, I'll take you up on your offer for my Wednesday trip."

"Good." Davis Lee smiled into her eyes.

She found him easy to be with, charming, a gentleman in every sense of the word. "Thank you for today."

He took her hand and pressed his lips to her knuckles. "I had a fine time."

"So did I." She waited for the butterflies in her stomach, but they didn't come. Her palms were dry, her heartbeat steady. And she knew that the fine tremor working through her wasn't due to his attention, but to Jericho's intense regard. She gently slid her hand from Davis Lee's. "I'd best see about supper. I'll see you Wednesday."

Without a glance at Jericho, Catherine left the two men. She walked into the house feeling as if she were about to come out of her skin.

Their low tones followed her. She wanted to watch them, stare at the sharp lines of Jericho's newly bared face, the high cheekbones and the hollows beneath. His sculpted lips. Lips that had turned her inside out.

Frustration welled within her. She had enjoyed her time with Davis Lee. She liked him very much, but he didn't start her pulse racing. Didn't make her breath catch with just a look.

She walked into her bedroom and stuck her parasol into her wardrobe, resting her head against the door's dark wood. Davis Lee didn't do any of those things, but Jericho did.

Jericho wasn't going to ask Davis Lee what he and Catherine had been doing the whole time they'd been gone. Both of them had already said, more than once, how much they enjoyed each other's company, and it was none of his concern. He was only watching the slender line of her back and the sway of her hips so he would know when she was out of earshot.

The woman had no place in his thoughts. If he weren't so spent, he'd be totally focused on what he had learned today.

His gaze shifted to his cousin, who watched him with a measured intensity. "While y'all were gone, I went into town and saw Jed Doyle."

"You walked all the way to town?"

"It's just down the hill."

"It's nearly a quarter of a mile and you've only got one good leg."

He had needed something to occupy his mind, block thoughts of Catherine sitting in the buggy with Davis Lee, eating lunch with him. Focusing on making it all the way to town without falling down had gone a long way toward keeping her out of his mind, though it did nothing to blunt the taste of her. The hot sweet honey of her tongue on his.

Think about walking. The sooner he got his strength back, the sooner he could finish what he'd come here to do. "A couple of days ago, I found a rifle cartridge in the barn, and I wanted to see if Jed could identify it."

Davis Lee folded his arms. "There could be cartridges in my barn, too."

"Jed recognized it. Said it matched the ones stolen from his shop last week. The Donnellys have a shotgun. Why would they need rifle cartridges?"

"Good point." His cousin turned thoughtful.

Jericho glanced around, checking to see that they were alone. "I made sure Andrew knew I had it, and he was mighty nervous."

"What about Catherine?"

"The kid is the one I saw at the ambush, and now I know he's the one stealing from Whirlwind's businesses."

"Maybe you ought to show it to her, see if she has any reaction." Davis Lee's eyes narrowed. "That is, if you still believe she's involved with the gang."

"You don't?"

"No."

"Why? Because that telegram you got on Friday from those nuns confirmed she was raised by them?"

"No. Because I've spent some time with her. So have you. Why do you still suspect her? My gut says she isn't involved with those outlaws."

"From what I just saw, you're not thinking with your gut," Jericho said bitingly. "But yeah, I don't suspect her anymore, either."

Davis Lee's gaze sharpened and he studied Jericho hard. "If something is going on with the two of you, then say so."

He worked to relax the rigid stretch of muscle across his shoulders. "Nothing is going on."

"Then why are you looking at me like I just shot your horse out from under you?"

Hoping Catherine couldn't hear them, Jericho glanced at the house, saw that the front door was still open. He lowered his voice. "It would be better if she weren't stepping out with you. Thanks to my damn leg, it's all I can do to keep up with her brother. I don't need to wonder about her comings and go-ings, too."

Davis Lee eyed him doubtfully. "Uh-huh. If you know she's with me, you don't have to wonder."

Jericho had told himself exactly that the whole time Catherine had been away this morning. But he *had* wondered. And imagined. Frustration had him clenching his good fist. "Don't you wonder why she suddenly said yes to you after so many no's?"

Davis Lee rocked back on his heels. "You want her."

"I'm not involved with her. That would be stupid."

"I didn't say you were involved with her," the other man said quietly. "I said you want her."

Jericho gave his cousin a flat stare, but Davis Lee didn't

back down. His eyes glittered with speculation. "She's beautiful and kind and intelligent. A hell of a nurse."

He didn't need Davis Lee pointing out Catherine's attributes. "Are you trying to convince me to admire her? I thought you were the one interested in her."

"She's here alone with you the majority of the time," Davis Lee mused. "You had to have noticed her fine figure, those perfect breas—er, blue eyes. Her other qualities."

"She hasn't been compromised." Jericho had not only noticed, but felt those fine qualities right up against him. "I'm sleeping on the porch now."

"I didn't think you had tried to seduce her." Davis Lee grinned. "Interesting that her virtue would be your first thought."

"It should be yours, too," he growled.

"And even if you wanted more, you wouldn't get involved with her because of your investigation."

Jericho swallowed a curse. "That's why you shouldn't get involved, either."

"It's *your* investigation."

"You want to catch those bastards as badly as I do."

His cousin stared at him, so hard Jericho thought he might pop a blood vessel. "If Catherine wants to accept my invitations, then I'll continue offering them."

Which did not concern Jericho. But his good hand curled into a fist.

"Tell me straight out. Is my seeing Catherine going to be a problem between us? Because no woman is worth that."

Hadn't Jericho told her only two days ago that he shouldn't have touched her? That he wouldn't do it again? He had no business feeling anything for her. "No. There won't be any problems."

"He said while taking aim at my back," Davis Lee muttered.

Jericho wanted to laugh, but could only manage a smile.

Never mind the itch that had been under his skin the entire time she'd been with Davis Lee. Or the relentless urge to know every single thing they did together. What mattered was catching her brother with the McDougals.

Imagining the hate in her eyes when he finally caught Andrew in the act should've hardened Jericho's resolve to keep a distance from her. Knowing she liked his cousin should've reined in his hard-driving impulses about her, but the urge to touch, to *take* burned deeper than ever.

His mind tortured him with images of Catherine and Davis Lee all through the night.

Catherine buttoned up the front of her gray dress. The soldier sent by Dr. Butler would be here shortly, and she wasn't ready. She'd spent a restless night trying to escape thoughts of Jericho. Even though that kiss had happened three days ago, she could still feel his lips on hers, the hard lines of his body against hers. Being away from him today was a good idea.

As soon as Andrew finished breakfast, she confiscated his lunch pail and they left for school.

Sums were on her brother's mind this morning and he recited his multiplication tables as they walked. The sun warmed her neck and the scent of bruised grass followed in their wake. The pleasure she took in the lovely morning was dimmed by the fact that she had barely spoken to Jericho since rising, or he to her. She wanted to know what he and Davis Lee had talked about yesterday. Why Jericho had looked so haggard when she returned home. His limp seemed more pronounced, and his neck and newly shaved face were a deeper brown. As if he'd been in the sun all day.

She should be thinking about Whirlwind's handsome sheriff, who was kind and charming. Who took pains to put her at ease. Who liked her.

Dr. Butler's request for her to return to work had come at the perfect time. She didn't feel completely comfortable leaving Jericho alone for these few hours, but the chance to escape this simmering awareness of him, to clear her head, was more than welcome.

After delivering Andrew to school, she rushed home. A wagon hitched to a placidly waiting bay sat in front of the house. Catherine hurried up the porch steps, noting the U.S. brand on the horse's flank. The soldier was here.

Jericho's empty chair and the bedroll neatly placed beneath his saddlebags meant he must be inside with the man. With a welcoming smile on her face, she opened the door.

The front room was empty and quiet. No one sat at the kitchen table or on the bench Catherine had moved to the corner by the rocker. The faint scent of leather and soap drifted to her. Jericho. Where was he? Where was the soldier who'd been sent to fetch her? Maybe the wagon wasn't from Fort Greer. Maybe—

A gunshot ripped through the morning stillness, and she jumped, pressing a hand to her chest. Bless the saints!

Picking up her skirts, checking that the shotgun was in its place behind the door, she ran outside and around the house. Who had fired that gun? What had happened? Where was Jericho?

Through the panicked thunder of her heartbeat, she heard the murmur of voices. Male voices. She ran past the root cellar and garden, lurching to a stop. Between the house and the barn stood Jericho and a soldier. Her frantic gaze skimmed Jericho's wide shoulders, lean legs, the ground. He wasn't shot. Neither was the brawny, dark-haired man beside him. No one was wounded. No one was bleeding.

Dragging in air, trying to calm her pulse as she walked toward them, she pressed her hand to her aching side. "What happened? What's going on?"

The men turned and the soldier snapped to attention. Flipping the rifle barrel-down against his leg, he saluted.

"Sergeant Lucas Ryan, ma'am." Cobalt-blue eyes shone in a young, handsome face. "Dr. Butler sent me."

Jericho's gaze slid to the man in uniform, but he said nothing.

The sergeant, who looked to be about Catherine's age, sent an uncertain glance toward Jericho. Though tall, he lacked the older man's height by three inches. The dark blue of his frock coat and trousers was spotless. He was polished and perfect from the brim of his black felt hat to his unbelievably shiny boots.

"I heard a gunshot," she stated, her gaze going to Jericho.

"Lieutenant Blue wanted to see if I could hit a target, ma'am."

"He did?" She frowned. Over the sergeant's shoulder she spied a bucket on its side sporting a hole the size of a fifty-cent piece. "That had better not be my water bucket."

"No, ma'am."

Jericho's cool gray eyes watched her steadily, unapologetically.

Heat curled through her. Refusing to let him fluster her, she said to the sergeant, "And it appears you hit it."

"Yes, ma'am." He still stood at attention.

She smiled and stepped toward him. "Well, then. I'm sorry to keep you waiting. I got a late start this morning, but I'm ready now."

"At your service, ma'am."

"Dr. Butler will wonder where we are." She turned toward

the house, expecting the soldier to follow, but he didn't. She looked back. "Sergeant?"

His gaze cut to the big man beside him. "I don't think the lieutenant is satisfied, ma'am."

Satisfied? Catherine searched Jericho's eyes, but could read nothing. What was he about?

His jaw, shadowed with morning whiskers, tightened. "I'm sure Doc wouldn't mind us taking a few minutes to make certain of your safety."

"The doctor said he would send the fort's best marksman," she said brightly. "And here he is."

Jericho eyed the other man. "The Rangers set great store by accuracy."

"As does the Army, sir."

"Can you shoot the bloom off that flower over there?" He pointed past the barn into the field beyond, where, dozens of yards away, a lone yellow sunflower waved above the prairie grass.

Catherine could only just make it out.

Confidence shone in Lucas Ryan's eyes as he lifted his rifle and blew the flower to kingdom come.

"You're a marvelous shot, Sergeant," she praised.

Jericho crossed his arms over his chest, his brow lowering. "You hesitated right before you pulled the trigger. Can't hesitate."

"I did?"

Jericho gave a curt nod. "Try something else."

Catherine didn't know what was going on, but she didn't like it. "The doctor is expecting us."

"I'm sure he won't mind waiting a few more minutes."

What did Jericho want? For the sergeant to fire every bullet he had? She could read nothing in the Ranger's face as he tossed a hole-riddled tin can in his hand. "How are you at moving targets?"

He threw the can high into the air. In one smooth motion, Ryan sighted his target, followed it, then squeezed the trigger. The bullet pinged the metal and the can fell to the ground with a soft thud, sporting a new hole.

Ryan grinned.

"Humph." Jericho pointed past the barn into the pasture. "See that mesquite tree?"

"Yes."

Catherine stepped up close enough to see the sheen of perspiration on the sergeant's neck.

"Knock off that lowest branch."

"That's practically to Abilene," she protested.

"It's only about a hundred and fifty yards." Jericho looked at the other man. "To test your accuracy with distance."

Ryan took the challenge, lifted his rifle and fired. The lowest branch fell cleanly to the ground.

A smile broke across his face. "You have to admit that was an excellent shot, Lieutenant."

"Could've been lucky."

The sergeant's smile slipped. "It wasn't."

"Hmm. Just to be safe I think I'll ride along with y'all."

"What?" Catherine's mouth dropped open.

"That isn't necessary, sir—"

"With the McDougal gang running around, it's a good idea to have someone at your back."

The other man eyed him uncertainly. "I guess so."

Catherine stepped between them, her hands on her hips as she faced Jericho. "You don't even have full use of your gun hand yet."

"I can use a shotgun. Don't have to be too skilled with that."

What was he doing? "You said you were a lousy shot with your left hand. What if you shoot one of us?"

He chuckled, amusement glittering in his eyes. "I didn't know you had such a sense of humor."

The sergeant watched them intently.

"Well, I hardly see how you'll be able to get in and out of the wagon. And all that bouncing will not be good for your leg."

"I can ease myself into the bed. I'm going to have to start riding in a wagon sometime. And riding my horse, too."

"You still have stitches. You could rip them open."

He smiled, his teeth flashing. "I think Sergeant Ryan will probably drive as gently as he can, seeing as how he has to deliver you in one piece."

She did not want to be with Jericho today. Crossing her arms, she demanded, "What are you going to do while I'm helping Dr. Butler?"

"Same things I do here." He shrugged. "Work my hand, exercise my leg, practice with my gun. Sergeant Ryan might even want to practice with me."

The young man frowned.

Catherine pressed her lips together, choking back further arguments. The doctor probably wouldn't care if Jericho accompanied her to the fort, but she cared. She needed some time away from him. But she had come to know that steely look in his eyes. He had made up his mind to go.

Ryan glanced from Catherine to Jericho. "So we'd better get going then?"

"Yes, we had." Jericho gestured for her to precede them.

Lucas Ryan looked distinctly uncomfortable, and she let her own confusion show as she swept past Jericho. Yes, the McDougals were dangerous and yes, two guns probably were better than one. But there was something more, something deep in his gray eyes that she couldn't decipher.

She didn't know what to make of him, first telling her he shouldn't have *overstepped* with that kiss, then declaring he would ride with them to the fort. As if he cared for more than her protection. Which he did not.

She glanced back, saw the smug satisfaction glinting in his eyes, and pressed her lips together. And she thought Andrew was hard to figure out!

Chapter Ten

Jericho was not letting Catherine go to Fort Greer without his protection. Lucas Ryan was a good shot, but he was just a kid. Jericho didn't understand the ferocity that had risen in him upon seeing the soldier's discreetly admiring glances, but it had come from his gut. As he had done his entire adult life, he followed his instincts.

During the thirty-minute ride out, he bounced around in the back of the wagon like corn in a popper. His leg hurt like bloody hell, and Catherine seemed to have forgotten he was even there. Ryan drew her out and she talked about her upbringing and how she'd come to Whirlwind. Jericho had heard some of it before, but she talked in more detail about her father, about her parents' lives here before she came. Enough so that Jericho itched to know more.

Fort Greer was still a relatively young encampment, one of the few not established on a stage or cattle route. Concern from citizens in the western part of Texas had prompted the government to offer more protection. Indians weren't the problem now; outlaws were. No high walls made of split rails encircled the fort. There were no gates. Nothing enclosed the place at all. Rather, the fort was a series of tents and build-ings laid out in an open-ended rectangle.

The yard where the men trained was well trampled, the grass flattened from hours of marching. Long frame buildings made up two sides of the rectangle; they were raised on foot-high pyres, and housed the officers and Dr. Butler. The hos-pital took up one room at the far end of the west building. Tents set up behind the quarters were reserved for the enlisted men. The laundry and kitchen shared a building and con-nected the two barracks to form the third, shorter wall. Set away from the barracks, behind the tents, were the stables.

Jericho's gaze shifted to Catherine. The way the sergeant eyed her, as if he wanted to lap her up like cream, sent a sharp heat jabbing Jericho's chest. He and Catherine would return alone.

Since she had to be home in time to collect Andrew from school, they only stayed at the fort until early afternoon. As she said goodbye to a stoop-shouldered lieutenant, Jericho spoke to Dr. Butler about driving the wagon back without Ryan. Any further trips could be made in Catherine's own wagon.

The doctor agreed easily, telling Jericho he had to ride into Whirlwind the next day to collect his wife, who was return-ing from a visit with her folks in Dallas. It was no problem for Butler to drive the wagon back to the fort then.

After informing Sergeant Ryan that he wouldn't need to make the return trip, the doctor had the younger man lead the horse and wagon to the front of his quarters. As Butler cau-tioned Jericho about climbing into the wagon, he lifted a wooden stepping block from the crawl space beneath the building and placed it adjacent to the rig.

Though the stitches in his thigh would soon come out, Jericho hadn't yet bent his leg as far as he would need to to climb up into the wagon. For the trip out, he had been able to sit on the edge of the wagon bed, then scoot back. The wooden block allowed him to step up, causing no more discomfort than walking did. He eased onto the smoothly worn wooden seat, glad he'd already gotten himself used to sitting in a chair for the past week.

He braced the shotgun on his left, butt-up against the foot-board so it would rest between him and Catherine. His Peace-maker was snug against his belly in the waist of his trousers, where he had put the six-shooter for the trip out.

Sergeant Ryan carefully helped Catherine into the wagon, one hand on her waist longer than Jericho saw fit. At least that pup wasn't going back with them.

Dr. Butler passed her a wool blanket and she folded it into a thick pad. Without so much as a by-your-leave, she leaned over Jericho and lifted his right leg, shoving the blanket beneath his thigh. "Maybe that will help buffer the rough ride."

He grinned. "Thank you."

"You shouldn't even be here," she said in a low voice. "You are a stubborn, stubborn man."

She reached for the reins.

So did Jericho. "I'll drive."

"Your hand isn't healed nearly enough for that."

"She's right, Lieutenant." Dr. Butler wore a mildly re-proving look.

Jericho nodded, intending to take the lines once they were away from the fort. The wagon jerked into motion and they pulled away from the doctor's quarters, turning around in the yard to head back the way they'd come. The horse lumbered along, its mahogany coat gleaming in the hot sun.

Catherine ran a hand across her nape and stretched her back. The movement pulled her bodice taut across her breasts and Jericho curled his good hand against his thigh, studying the horizon. A faint whiff of verbena and her uniquely feminine scent drifted to him, along with the sweetness of prairie grass and flowers flattened beneath the wagon wheels.

Catherine's hair, up as usual, was hidden beneath a sunbonnet that protected her face from the rays, but not the tender skin of her neck.

Flicking a glance at her, he saw shadows under her eyes. He reached for the reins. "You look tired."

"I'm fine." She flashed him a smile. "Besides, you heard Dr. Butler."

"You've been working all morning, Catherine."

"If it weren't for these outlaws, I'd be driving myself, anyway."

"My mama did teach me to be a gentleman. Some of it didn't take, but I do know not to allow a woman to drive a wagon."

"You're wounded. I'm sure your mother would make allowances for that."

He tried again to take the reins but she pulled them across her lap.

"I can drive with one hand." He stretched his arm across her body. They weren't touching, but he could feel the teasing warmth of her flesh.

"And what if those outlaws did come upon us? Having the reins would slow you down when you went for your gun."

"I put the shotgun here between us so I could reach it easily."

"Any hesitation could be costly." She schooled her features into a stern mask and lowered her voice. "Can't hesitate."

She was imitating the way he'd spoken to the sergeant, and Jericho chuckled, withdrawing his hand. "All right."

She slid him a teasing look. He smiled, taken again by the clear blue of her eyes. She jerked her gaze away. Around the edge of her bonnet, he could make out the soft line of her jaw, the way it curved to a stubborn chin. Her small straight nose.

The delicate patch of skin between her nape and the collar of her gray dress.

His gaze slipped to the fullness of her breasts and held. He flexed his hand, imagining the feel of her in his palm. A low throb started in his blood.

When she cleared her throat and a blush spread up her neck, he realized she'd caught him looking. He couldn't find it in him to apologize.

"What did you do while I worked with Dr. Butler?"

She sounded slightly breathless, her voice evoking a response he could no longer stem. "Worked on loading and unloading my Peacemaker. Took some target practice out behind the fort."

"With Sergeant Ryan?"

He grinned. "I think he might've been there."

He would do better to think about the targets he'd missed rather than the softness of Catherine's breasts or the taste of her. Anything other than what he wanted to do to her. "I heard you telling the sergeant on the way out to the fort that your pa and uncle pooled their money to build your house."

"Yes," she said softly. "My uncle died about a year after my parents arrived here."

"When did your pa pass away?"

"When I was eight. Andrew was just a baby, three months old."

"I was fourteen when my pa passed on."

Sympathy darkened her eyes. "What happened?"

"He was a Ranger, too. He was killed when he tried to stop a bank robbery."

"And you were left to help your mother and sisters?"

"Yeah. A gunsmith took me on as an apprentice and he paid me a little bit. I did odd jobs where I could, but my ma took the brunt of providing for us."

"I would've helped my mother if I'd been here," Catherine said wistfully. "She took in sewing and laundry."

Jericho knew the responsibility she felt, but he also knew that his mother would've done the same as hers if it meant certain care for her children. "Your ma felt better knowing you had food and a solid roof over your head."

"Yes. Still, I would've liked to have seen her one more time."

Her sigh of regret tightened his chest. "Did you ever want to become a nun?"

"No." She smiled softly. "I never felt the calling."

"Didn't I hear you say that your pa worked for the stagecoach company?"

"Yes. He was in an accident."

Her voice was even, but Jericho knew about pain buried beneath the surface.

"He drank off and on all through his life." Her voice was distant, faint with memories. "After he and Uncle Colm bought the house, my father planned to buy some land and also bring me from New York City. But he spent all his money on this place. Then he started drinking again."

"He felt like he'd failed you?"

"I think so. He shouldn't have been driving at all that day. He took a turn too fast and hit a rock. The stage toppled and crushed him."

Jericho wanted to put his hand on her shoulder, console her in some way, but he stayed as he was. "The passengers?"

"There were none, thank goodness."

"Did he drive Whirlwind's stage?" He didn't recall Davis Lee or Riley mentioning that.

"No, for a company in Abilene. They paid higher wages."

"And after he passed on, your ma had her hands full trying to provide for Andrew?"

"Yes. I suggested once that she sell the house, but my father had set such store by it that she couldn't. And she said it was all of him she had left."

"But if she had, you thought you could've joined her," he guessed quietly.

Catherine nodded. "I could've found some way to earn money and help her, but she begged me to stay with the Sisters so she would know I was safe and fed. At first I was relieved, because I was terrified of coming out here alone. And then it was too late."

He resisted the impulse to pull her close, rubbing his thumb absently against his thigh instead.

Catherine straightened her spine and asked briskly, "How's your leg? Are you hurting?"

"I'm okay." The rough, jarring ride sent pain shooting through his thigh constantly, but he had to get used to it sometime.

The creak of wagon wheels and the occasional chirp of a grasshopper wove their way into the silence between them. After a moment, she asked, "What of your mother? Does she know about your wounds?"

"No." He'd meant to wire her this morning, but he hadn't been about to let Catherine go off alone with that sergeant.

"You should let her know." Her eyes were bright with hard-earned wisdom. "You never know when you may not see her again."

She touched his knee, her fingertips barely skimming his trousers.

He tensed, pushing away the dangerous thought that he wanted her hands on him everywhere. "You're right," he said gruffly. "I'll do it this afternoon."

"Good." She smiled as the wagon rocked along. "I miss the Sisters, but I'm glad to finally be with my brother. Even if we're getting off to a rough start."

Andrew was the only family Catherine had left, and Jericho had every intention of taking the boy away from her. He was coming more and more to dread that day, but the kid had killed his partner. Possibly lamed Jericho's hand for life. There would be justice for Andrew and the McDougals. Still, it tore Jericho up inside to think about the consequences for Catherine. And the way she would look at him afterward.

Her hands seemed so tiny on the reins, yet he knew they were adept and capable. Before he realized what he was about, he ran his thumb over the back of one of them. Her skin was petal-smooth beneath his touch.

Her gaze flew to his and the air went still.

"You should've worn gloves," he said.

"Yes." Her blue eyes were wide, startled. "They'll burn, I know. My hands, I mean."

"And you may get blisters on your palms." He brushed his thumb the length of hers, to the inside of her wrist.

Her hands tightened on the reins and he withdrew.

She sent him a look from under her lashes. "It's really your fault."

"My fault?" He couldn't stop gazing at her, wanting to drown in her. "How's that?"

"I was flustered when we left the house, and forgot my gloves. I wasn't expecting you to come. I know Sergeant Ryan wasn't, either."

Jericho smiled though his body hardened with every sway of the wagon. She was so close. He could touch her if he wanted, probably kiss her. *And then what?* a voice inside his head taunted. *Arrest her brother?*

She glanced at him. "Why were you so disagreeable to him?"

Her mouth was perfect for his, soft and pink. Neither her upper nor lower lip was too full. He stopped that line of thought immediately and squinted across acres of spoke-high green grass. He could make out Catherine's house, small and yellow in the distance. "Was I?"

"You were." She drew her lower lip between her teeth. "I admit I'm no expert with a gun, but Sergeant Ryan hit everything you wanted."

"There's more to it than that."

"Like what?"

"Quickness, for one thing. He can't be so fast that he sacrifices accuracy, but he has to be fast enough to stop a bullet."

"He's a marksman in the Army. If that isn't good enough, what is?"

Jericho removed his arm from behind her, wishing she would talk about something else. "It was a good idea to have someone cover his back. You heard him. He thought so, too."

"I think you bullied him into it."

Jericho was sick to death of talking about the young sergeant, who'd shown more than a passing interest in Catherine. "He was flustered easily enough when I asked him to prove himself."

"He still didn't miss a shot."

"Only by luck." His jaw tightened. "He was plenty distracted."

She rolled her eyes. "By what? You had his undivided attention."

"He wasn't performing for me, Catherine," Jericho said evenly. Restless energy surged through him.

"Are you saying for me?" She threw him a quick look and laughed.

"He couldn't take his eyes off you." *Just like I couldn't.* He and Ryan had both been too concerned with her.

The admission twisted in his gut and he knew it was because she had noticed the other man. Seemingly enjoyed his company. As she had every right to, he reminded himself ruthlessly.

She waved a dismissive hand. "He did nothing untoward."

"It's a good thing," Jericho grumbled. This conversation scraped at his nerves.

"He has experience. He's been in the Army for some time. He fought Indians and um, other things."

Her admiration of the man ripped at Jericho's restraint. "I've had more experience with the McDougals."

"Still, why wouldn't you think he could protect me? He seems more than qualified, and Dr. Butler trusts—"

"Because he's not me," he said baldly, meeting her gaze straight on.

Her mouth dropped open and whatever she'd been about to say died on the wind. She dragged on the reins, stopping the wagon.

Jericho wished he could cut out his tongue.

Shy pleasure heated her eyes as her gaze drifted to his mouth. He was not going to touch her. No.

"I don't understand. If you—"

"Don't misread me, Catherine." He had to force the words out.

"*You* said you wanted to protect me," she reminded quietly.

"Only because I've seen firsthand what those outlaws can do." He couldn't bear the light in her eyes, the warmth in her voice. He made himself go on. "I won't take any chances that something might happen. My instincts said go, so I went."

"And that's the only reason?"

Hell, no. Every cell in his body strained for her, but his head knew better. He'd been on the McDougals' trail too long to allow any vulnerabilities now. "It's part of my job to provide protection to citizens."

"Oh." Her voice was small, but her eyes flashed. She snapped the reins against the horse's rump and the wagon lurched into motion.

He gripped the seat, clenching his jaw against the stab of pain that radiated up his leg.

"I guess it's good that you trust Davis Lee then," she said mildly. "Since he'll be taking me to the fort from now on."

Over my dead body. But Jericho didn't say the words. Didn't haul her to him and kiss her until she forgot every name but his.

Her blue eyes met his, full of challenge. *Tell me you hate the thought of me going with Davis Lee.*

But he couldn't. He wouldn't.

They reached the house in silence and Catherine positioned the wagon with his side against the porch. As she put her foot on the wagon step, he reached for her elbow to steady her, but she brushed off his touch.

She withdrew into herself, aloof and reserved, reminding him that she'd done the same that day in the barn when he'd sent her away. He rubbed a hand across his chest, which was aching dully.

She went around the back of the wagon, stepped up on the porch and reached for his arm expectantly. As he maneuvered himself out of the seat, she gripped his bicep to steady him, but as soon as he stood on solid ground, her hand fell away.

"I'll unhitch the horse and go after Andrew." Taking the sorrel's bridle, she disappeared around the house.

Jericho cursed. He could tell himself up and down that he had gone to the fort with her only because he wanted to protect her, but it wasn't the whole truth. He hadn't wanted her to be alone with that sergeant any more than he had wanted her to be alone with Davis Lee.

She had made a perfect fool of herself. Why had she let him see her reaction to his blunt announcement? *Stunned* was the only word to describe her emotions when he'd told her he had gone to the fort because he didn't trust anyone else to protect her. For one heady moment she had thought that meant something. That maybe he thought about her as often as she thought of him. That he wanted to kiss her as much as she wanted him to.

Idiot. She sighed. He didn't want her to believe more existed between them than actually did. One kiss. That was all.

But her body felt more; her heart certainly did. Maybe she didn't have the skill he preferred in a woman. Even as the thought jabbed through her, she couldn't believe it. Maybe she was too proud to admit otherwise, but she knew he wanted her. Even with her lack of experience, she knew that.

But he wouldn't act on it. She knew that, too. Neither would she. Not again. He had made himself clear in the wagon.

In a burst of irritation, she decided he was an idiot, too. She would gather what she could of her dignity and try to go back to treating him as a patient rather than a man she wanted.

Half an hour later, as she waited outside the hotel for Andrew to come out of the schoolhouse, she saw Jericho limping into the telegraph office next door, using his crutch. She hoped he was going there to wire his mother. And that the drive to the fort wasn't still causing him pain.

Back at home, she tried to avoid him. When she went out to the garden, he was on the porch. When she started a fire in the stove, he walked around her to the wood box, cradling an armful of kindling. She peeled potatoes for dinner. He watched her. She sat with Andrew to go over sums, and Jericho stayed nearby. His presence rattled her composure, but she wouldn't let it slip again.

Finally, after Andrew was in bed, she escaped to her bedroom. She had taken down her hair and unbuttoned her bodice when she heard the thunder of hoofbeats. Alarm spiked through her and she fumbled with the buttons again. More than one rider. What had happened? She rushed out and quietly opened Andrew's door to make sure he was still in bed.

Moonlight striped the near corner of his room, leaving his bed in deep shadow, but she could see that her brother was asleep on his stomach, his head turned toward her.

Relieved, she backed away and rushed to open the front door. Davis Lee and Jericho stood at the top of the porch steps. She noticed Matt Baldwin on the bottom stair at Davis Lee's shoulder, but her gaze snagged for a moment on Jericho. On his bare chest. Oh, my.

She swiftly shifted her attention to the other men. The sheriff's face was drawn and angry. And Matt, whom she'd only ever seen with a smile, looked like murder.

All eyes turned to her in strained silence. She stepped outside and closed the door. "What's happened?"

Davis Lee looked at his cousin as if to ask permission to tell her. Jericho scowled, obviously frustrated.

Annoyed, she moved into their small circle, closer to Jericho than she'd been since that afternoon. She studiously ignored the play of light across his strong shoulders and arms, the dark hair on his chest. "Tell me, please."

He jerked his head toward her as if telling Davis Lee it was all right to speak, but Davis Lee said nothing.

Muscle and sinew flexed in Jericho's arms as he braced his hands on his hips. Hating the awareness that lit her nerves, she sought out the big handsome man who had tried to court her when she'd first come to town. "Matt?"

"It's those damn McDougals," he said harshly. "Pardon my language, ma'am."

Her gaze flicked to Jericho, then she quickly focused on the sheriff.

"Matt's brother and pa found a steer butchered on their property," he said. "And a recent campsite."

"How do you know it's the McDougals?" she asked.

"It's them," Jericho said roughly, scrubbing a hand over his face. "I think they've been hiding nearby. It was only a matter of time before they came out of their hole."

"How near?" She looked at Matt.

He glanced at the other men for approval before answering. "Our ranch is four miles outside of town, Miz Catherine. On the other side of Riley's land."

That sounded entirely too close.

"We're getting a posse together now," Davis Lee announced to Jericho. "I knew you'd want to know."

"I'm coming." He turned and limped to the corner where he had dumped his saddlebags.

A protest rose on Catherine's lips, but she kept silent. He wanted nothing from her.

"Get his horse, Matt," Davis Lee said.

Matt Baldwin started for the barn.

"Damn." Jericho moved back into the feeble wash of light. "I can't ride. I only got in a damn wagon for the first time today. I sure can't shoot from a gallopin' horse."

His frustration was palpable, but Catherine feared the strain in his voice was due to pain.

"I'd slow you down." Anger and resentment pulsed from him.

"It's better that you stay here with Catherine, anyway," his cousin said. "We don't know which direction they'll ride."

"If you catch up to them—"

"They're yours." Davis Lee's gaze flickered to Catherine. "All of them."

She frowned, wondering what that meant.

Restless energy rolled off Jericho like waves of heat.

"Catherine, I'm sorry." Davis Lee turned to her. "I won't be able to drive you to the fort day after tomorrow. Jake will come for you."

"All ri—"

"No need for that," Jericho rasped. "She's not going."

Her gaze shot to him. Why did he think he could order her around? He would probably expect her to salute next. "I most certainly am."

A feral gleam came into his eyes as he looked at her fully for the first time. "Why would you do something so foolhardy?"

"I—" His gaze stripped her, probing, suspicious. Of her? "Dr. Butler needs me."

"He needs you alive, not dead."

Anger smoldered in his eyes, but she also glimpsed something else. Something soft and troubled. "And what if there's an emergency?"

"The gang won't ride toward the fort, Jericho. Not with the Army there." Davis Lee didn't flinch at the thunderous look on his cousin's face.

A muscle worked in his jaw. "If she goes—if—I'll take her."

"Dr. Butler might need me." Catherine kept her voice even with an effort, telling herself that Jericho was only concerned for her safety. He wasn't *trying* to be unreasonable.

"When he comes to town tomorrow, he'll hear about what's happened and probably agree that you shouldn't go." Tension coiled through his lean body, bringing the planes of his chest and shoulders into sharp relief. Shadows slid over the knuckled muscles of his bare belly right above the waist of his denim trousers. His face was unyielding. He laid down the law as if he were her husband.

A slow burn started inside her. "There are others who might need attention just as you did, *Lieutenant*."

His eyes narrowed into silver slits. "We'll discuss it later."

"We oughta go." Matt walked to his horse and swung into the saddle, tipping his hat to her.

Davis Lee took Catherine's hand. "I do apologize. I'll make it up to you."

"It doesn't matter right now." She smiled up at him, though

her lips trembled. Why was she about to cry? Certainly not because of the taciturn Ranger beside her. "Thank you, though."

The sheriff squeezed her fingers before he walked down the steps. He reached his horse, gripped the saddle horn and vaulted onto the animal's back.

Beside her Jericho seethed, resentment written in every taut line of his body. She eased away from him. "Be careful," she called as Davis Lee brought his horse alongside Matt's.

He tipped his hat to her, gave his cousin a long, strange look, then galloped off into the night with the other man.

She fingered the buttons at her bodice, realizing only now that she had missed the top two. Jericho watched the men go, his face hard in the pale light.

Maybe it came from her earlier embarrassment. Maybe it was because of his high-handedness, telling her where she would and wouldn't go. Her own anger flared again.

"You will take me to the fort." She'd meant it to sound confident; instead, uncertainty shook her voice.

He turned his head, his gaze impaling her. "Why are you not afraid, Catherine?"

She blinked. "What?"

"Why are you not afraid of the McDougals?" He took a halting step toward her. "You know what they've done to me. To others. Yet you take no precautions."

"I do. I have." She backed up once, then again as he kept coming. Her fingers fluttered at her chest, searching for buttonholes. The wall met her back and she pressed into it. "What is wrong with you?"

He stopped, his massive chest a fraction of an inch from her. Silver eyes burned into her and she heard his breathing turn rough.

"I only want to see you safe, Catherine. And yet you seem not to care."

"But I have you." The dusting of dark hair across his chest ran over his breastbone, then formed a thin line below his navel. Bless the saints. "Even if they tried to hurt me, you'd stop them."

He made a rude sound, his gaze piercing.

She stared up at him, her own breathing shallow as she clutched the open edges of her bodice together. At most, only two inches of her skin showed, but she felt stripped in front of him, her nerves, as well as her body.

Heat poured from him, his chest rising and falling. His stare was so intense that she squirmed. "Jericho?"

"I can't even get on my horse," he muttered. "What kind of protection is that?"

She frowned. "It's all I need."

"It isn't." Something flared in his eyes, something tender and wanting.

Her heart wheeled crazily in response. She dropped her gaze to the burnished skin stretched smoothly over his chest, his wide shoulders. If she put out her hand, she could touch the hewn muscles in front of her, his warm flesh.

Every pore drank him in—the tang of his shaving soap, his dark male scent tinged with a hint of sweat and salt.

"You wouldn't let anything happen."

He opened his mouth, clamped it shut.

His warm breath teased her lips and desire stabbed deep in her belly, between her legs. That had never happened before! She gasped and closed her eyes, trying to control her breathing, chase away her stupid thoughts. *Kiss me. Please kiss me.*

They stood like that for long seconds, merging shadows in the night. Braced against the wall, his heat stroking her, surrounding her, Catherine melted against the hard planes of his chest.

He turned away, saying harshly, "You trust too easily."

She opened her eyes and stared at the fluid flex of muscle across his broad back, the hand that fisted against his thigh. Shaken by the accusation in his tone, she felt a shudder ripple through her from head to toe. "I didn't think that was a fault."

She turned and went inside, closing the door against him.

Chapter Eleven

⁓⁓⁓⁓⁓

Even after Catherine went inside, frustration seethed in Jericho. He was damn tired. And mad. And hot.

He wanted to get Cinco and race after Davis Lee, but what help could he be? With the night closing in around him, Jericho eased himself down the porch's planed pine wall to the floor. Sharp, brittle pain chewed into his thigh.

Some of his anger abated, but not the grating sense of helplessness. Or the fiery sting in his blood. With the wooden wall at his bare back, he managed to get his boots off, not caring that his wrist hurt worse than it had in days. He was useless to Davis Lee right now, but at least he was here to provide some measure of protection for Catherine in case the Mc-Dougals rode close to the house. Andrew's involvement with the gang made that a real possibility.

He pulled his saddle over and balled his shirt into a pillow. Leaning back on his elbows, he lowered himself down to rest his head in the leather cradle. He told himself he was on the road to recovery, that he would regain full use of his hand and leg. The encouraging words from Catherine and Dr. Butler about the time it took to heal the body swirled through his mind, then his thoughts turned to Catherine.

Earlier, she had been so earnest in her belief that he could protect her, and what had he done? Backed her into the wall. Still, she hadn't cowered. It would've been far better if she had. Instead, she had studied his chest with a feminine appreciation that widened her eyes. The flash of hunger had made him want to peel that dress off her and kiss every inch of that creamy skin. He rested his good arm on his chest, working to ease the tangle of emotions inside him.

He focused on breathing, on the chirp of crickets. On the smells of dirt and grass, and the sultriness of the night. A puff of wind drifted along the porch, blowing across his damp chest. And still he pictured Catherine, looking at him as if she wanted to climb him. He didn't think she knew how easily he could read her face. Those blue eyes lingered in his mind as he fell asleep.

Some time later, something woke him. He lay still, registering a thud and a soft grunt. The sounds came from inside the house. Was Andrew sneaking out?

Jericho planted a hand on the wall to help himself up, then limped down the steps. On bare feet he hobbled toward her bedroom window and peered inside.

Yes, she was there, lying on her side facing him, her hair falling over one pale shoulder half-bared by the capped sleeve of her nightdress. He moved on to look into Andrew's window, but the boy's bed was shoved into the dark corner on the near wall. Jericho couldn't see anything. He opened the window and leaned in. Andrew's bed was empty and the boy wasn't in the room.

Jericho was pretty sure the kid had made the noise he'd heard, but had he been coming or going? The sounds had originated from the front part of the house, but no one had left by that door. Andrew had probably woken just as Catherine had, after hearing Davis Lee and Matt ride up. If so, the kid might have listened in on their conversation. Had he gone to warn the McDougals about the posse?

Usually the boy climbed out his bedroom window for his midnight trips, but this time he'd used the back door. Jericho stumped around behind the house. Was the lad outside or inside? Once on the stoop, Jericho opened the back door silently and stepped inside. The darkness swallowed him as he felt his way through the narrow space, moving toward the fireplace and kitchen. Once there, he could make out the stove, the dry sink and the rest of the front room and its contents. A small amount of moonlight leaked around the window curtains. The table and chairs were as Catherine had left them. No one was in this part of the house.

As quietly as he could, he groped his way past the stove. Recalling the last time he'd walked through this house in the dark, he put out a hand and followed the edge of the kitchen table, carefully skirting it. Favoring his leg made it difficult to avoid creaky floor planks, but no one stirred in the thick silence broken only by the sound of his breathing and the drone of night insects. He reached Catherine's bedroom door, already angling toward her brother's. It happened in a split second.

Her door flew open. She ran headlong into him, the surprise impact causing him to grunt. Reflex had him gripping her arms and pulling her hard into him to save them both from a fall. "Whoa."

Before the word left his mouth, she went wild, twisting away from him. Her arms flailed and one small fist caught him on the chin.

Stunned, he tightened his grip on her arms.

"No, no! Let me go."

"Shh, Catherine—"

"Get off!" She fought desperately, kicking, scratching, pummeling his chest with stinging blows.

He couldn't release her. She would fall if she suddenly lost his support.

"Get off of me!"

He clasped both arms around her and stilled her hands. She bowed her back, her hip banging him dead center. Oh, hell. He locked her against his chest so she couldn't knock into him again.

"Catherine." He grunted as her knee came perilously close to his manhood. "Stop. It's me. Jericho."

Her eyes were frantic and she shoved at his chest. "Please don't do this. Please, please, please."

She was panting the words. Her eyes were unfocused, her face a mask of fear. The obvious terror there jerked his mind back to the night he'd fallen against her.

He gentled his hold. Her spine felt fragile beneath his hands, her body so stiff it seemed she might snap at any moment. "Catherine, it's okay. I'm letting you go. See?"

He released her, pain shooting through his wrist. "Catherine?"

She blinked, staring at him uncomprehendingly for a moment.

"It's all right. I'm not touching you." His chin still tingled from the blow she'd landed. "You're okay."

He didn't know what else to say, but that seemed to help. He looked into her eyes, willing her to recognize him. Finally realization dawned. The fear faded and was replaced by confusion, then tears.

She looked so raw that he wanted to gather her back into his arms, but he didn't. "I'm sorry."

"No, I—" A choked sob escaped her. She bent her head and walked straight into his chest, her arms going around him, so tightly he felt her touch all the way to his heart.

Assaulted by the feel of her softness against him, the teasing scent of warm flesh, the uncertainty of what was happening, he stood unmoving for long seconds, his arms suspended at his sides. Touch her or not? A silent sob shuddered out of her and his arms wrapped around her. He rubbed her back, murmuring soothing words to her the way he had to his sister, Deborah, when she'd gashed her knee on a rock one summer.

Still Catherine trembled violently against him. "What just happened, sweetheart?"

She shook her head and looked up. Tears spiked her lashes, wet her cheeks in silver trails. His heart twisted. He lifted his hand, wiped away the wetness with his knuckles as he started to step away.

She buried her face against his chest and held on. "No."

A tightness squeezed his lungs and he knew he couldn't leave her like this. Still, her breasts against his chest and her hips between his thighs were starting to affect his body. He forced himself to lighten his hold on her. "I won't go. It's okay."

She sagged into him, her head falling against his shoulder. Concerned, he curled his arm around her and lifted her, bearing as much of her slight weight on his good arm as he could. His wounded hand could barely cup her knee. Pain burned through his wrist, but he didn't care.

He expected her to protest. Instead she hooked one arm over his shoulder and snuggled into his neck. Hell for breakfast.

He hobbled into her room, hating the drag and throb of his leg as he headed toward her bed. Sitting down, he braced his shoulder against the headboard for support. She clung to him like moss on a stone.

With an unsteady hand he stroked her shoulder, her hair, her arm, trying to keep his touch gentle. Deep, dark need sawed through him. The musky scent of her skin was underlaid with verbena and slipped inside his pores, insidious and tempting.

A ragged breath shuddered out of her and warmth washed against his neck.

Her unbound breasts rested softly against his bare chest, her position offering him a view of the satiny swells and the shadowed cleft between. He looked at the floor. "Are you all right?"

"Yes." Her voice was muffled against his bare chest.

"Can you tell me what happened?" He'd never seen such stark terror on a woman's face. On anyone's face.

"You startled me and I—" The words came reluctantly. Still looking dazed, she lifted a hand and stroked his cheek. "—I hit you. Where?"

"It's nothing."

"I'm so sorry." Her gaze searched his, her fingers sliding gently down the side of his face. "I don't know what happened. Something came over me."

"Tell me," he urged quietly.

She stared into his eyes, searching, considering. Uncertainty warred on her delicate features.

His thumb made small circles on her arm, foreboding and rage tangling inside him. She had been completely beside herself. He dreaded what she would say, but somehow he knew she needed to tell him.

"There was a man, a patient at the hospital in New York." She huddled against Jericho as if his body could break any wave of emotion that hit her.

His arm curved around her, his hand resting on her hip.

"I had assisted during his surgery. The doctor said he should've died, but he didn't. And he started calling me his angel." Her voice was remote and dry as dust, yet she shook violently. "During his recovery, he was charming and sweet, but after he was allowed to go home, he would appear in places where I was. Showing up at the market or the hospital. Once I saw him walking past the convent."

Jericho rested his head atop hers, trying to calm the fury gathering inside him like the winds of a twister.

"One evening, I went with Sister Clem to a rough part of the city to help a woman who was having a difficult labor. She was dying and she wanted her baby to be raised by the nuns. I went out to the buggy to fetch something. I don't remember now—oh, yes, she wanted a prayer book. I didn't even see him until I started back inside."

Her body was tighter than strung barbed wire, her slender shoulder pressing into his chest, her hip into his arousal. He ignored the effect she was having on his anatomy.

"I saw him and I spoke. I thought he had only happened by the place but he had followed me there. When I tried to go inside, he dragged me around the building. He said I'd been leading him on, which I *hadn't* been."

She said that part fiercely, and Jericho rubbed his hand up and down her arm.

"He tried to kiss me. I—I pushed him away. He knocked me into the wall and started tearing at my clothes." Her hand crept to her throat, gathering the thin fabric of her nightdress. "I hit him, I think. He pulled my skirts up, tore my underthings and my bodice."

A shudder rippled through her and Jericho blinked his stinging eyes. This was why she had been so terrified of him that night.

"Did he—?" The words stuck in his throat, scraping and raw. "Catherine?"

"No." She looked up at him, her eyes bright with pain and relief. "A group of boys were roaming the streets and heard me scream before he covered my mouth. They were a little older than Andrew, and they managed to get him off of me and chase him away, throwing rocks and whatever they could find."

Jericho worked to steady his breathing, trying not to crush

her to him. Fury blazed through him in a white-hot flash. "And did you tell the Sisters?"

"Yes, and the authorities. They chased him up to the roof of a tenement building and he jumped." She bent her head and Jericho had to dip his head to hear her. "Even though he was dead, I thought I saw him for weeks after that. Thought I heard someone following me, but there was no one."

"And tonight when I grabbed you, it all came back."

"I—I guess because I was awakened so abruptly. I'm sorry I hit you."

He pressed his lips to her temple, inhaling her fresh scent. Stray wisps of hair tickled his hand and he clumsily tucked a strand behind her ear. "No one is ever going to hurt you again."

Even as he said the words he knew they were a promise he couldn't keep, but he wasn't taking them back.

Her gaze locked on his, searching and soft. The trust in her eyes, the light wash of her breath against his lips had need punching him like a heavy fist. He was fair to bursting with it, and his timing made him sick.

He couldn't look at her. Gently he tucked her head under his chin.

"Thank you."

Her teeth chattered and he hugged her close. "You're shaking. Am I spooking you?" He loosened his hold to slide her off his lap.

She clutched his arm to her stomach. "No."

The strength of her grip surprised him. Her fear was palpable and it was clear she had only a tentative hold on her control. Just a few minutes more. He'd stay until she felt steady again. He angled himself so that he leaned back against the headboard, her body in the cradle of his thighs. He held her that way, his arm under her breasts, tight around her slight frame.

After long minutes, she relaxed into him and her clamp on his arm eased. But she didn't release him. Her breathing evened out. His gaze traveled slowly over the paleness of her skin and gown. In the haze of moonlight filtering through the window, he could see her small feet with their delicate arches. The neat turn of her ankle, a slender calf. Her gown had ridden up to her knee. Far enough to make his hands itch to slide beneath the garment and between her legs.

She had to be asleep. Otherwise she would feel his erection and bolt out of his lap. Savage need pounded through him. His hand crept over the thin cotton at her hip and he rubbed the soft fabric between his thumb and forefinger. He reached for her hand and lightly slid his fingers over hers.

After a moment, the urge to take her ebbed into a manageable state and his hands steadied. Touching her like this, without her knowledge, her *permission,* was a violation. He couldn't help himself. She stirred against him and he throbbed painfully. Lifting her hand, he softly kissed her knuckles, then the center of her palm.

There had been women in his life before, but he had never felt anything like what he felt for her. He didn't understand half of the emotions tearing through him, but he knew he could never touch her the way he wanted.

She didn't know the truth about him, what he'd come to take from her. And if he pursued this lashing, savage need and claimed her body the way he burned to do, he would be stealing everything from her. Trust, innocence. Jericho stared at the dance of moonlight on the wall, tortured by what he knew and what she didn't. But he couldn't leave her yet. She had touched something deep inside him and he had answered with his instincts, the only way he knew how. For better or worse.

Something warm grazed the hollow of his throat. Before

he could identify it—tears? her hair?—the sensation came again. A featherlight caress, but longer this time. Hot and wet. As Catherine laid a hand on his chest, he realized what was happening.

Her tongue. She had kissed him, *was* kissing him.

Need shot through him like lightning, and so did alarm. After the horrible memory she had just shared with him, he could not fathom giving in to the temptation of putting his hands on her the way he wanted. He reached up and covered her hand with his wounded one. She had been shaken earlier. She didn't know what she was about.

But when she looked at him, the quiet certainty in her eyes told him she knew exactly what she was doing.

She sat up, her hair tickling his chest. He took advantage of the movement, dropping his hand from her waist and scooting her down his thigh to his knee. He didn't want to push her off, but he had to get out of here. "Catherine, I don't want to leave if you're not all right, but—"

"But?" She stared transfixed at his mouth, and lust roared through him.

Lust and panic. "I can't stay. But after what you've told me, I don't want to hurt you."

"Then kiss me," she whispered.

He already didn't have a thimble's worth of restraint, and his trousers were too snug by far. He grabbed her waist and lifted her, setting her feet on the floor.

She blinked at him, looking startled, then wounded. Hell, he didn't want that, but he couldn't allow himself to reach for her. He got to his feet in turn, biting back a groan as blood rushed in a fiery tingle to his feet.

Concern flared in her eyes. "Are you all right?"

"I'm fine." Amazing that his voice didn't betray the fierce need clawing through him. He started for the door, damn near bent over from the pounding in his groin. "I'll be just outside if anything happens."

"All right," she said softly, tentatively.

He wanted nothing more than to go back and kiss her. Touch her. *Take her.*

"You shouldn't have felt you needed to stay," she said defensively.

He turned his cowardly butt around, refusing to let her think he didn't care about her feelings. "I didn't do anything I didn't want to do."

Searching his face, her eyes darkened with gratitude and some emotion that sucked the air dangerously out of his lungs. "Thank you."

Looking into those eyes, he could see clear to the core of her. She was so good, so trusting. He suddenly wanted to be worthy of that trust, and in the next instant, he didn't. Lives depended on his not being worthy of it, on staying true to his purpose for coming here.

"You're welcome." He limped out, aching for relief in his heart as much as his body. He didn't know how he would keep his hands off her now, but he would.

His erection throbbed. He headed straight for the barn, heedless of sharp pebbles hurting his feet, the occasional stab of grass between his toes.

Hot, reckless impulses surged through his blood, and Jericho knew he wouldn't get a wink of sleep. Not while knowing she was steps away, or remembering the way she'd curled against him, pressing shy kisses against his chest.

Bending his stiff right hand into a fist, Jericho let the shattering pain slice sharply through the haze of desire. He grunted, welcoming the discomfort for a moment. But at the barn, he stopped. He already felt suffocated; he couldn't go inside, where the walls would press in on him. He leaned one shoulder against the shadowed wall, wishing he could leave thoughts of Catherine behind as easily as he'd stepped out of the moonlight.

The darkness was his refuge as he struggled to calm the pounding of his blood. He didn't know how much time passed. A stray cloud covered the moon, then scudded past. The stars glittered in the midnight sky. He stilled his thoughts, as well as his body. Braced against the rough wood, he balanced his weight on his uninjured leg. The rush of his blood finally slowed, but he couldn't block the images of Catherine, the feel of her moist lips on his chest, her hip pressing against his erection.

He scrubbed a hand down his face. Hell.

A sound caught his attention and he glanced over his shoulder toward the house. In the moonlight, he recognized a blurred but familiar profile moving stealthily onto the back stoop. The door opened with a squeak, the noise that had alerted both him and Catherine.

Andrew.

Jericho stood motionless and watched as the boy slipped into the house. He took two limping steps out of the shadows, then one more, listening hard to the night sounds outdoors, and focusing on the muffled ones inside the house. A floorboard creaked, then another. Likely the same ones he had stepped on earlier. The kid was home safe, but how long could he keep this up?

Jericho didn't like knowing that Catherine would worry herself sick if she knew her brother was still sneaking out. He couldn't forbid the boy from going anywhere, not only because he had no right to but also because he needed the kid to lead him to the McDougals.

Frustrated over that for the first time since arriving, Jericho wondered if he could get Andrew to admit that he was in contact with the outlaws. If so, maybe Jericho could figure out a way to get to them without having to use the boy any further. The idea held far more appeal than it should have, until Jericho reminded himself that he had seen Andrew shoot him and his partner.

He had to face her sometime. Best just to get it over and done. The next morning, Jericho gave the pump handle three sharp jerks, then stuck his head under the spout. When the cool water hit the warmth of his neck, he winced at the change in temperature. Maybe he should've done this last night, he thought ruefully. It might have served to douse the fire in his blood and clear the fog of desire that had overtaken his mind.

He splashed water over his face and neck, scrubbed at the bristle of his whiskers. Walking away from her had been the right thing to do, the only thing.

Straightening, he dragged his hands down his face. He needed another shave. Water dripped onto his bare chest, sluiced down his back and into the waistband of his trousers as he shoved his hands through his hair. Steering his thoughts to Andrew, and the recollection of watching him sneak back into the house last night, Jericho reached for the towel hanging over the handle and passed it over his chest, turning as he did so.

The boy stood there, solemn and pale, with shadows under his eyes. No doubt because of his late night.

Jericho narrowed his gaze. "Doing all right?"

Obviously nervous, Andrew stepped in front of him and worked the pump handle a couple of times, washing his hands.

Surprise might be the way to trip up the kid. Spearing him with a look, Jericho said, "Your sister heard a noise last night. So did I."

He waited. Nothing. "Did *you?*"

Andrew shook his head.

Jericho thought the boy's chin quivered. "Sounded like somebody went out the back door, but I didn't find anyone." He drew out the silence for a bit, wanting to see how Andrew would respond.

Pressing bloodless lips together, Catherine's brother wiped his hands on the towel Jericho had used. He had to admire the boy. Even though his pulse beat wildly in his throat, he looked Jericho in the eye. "Maybe that was when I went to the outhouse," he mumbled.

"Hmm." Of course the kid was lying, but Jericho wouldn't get anywhere by pressuring him. His best bet was to follow Andrew the next time he left the house. Regardless of how his leg was, Jericho would trail the kid.

He glanced over and saw Catherine in the doorway, watching them. She worried the hem of her apron until he caught her eye. She gave him a tentative smile—a truce—and went back inside.

Regret flayed Jericho. If she knew he was trying to intimidate her brother into giving him some answers, she wouldn't want a truce.

Andrew seemed to be mighty interested in the pump handle. "What would you do if there was a girl—"

Aw, hell, the kid wasn't going to ask him how to cozy up to some girl, was he? Jericho had all he could do to *resist* cozying up to Andrew's sister.

"—and someone was trying to hurt her?"

That got his attention. "Trying to hurt her how?"

"Just threats." Andrew wiped jerkily at his face with the towel. "Saying they're going to do stuff to her."

"Have they done anything yet?"

"No."

"Are they your age?"

"Older. Bigger."

"Have you tried to get them to back down?"

Andrew hesitated, then nodded. "They just laughed."

"But you take them seriously?"

He nodded again.

"Is this taking place after school?"

"Yes."

"I can go talk to the teacher."

"No!"

Jericho frowned at the boy's vehemence.

"Uh, that would just make things worse."

Was that sweat on the kid's temple? "It's not Creed and Miguel, is it?"

"No, sir. No."

He threw another look toward the house. "What does your sister say?"

If possible the kid went even whiter. "I wanted to ask you."

"Do you want *me* to talk to them?"

"No." Andrew's eyes widened in protest. "I just wondered if there was something I could do."

"If you don't think the teacher can handle it, maybe you should tell the sheriff."

Tension coiled in Andrew's stocky body and his gaze darted nervously around the yard. The kid was as jumpy as a grasshopper outrunning a prairie fire.

"What is it?" Jericho asked softly.

The boy released a shaky breath.

"It's okay, Andrew." He clasped the kid's shoulder.

Worry lines were etched on his young forehead. He looked off into the distance, chewing his lip. Catherine did the same when she was nervous, Jericho noted absently. Her brother turned and opened his mouth, then clamped it shut, looking tortured.

"If you have a problem, you can tell me. I'll try to help."

"I don't." His voice was thick and guttural as he pivoted away. "Thanks."

Jericho followed the boy inside. He was disappointed that Andrew hadn't given up any information about the McDougals, but the kid was running scared from something. What could've happened to make him ask for Jericho's advice about anything? Did it involve the McDougals or not?

It was a shame Andrew had gotten tangled up with those outlaws. Jericho was starting to like him.

Inside, Catherine rushed around, pouring coffee and milk and pushing a plate of day-old biscuits and ham to the middle of the table. Andrew wolfed down two biscuits in short order, and Jericho diligently kept his eyes on his coffee, the honey he drizzled on his biscuits, the dust motes floating in the strip of sunshine coming in the window. Everywhere but on Catherine.

Her hair hung down her back in a neat plait and she had scrubbed her face, all pink and creamy. Her blue gaze met his, then skittered away as she sipped her coffee. Regret pinched him. He hated that she felt uneasy, but he couldn't afford to breach the distance he'd put between them last night. Run away. That's what he had done.

Andrew cleared his crumbs from the table and grabbed his lunch pail, holding it out to his sister. "Here ya go."

She took it and he picked up his books, tightening the leather strap holding them together. He balanced them over his shoulder and moved toward the door.

Catherine stared after him. A smile curved her lips as, lifting the lunch pail, she turned and met Jericho's gaze. "What do you think about that?"

He wanted to drink her in, kiss the pulse fluttering in the hollow of her throat. "I think you're gonna be late for school."

She came around to his side of the table on her way out. "You'll be ready when I get back?"

He knew she meant to work his hand. But he was ready now, Jericho wanted to grumble. With the feel of her body burned into his, he figured he'd be ready from now till hell froze over. And hell was likely where he was going for what he wanted to do to her. With her.

He was coming dangerously close to forgetting why he was here. No woman had ever made him want to stay until now. And this was the one place on earth he would never be welcome after he showed her the truth about her brother.

Chapter Twelve

Catherine had watched Jericho and Andrew having what looked like a serious conversation. But when they came in for breakfast, neither of them volunteered the topic of their discussion. What surprised her was that the two of them seemed almost comfortable with each other, while she and Jericho didn't.

She sighed. The strain didn't stem from the awful story she'd told him last night. No, the unease closing in like a press was due to the kiss she'd given him. He had held her, protected her and listened. And while she snuggled in his lap, she'd felt his arousal against her hip. She had waited for the fear, expected it, but rather than make her want to run, the feel of him against her had piqued her interest. And excited her.

For the first time since her attack, she had felt something stronger than fear. She'd experienced desire, and a soaring relief that she had finally put the incident behind her. The soft kiss he'd placed in her palm had encouraged her to follow a wild impulse to do the same, but *her* attempt at kissing him had gone badly. The taste of his skin, a warm blend of soap and salt and male, still lingered on her lips, interfering with her chores, her time with Andrew, her concentration.

Sensations she had never noticed before unfurled inside her. The rub of her breasts against the linen of her chemise, the silkiness of her hair drifting across her neck and shoulders. She wanted him to touch her. This awareness, acute and strange, was especially strong when she looked at him. Which was too frequently.

He, on the other hand, hardly looked at her at all over the next couple of days. He was still polite, continuing to help with the chores, but his face and eyes were carefully blank. Despite that, she felt a curious anticipation, an expectancy charging the air between them.

On Wednesday, he rode with her to the fort and pestered her into letting him drive the wagon. She finally relented, pleased to see that he managed the reins fairly well with his left hand. In an effort to fill the thick silence between them, she asked about his years as a Ranger, and about his friend, Hays.

She hoarded every bit of information he gave her. The men had met when Jericho secured a commission with the company of Rangers, and the two had become fast friends after getting caught in a hail of gunfire on their first assignment, escorting two prisoners to Austin. Hays had saved his life by picking off a pair of bandits who had Jericho in their sights. Jericho had returned the favor a couple of times in their twelve years together, but he hadn't been able to help his friend on the day of the McDougal ambush. Catherine knew that weighed heavily on him. His eyes hard, his voice even harder, he told her he would bring every last one of them to justice, and she believed him.

Even though he shared parts of his past with her, there was a reserve in him that hadn't been there before she'd stupidly

touched her tongue to his throat. She had seen more than desire in his eyes that night, but she'd seen nothing since.

Had she thrown herself at him? Should she apologize or
just follow his lead and try to dismiss the incident? But how
could she dismiss it when it had melted her fear? Maybe that
was it. Maybe he thought she was afraid. She wanted to tell
him she wasn't, but his polite detachment kept her silent.

Except for appearing at the times they had agreed to work
on his hand, he stayed to himself. He spent his mornings behind the house practicing with his revolver. On Thursday, she
heard an explosive blast and ran out to find him cocking his
rifle awkwardly with his left hand.

That evening she found him on the porch attempting to
shave himself. Hurt that he would rather cut his face than ask
for her help, she firmly took the straight-edge and imperson-
ally finished the job. Then she handed him a damp towel to
wipe the shaving soap from his face, and walked off.

For a couple of days she secretly believed that he would
bend, and confess that he wanted her with the same desperation she wanted him. Her mind conjured all kinds of scenar-
ios. As they drove back from the fort, he would pull her to him
and kiss her. Or when they worked on his hand. Or maybe he
would just walk into the house and do it. But none of those
things happened. *Nothing* happened.

The whole business was highly exasperating.

Finally on Friday, four days after he had sat on her bed and
comforted her, she was forced to admit that the wall between
them was one she couldn't breach, and Jericho didn't want her
to. Though his deliberate distance stung, she struggled to
carry on the way they had.

Since Dr. Butler hadn't needed her that day, she had been
doing the wash. Now, with the sun starting its descent, she was
nearly finished, her hair wilted, her arms aching. Andrew had

asked if he could go to Creed Carter's until suppertime. Catherine thought Jericho was behind the house, working with his gun. The wash water boiled in the kettle over the fire; a nearby barrel held cool water for rinsing. She always rinsed thoroughly, hating how the lye soap made her skin itch.

Steam from the hot water misted her face as she scrubbed at a pair of Andrew's grass-stained trousers, the last garment in her pile of laundry. With the back of her hand, she wiped away the perspiration on her brow, pushing damp hair off her forehead. The loose bodice of the threadbare dress she wore on laundry day stuck to a patch of damp skin between her shoulder blades and clung to her breasts.

A breath of wind circled the house and she stepped away from the fire to enjoy the welcome relief. Lifting her braid, she put a hand to her aching back and stretched. The pungent scents of wood smoke and strong soap drifted through the air. A pair of crows cawed hoarsely, their shrieks joined by a sound she didn't recognize.

It sounded like a moan. She glanced around, but saw nothing. She dunked Andrew's trousers into the barrel to rinse them, then heard the noise again. What was it? After wringing out the trousers and hanging them on the clothesline, she walked to the corner of the house and listened. It came again, louder. A groan. From behind the house.

Jericho. Picking up her skirts, she ran past the garden and root cellar. Jericho wasn't in the backyard or in the pasture beyond, so she headed toward the barn, her heart banging hard against her chest at the thought that she might find him hurt. She paused in the doorway, squinting into the dimness, but didn't see him. The groan came again.

Behind the barn? She raced around the back, her shoes silent on the short grass. She rounded the corner and saw

Cinco standing in a slight hollow in the ground. Jericho sat on the horse's back without a saddle. Or bridle, she could see now. And he wasn't sitting; he lay slumped over the horse's neck, his dark head visible between the animal's black-tipped ears. Struggling to catch her breath, she slowed. The Appaloosa stared at her with big dark eyes.

Her heart skipped a beat as she moved toward horse and rider. What was wrong? What had happened?

She was within arm's reach when Jericho swore violently and pushed himself to a sitting position. His gaze crashed into hers. His face was taut, his lips thin with pain, but she saw no blood, no awkwardly twisted limbs.

"Are you all right?" Alarm made her voice husky. "What is it?"

"I'm okay." He scowled. His shoulders blocked most of the sun as it sank to the horizon.

Her heart beating sharply in relief, she put her hands on her hips. "What are you doing? How did you get up there?"

He glared, muttering something she couldn't understand. He looked like Andrew had the first time she'd walked him to school, furious and embarrassed.

"You shouldn't be on that horse."

"It's time," he said shortly. "I need to ride."

"You've hurt yourself."

"My muscles just aren't used to this. I'm fine."

She refrained from pointing out that he had just groaned loudly enough to be heard in the next county. He shifted on the mare's back and his face creased in pain. She could see the sheen of sweat on his neck.

"What about your stitches?"

"I took them out."

"You what?" She shouldn't have been surprised. "What would make you do such a thing?"

"I didn't want to rip them."

"You would rather tear your wound?" she asked hotly. She moved to the horse's shoulder, tipping her head back to give Jericho an irritated look. The Appaloosa bumped her chest with a warm muzzle. "Come down from there right now."

One dark eyebrow arched. "Or what?"

She frowned.

"You gonna come up here and get me? Pull me off?"

"Don't be ridiculous."

"I have to get back in the saddle, Catherine. I should've gone with that posse the other night. Next time I will."

She understood how badly he wanted to capture the McDougal gang, that he had promised to avenge his friend's death. "I'm worried about your leg."

"It's a little sore, but okay."

"Let me look at it."

"You want me to just drop my trousers right here?" he asked dryly.

"Well, how else will I be able to look at it?"

His mouth fell open, but he quickly recovered. "No."

She waved a hand dismissively. "It's not like I haven't seen your…that…you naked before."

"I was unconscious," he muttered. "And couldn't be affected by you."

He was affected by her? She hadn't only imagined it? A wild, stupid flare of hope leaped in her chest. "Come down."

He stared at her mutinously.

"Didn't your mother teach you not to keep a lady waiting?"

A smile tugged at his lips, but it was completely at odds with the dark seriousness of his gray eyes. "All right."

He leaned forward and held tight to Cinco's thick neck, then dragged his right leg over the animal's back. His tall, lean body draped over the horse and he hung there for a moment, his booted feet dangling close to the grass. Catherine knew he was gauging the distance, trying to avoid jarring his leg when he touched the uneven ground.

She lightly placed her hands at his waist.

He froze. "You'd better move or I'll fall on you."

"I'll just help you find your footing. Slide on down." The heat of his skin reached her through his shirt, warming her palms.

Without thinking, she put a hand on the back of his left thigh to guide him. A breath hissed out of him as he set his feet on the ground. His breathing was rapid, his jaw drawn tight.

"How bad does it hurt?" she asked quietly.

"I'm okay." His voice was strained as he faced her.

"I'll get your crutch." She turned to look for it.

"I didn't bring it out here."

"That's all right. I can help you in."

"I don't need help, Catherine." A desperate light, close to a plea, shone in his eyes. "I need you to leave me alone."

"Which I would do if you would let me help you back to the house," she said tartly, determined to keep her gaze from the wide expanse of chest in front of her.

The open placket of his shirt revealed the hollow at the base of his throat, a swath of burnished skin, a smattering of dark hair on the flat planes of his chest.

He stared hard at her, scowling.

She ignored the flutter in her stomach and folded her arms, staring back.

"All right," he said gruffly. "But you're still not looking at my leg."

"I really should—"

"No."

He would stand here arguing until midnight, so she didn't answer, just slipped an arm around his waist and tugged gently. "Come on."

He didn't budge.

She rolled her eyes and glanced up. An intent look had settled on his face; his eyes burned with silver light. "We'll get there a lot faster if you'll help me," she chided softly.

A muscle ticked in his jaw. After a long hesitation, he carefully put an arm around her shoulders and they started across the uneven ground. She tried not to think about the last time she had felt the corded strength of his arm around her. Or wonder if his skin would taste the same today.

He was heavy. She reached up and grasped the wrist that hung over her shoulder, realizing she fit next to him as if they were a whole that had been separated into halves years ago. She belonged there. Why couldn't he see it? His heat pulsed against her and his heady male scent surrounded her, reminding her of questions she had been asking herself for the last four days.

"Do you find me…" She *was* going to ask. Catherine forced herself to look at him. "Is there something wrong with me?"

Perplexed, he stared down at her.

She could've quit right there, but she gathered her courage and plowed on. "I mean, why don't you want me?"

The words cut the air like a blade. He went perfectly still.

She couldn't take back what she'd said, but as the seconds stretched awkwardly, she wanted to. *Oh, please don't make me ask again.*

He shook his head as if trying to clear it, saying hoarsely, "There's nothing wrong with you. Not one thing."

Her face burned, but she had to know the truth. "Then is there someone else?"

"No." He expelled the word like a curse, dropping his arm from her shoulders and stepping back.

"I don't understand." Her voice thickened, but she made herself press on. "That night in my room, you wanted me. I felt it and I wasn't afraid."

Dark color flushed the strong column of his neck. His good hand flexed at his side.

"I'm so inept at these kinds of things." She wrapped her arms around herself, ready to chew her nails to the quick. "I don't know what to say or do."

"You're doing just fine," he said gruffly.

"But you don't want me. I don't know how to—"

His hand closed gently over her upper arm and he backed her up a step until she was pressed against the barn wall. "I want you more than I want my next breath."

She blinked. His voice was strained, tortured. He sounded as if he was in agony, while she was elated. He removed his hand, just held her in place with the welcome nearness of his body.

"Then why won't you touch me? Kiss me like you did before?"

A muscle worked in his jaw. Hesitantly, he cupped her face. "Because I'll be leaving."

"I don't care." She felt his hand tremble against her cheek. "Is it because you think I'm afraid? I'm not. Not of you."

Despite the tenderness in his eyes, a pained look crossed his face. "We shouldn't be talking about this. It can't happen."

"It can if we both want it," she whispered.

He looked at her as if he were committing her to memory, one finger gently tracing the shell of her ear, touching the sensitive hollow below. She should've been ashamed of her boldness, but she wasn't. Mortified that she was baring her soul to him, maybe, but not ashamed.

His silver gaze was soft. "I can't take you like that and walk away."

"Then don't go," she begged quietly.

"If we did this, I would still have to leave and you would be here, changed. Ruined."

"No, not ruined."

She could tell he was struggling with something, and he seemed to have trouble speaking. "I don't want you to hate me when I go, Catherine."

"I could never hate you."

"You don't know everything about me."

"I know enough." She touched his face then, as she'd been aching to—the strong jaw rough with stubble, the scar high on his left cheekbone. "I know you're kind and noble and would never let anyone hurt me."

He stiffened as if bracing for a blow. Every careful word seemed to take a measure of control as he answered, "Someday you'll meet someone and you'll want him to be your first."

"You're the one I want, the only one I'll ever want."

He shook his head and turned his face into her palm, pressing a kiss there. "Must you make it so hard on a man?"

"I want to give myself to you. No one else."

"Woman, you try me," he muttered.

She read desire in his eyes, saw it battle with restraint. He brushed his thumb down her cheek, across her bottom lip.

She held very still, trembling as a hot restlessness churned inside her.

His head descended and a thrill shot through her. Then he froze. Her heart thundered in her ears and she stared into his eyes, willing him to touch his lips to hers.

He turned his head away and closed his eyes. "Andrew."

"Andrew!" The anticipation that had arced between them disappeared. How could he be thinking of her brother at a time like this? "What does he have to do with this?"

Jericho swallowed hard. "He's yelling for you."

Completely absorbed by the man in front of her, she hadn't heard a thing.

"Catherine?" She heard Andrew now in the distance, his voice sharp with impatience.

Jericho's eyes glittered with savage need as he stepped back. Frustration and disappointment tore through her.

"Catherine!" Her brother's voice was filled with a panic she'd never heard before. "Catherine!"

"You'd better go," Jericho said quietly.

Confused, her emotions tangled and bruised, she turned, heat stinging her cheeks as she moved to the corner of the barn.

Just as she started up the side of the building, a small dark blur barreled into her. Andrew, she realized, closing her arms around him. "What is it? What's wrong?"

Worry carved a deep frown in his forehead. "I couldn't find you. I thought something had happened." His words tumbled out in a frenzy.

"It's all right. I'm here." She hugged him tightly, smoothing a hand over his hair. Ignoring the hollowness in her stomach, she focused on her brother.

He was shaking, and Catherine stroked his back. After losing their mother so suddenly, she shouldn't have been surprised that her brother would fear she might disappear, too. "I won't leave you, Andrew."

He squeezed her hard. At least one male in her life wasn't pushing her away.

Then he drew back and looked at her, his eyes suspiciously bright. "I thought you were gone."

"Now, where would I go?" She kept her voice light, trying to ease his agitation.

"Just… You can't go anywhere alone. All right?"

"Has something happened in town?" Perhaps his fear had nothing to do with their mother's death. "Have the McDougals done something else?"

She was sure it was guilt that flitted across his features. "Have *you* done something?" she pressed.

"No. I swear." His blue eyes were earnest as he released

her. "It's just not safe around here. You shouldn't go out alone."

Behind her, she heard a movement in the grass and half turned. It was Jericho with the horse. Facing the man whom she understood so little about was the last thing she wanted. She hugged Andrew to her, then tugged him forward. "Let's go to the house."

"What were you doing back there, anyway?"

Her brother's question was innocent, but Catherine's entire body burned with embarrassment. She still hadn't been able to calm the staccato beating of her heart. "Helping Lieutenant Blue off his horse. He was trying to ride."

Her brother glanced back, looking relieved. "I'm glad he's here and you weren't by yourself."

He didn't shrug away from her hand on his neck. Since when had he been *glad* Jericho was here? "Are you sure you're not in any trouble? You'd tell me if you were, wouldn't you?"

"I'm not in trouble. I just don't want you to go off anywhere unless me or the Ranger know where you are. Since school's now out for the summer, I can go to town with you or wherever you need to go."

What had come over him? Making certain she was escorted to town, warning her not to go anywhere alone? "All right, I'll be sure and let you know—"

"Hello?" Davis Lee's voice interrupted them, and a moment later he strode around the house. "Ah, here you are."

The sheriff pulled off his hat and slapped it against his thigh, sending dust flying. He looked tired, dirty, and sunburned, which didn't make him any less handsome. His smiling gaze encompassed both of them. "You're a sight for sore eyes, Catherine."

"Are you only now returning from chasing the McDougals?"

"Yes." He stared intently at her and a quizzical expression

crossed his face. She didn't recall that the sheriff had ever looked at her that way before.

Feeling a little wary, she asked, "Have you eaten? Can I get you something to drink?"

Jericho limped around the side of the barn, leading his horse. As the two men greeted each other, Davis Lee's gaze shifted to his cousin, then came back to rest on her knowingly.

"I just came by to tell Jericho that we didn't catch the gang. They headed west, but we think they doubled back. We can't find any sign of them in any direction past Big Spring."

Jericho's face hardened and he said something under his breath.

Flanked by the two large men, Catherine suddenly felt the need to escape. "Will you be going out again soon?"

Davis Lee knew she had been behind the barn with Jericho. She could tell by the faintest flare of surprise in his face when he eyed his cousin.

The sheriff smiled at her without a trace of censure. "Not unless we hear something or pick up another trail. The Baldwins are checking their herd for more dead cattle and making sure there are no new campsites on their land."

Heat flushed her entire body, but embarrassment wasn't what had her stomach tightening. When Davis Lee had left with the posse on Monday night, he'd had every intention of returning and escorting her to the fort.

Her nerves jangling, all Catherine could think about was having a word with this man who had been so kind to her. "I've got some pie. Let me get you a piece."

"That sounds good, but I can't stay."

"I'll wrap it up." She squeezed Andrew's shoulder and moved toward the sheriff.

Jericho stood by the barn, his face impassive, his gaze burning with that silver light.

Davis Lee looked past her to his cousin. "We're having a town meeting tomorrow night. It would help if you were there."

"About the McDougals?"

The other man nodded. "We should be able to come up with a good plan."

"All right. I'm all for that."

Catherine fell into step with the sheriff, and Andrew trotted behind.

"Hey, Andrew!" Jericho called. "Would you mind helping me with Cinco? I plumb wore myself out."

Since he had used neither saddle nor bridle and could brush down the horse himself, Catherine knew he was giving her a moment with Davis Lee.

Andrew hesitated, then seemed to decide that Catherine would be all right, since she was with the sheriff. "Okay, yeah."

She watched her brother jog back to the barn, carefully keeping her gaze from Jericho's. Relieved that Andrew was staying behind, she continued with Davis Lee along the side of the house and to the front. She started up the porch steps.

He put a hand on her arm. "Wait."

She stopped, giving him a smile.

"I—We— Aw, hell, there's no way to ease into this, so I'm just going to say it." He shoved a hand through his hair, looking distinctly uncomfortable. "I can't help noticing there's something going on between you and my cousin."

Her cheeks flamed. So Davis Lee had known that she and Jericho were behind the barn together. What the sheriff didn't know was that his cousin wanted her, but had no intention of acting on that. Her confusion deepening, Catherine shook her head. "You mustn't think that. It isn't true."

"If you're trying to spare my feelings, I appreciate it," he said gently. "But it isn't necessary. I've known for a while that you're interested in my cousin."

She wanted to deny it; the interest would certainly never lead to anything. "If I did anything to injure you—"

"Hush now. We had no understanding between us. I enjoyed our time together."

"So did I," she said sincerely, plucking at the folds of her skirt. "You're one of the kindest men I've ever known."

"You were raised in a convent, Catherine," he said dryly. "There *were* no men."

She laughed softly, her unease fading. "I'll get your pie."

"Can I take you up on that offer later? Right now I'd sure like to get a bath."

"Of course. Anytime you want."

He swung into the saddle, smiling down at her fondly. "You know you can come to me if you ever need a friend."

"Yes, thank you."

"You okay?" His blue eyes were kind.

She smiled. "Oh, yes. I'm glad you're home safe."

"Me, too." He grinned and touched his hat to her as he clucked to the horse.

Jericho might want her, but he wasn't going to do anything about it. Catherine watched Davis Lee ride off, thinking she was a fool to want his cousin rather than him.

Chapter Thirteen

Why don't you want me? Catherine's question seared him all over again the next day, and Jericho felt like groaning in frustration. How could he *not* want her? Her declaration that she wanted to give herself to him had him hard and aching still.

Kissing her would've been a dozen kinds of wrong, but he hadn't stopped wishing he'd given in and done it. He could still taste the dark honey of her mouth from their first kiss, feel the shy touch of her tongue on his neck from the other night. The memory of her soft bottom in his lap and her hip pressing into his erection had him seeing double. Hell, he should just shoot himself right now.

His restraint was starting to fray like bad rope. The temptation to take what she offered, to possess her, rode him hard, but he couldn't take her innocence. Not after the assault she'd suffered. Not with what he was planning to do to her brother.

Which left him in the same rock-hard place regarding Catherine that he had been in before Davis Lee had left with the posse. He wanted her, but couldn't have her.

The strain between him and Catherine was noticeable enough that at supper Andrew eyed them both curiously. The

boy rattled on about the school session being over, the trip he
and his friends planned to take to the creek by Eishen's pecan
grove. Jericho and Catherine both talked to Andrew; they
didn't talk to each other.

Though there were still signs of worry in the boy's face,
he hadn't said anything else to Jericho about the girl who was
being threatened. With school letting out, maybe those bul-
lies had decided to leave her alone.

After the meal, Jericho reminded Catherine that he was
going to the town meeting. She nodded, saying nothing as she
bent over a shirt she was mending. All day she had avoided
his eyes and him whenever possible. The same thoughts that
had been circling through his head since yesterday still chased
him as he walked to town.

He was closing in on Andrew. All he needed was for the
kid to sneak out one more time, and Jericho would be on his
trail. That realization didn't bring the satisfaction it should
have, just a hollow ache in his chest. The murders of Hays
Gentry and Ollie Wilkes and the others made it impossible for
Jericho to let the kid and the outlaws walk away.

The men of the town met in the schoolhouse. Davis Lee
delayed the meeting, waiting on Riley and the Baldwins, as
well as some others, but after thirty minutes he began. Riley
finally arrived, announcing that two of his horses had been
stolen. Jake Ross came in right behind him, saying the same
thing. Three of his chickens were missing, too. J. T. Baldwin
said his housekeeper had reported two blankets missing from
the clothesline. It was the McDougals; it had to be.

By the end of the meeting, the men had divided into
teams of two, working six-hour shifts to watch both ends
of town. Davis Lee and Jericho planned to ride out to
Riley's and Jake's to see if they could pick up any tracks
from these new thefts. While his cousin went to saddle his

mount at the livery and get a lantern so they wouldn't destroy any evidence they found, Jericho went back to Catherine's for his horse.

Davis Lee rode up as he brought a saddleless Cinco around to the front of the house. After drawing the gelding next to the porch, Jericho limped up the steps to the door. Catherine answered his knock, looking disturbed when he told her about this latest rash of incidents. He didn't want to leave her and Andrew alone, but it wouldn't be for long.

Hating the way her eyes were shuttered against him, he clenched his fist against his thigh. She answered all his questions in a quiet, flat voice. Yes, Andrew was already in bed. No, she wouldn't let anyone in. Yes, the shotgun was loaded and behind the door.

She stood in the doorway, looking at him as if she wanted to escape. Lamplight brushed one side of her face and he suddenly ached to trace the line of gold with his lips, across her cheek to her mouth. He moved to the edge of the porch, using it as an aid to mount, the same way Dr. Butler had suggested he get in and out of the wagon. Mounting from the left didn't spook his horse, so he put his good leg over Cinco's back and sank down gingerly to straddle the animal.

Catherine's gaze flickered to his leg and her lips tightened, but she didn't speak.

"I won't be gone long."

She nodded, her face impassive, her blue eyes unreadable in the darkness. "Be careful, both of you."

Davis Lee's buckskin pranced impatiently and he threw an expectant look at Jericho. Finally dragging his gaze from her, Jericho turned Cinco and rode with his cousin toward town and Riley's ranch.

The guarded look in Catherine's eyes hollowed out his gut. He had to stop thinking about her. To that end, he focused on the painful muscles stretching in his thigh, glad he had not waited until now to get on a horse.

They were through town and heading for Riley's ranch when Davis Lee spoke. "What are you going to do about Catherine?"

"What do you mean?" Jericho leveled a look at his cousin.

The other man took his time in answering. "I've got a pretty good idea what the two of you were doing behind the barn last evening."

"We weren't," he said flatly. "Even so, I know what it looked like and I'm sorry for that—"

"I already knew which way the wind was blowing. Catherine and I worked it out, but things didn't appear too rosy between you two back there. She seemed ready to bawl and you looked like you could kill a buffalo with your bare hands."

Jericho set his jaw. He had seen how miserable he'd made her. He didn't need his cousin going on about it. "It won't be long until we catch the McDougals and I'll be gone."

"So you really are going to leave?"

"I won't be able to stay," he said gruffly.

"You don't think you and Catherine—"

"You know it doesn't matter what I want. I came here to arrest her brother and catch those outlaws. When she learns about that, she isn't going to want to be within a hundred miles of me."

What twisted at his conscience even more was the closeness he'd seen developing between her and Andrew. She would be more than angry because of Jericho. She would be devastated.

Davis Lee slid him a sympathetic look. "I'm very glad I'm not you, cousin."

Jericho grunted, his gut a mass of knots. His path was clear, but instead of asking himself if he could find a way to bait the kid into visiting the gang, he was trying to figure out a way to keep from hurting Catherine.

And that was when he knew. He didn't just want to take Catherine Donnelly to bed. He wanted a little piece of her heart, just like she'd taken from him.

Catherine sat on the top step of the porch, her arms hugging her knees into her chest. She hadn't been able to sleep, so she had quietly slipped outside, careful not to wake Andrew. For the last half hour, she had been telling herself that it wouldn't be long before Jericho was well enough to leave. She only had to keep up her guard until then.

From the corner of her eye, she caught a movement and turned her head. The dark shape of one short leg swung out of Andrew's open window. Where did he think he was going? She started to rise, then stopped as he eased to the ground and took off running toward town. She would follow him and see where he went, what he did during these late-night trips.

He had better not be meeting Creed and Miguel for more smoking or any other kind of mischief.

She let him get more than twenty yards away before she slipped quietly off the porch and hurried after him. There was no hiding place on the rippling prairie between her and Whirlwind, so while she could easily keep Andrew in sight, she would also have no cover if he turned around.

Being careful, she stayed near enough to see him, but not so near that he could hear her skirts swishing through the grass. Moonlight shimmered around them, making him easy to follow. He never turned around. Either he was too intent on his destination or he had done this so often he didn't fear getting caught.

He darted behind the schoolhouse, then across North Street to disappear behind Cal Doyle's law office. The town was dark and quiet, and being a weeknight, so was the saloon. Catherine eased around the corner of the law office in time to see Andrew duck down and disappear into the wall of Haskell's General Store. The wall? She moved closer and spotted a ragged gap sawed in the wood, just big enough for her brother to crawl through.

Was he the one stealing from the store? Why? First appalled, then angry, she folded her arms and waited. Several minutes later, she heard a grunt, then saw a pair of hands holding a lumpy bag emerge.

He dropped the bag to the ground and stuck out his head, level with her ankles. Slowly his gaze traveled up to her face. "Oh, no."

"Come out of there right now," Catherine whispered furiously.

He scrambled to obey, keeping his gaze on the ground.

"Are you the one who's been stealing from Mr. Haskell?"

"Yes," he mumbled.

A pain stabbed through her chest as she gestured toward the gunsmith's shop next door. "And the cartridges from Mr. Doyle?"

He nodded.

"Why?" Catherine was assaulted with anger and sadness and guilt. Why was he stealing? For thrills? Because he was lashing out at the death of their mother? Rebelling against his sister?

He still hadn't answered, and irritation flared in her. She picked up the bag and opened it. Moonlight glinted off the metal of several tinned goods. She felt the smooth skin of apples and a wrapped wedge that she identified as cheese. "I know you do not need this food."

He didn't speak, just looked up at her with a mix of agony and stubbornness in his expression.

"Take this back inside right now."

"But Catherine—"

"Do it. And come right back out the way you went in. Don't even think about using the front door."

He hesitated, uncertainty turning to fear on his face. "I can't," he moaned.

"Andrew," she warned. "You return those things, then we're going to tell Deputy Ross what you've done. And when the sheriff returns, you're going to tell him, too."

"No, Catherine! I can't." Andrew's voice trembled with panic and she was surprised to see tears in his eyes.

"Don't think to play on my sympathy."

"I'm not." A tear dropped onto his cheek and he swiped it away with the back of his grubby hand. He looked conflicted and she saw terror deep in his eyes.

Concern edged in with her anger. "Andrew?"

"I can't tell, Catherine. They'll kill me and maybe you, too."

His words were so unexpected that she drew back, asking sharply, "What are you talking about?"

He dragged his arm under his nose, his words broken as he tried to stop crying. "I didn't want to do it."

She gave him a narrow-eyed look.

"I didn't! When I said no, they said they were going to kill me if I didn't help them. And they said they would get you and the Ranger. I didn't know what else to do."

His words poured out with a raw desperation. Catherine struggled to make sense of them. "Who, Andrew? Who threatened you?"

He wiped his face against his shoulder, his voice a mere whisper. "The McDougals."

"The…" Shock washed the starch right out of her legs and she put a hand against the wall for balance. She didn't want to believe it, didn't want to hear anything else about it, but she could see by the icy whiteness of her brother's face that he was telling the truth. "How long has this been going on?"

His gaze slid away. "Since before you came."

He had been running errands for the McDougals. "When you sneak out of the house, is it to steal things for them?"

"Sometimes. At first I just wanted to be with them."

"Why would you ever want to be with men like that?"

"Ma was sick and I didn't have nobody." He snuffled. "They told me stories and taught me to play cards. I didn't see the harm. I fetched things for them and cleaned their guns, stuff like that."

"How did you even meet them?"

"One day I saw Ian—he has consumption—in the alley between the Pearl Restaurant and the telegraph office. He gave me some money and asked me to go to Haskell's and buy him some medicine."

One of the McDougals had tuberculosis?

"When he left, I followed him, and the others saw me. Since I had helped Ian, they didn't mind having me around." Andrew shrugged. "After that they asked me to bring 'em stuff and they took me to their camp a couple of times."

"And when did you begin stealing?" Her brother had felt so alone that he had tried to make a place for himself among outlaws? "After I arrived?"

He nodded. "I know I should've quit going there, but I was mad that you tried to boss me around. I didn't even know you. And I didn't like the Ranger being in our house."

Incredulous, Catherine inhaled sharply. "You knew he was after them and you said nothing? Oh, Andrew. They killed his friend. And Whirlwind's stage driver."

"I know," he said miserably.

She understood how lost and lonely he had felt after their mother's death. Then he'd been thrust into the company of a sister he had never met before. Their father was dead, and because their mother's illness had taken all her strength, Andrew had probably received little attention during those months before she passed away.

Her brother edged up to her, his expression earnest. "I didn't want to tell them things anymore or steal for them, but when I let them know I was finished, they got mad. They thought I'd told Sheriff Holt where they were camped. That's when they—" His voice broke.

"They what, Andrew?" Her own voice was ragged with apprehension.

His face twisted in a grimace and he lifted his shirt, turning so she could see his side. In the darkness, she could only make out a black blotch. "What is that?"

"They burned me."

"Oh, no." She immediately pulled him close. His arms went around her and he shuddered. "Are you burned anywhere else?"

"No."

She set him back and drew up his shirt, running her fingers lightly over the mark. "It's scabbing, but I need to look at it, make sure it isn't infected."

"I doctored it with some of that ointment you use on the Ranger's hand."

"It's not really for burns, but I guess it's done no harm. I wish you had confided in me. I could've helped you."

"There's four of 'em, Catherine. They would've hurt you, too. Just like they said."

"It will be all right now. We'll tell Jericho—"

"No!"

"The sheriff then. He'll protect you."

"No." Andrew pulled away, terror etched on his face. "They'll do what they said, Catherine. They'll hurt you, too."

"We have to do something, Andrew. We can't allow them to keep bullying you into helping them."

"If you tell, they'll come for me. And you. And the Ranger." His voice thickened with fresh tears. "I don't want you to go, Catherine. I finally like you and I don't want anything to happen to you."

He liked her. In spite of the situation, she smiled at his wording. "I like you, too."

"Please promise you won't tell the sheriff. Or Lieutenant Blue," Andrew pressed.

"You can lead Jericho and Davis Lee to the gang's hiding place. Then they won't be able to hurt you anymore."

"But I don't know where they're hiding. I haven't known since the posse went after them. They told me to leave the food in the usual place."

"You can tell that to the sheriff. He can go with you and set a trap for them."

"Only one comes, and if something happens to him, they'll know I told. They'll hurt you, Catherine. Please don't say anything. If something happens to you, it will be just like when Ma died. Then I won't have anyone."

He touched her heart with that. She knew he had suffered far worse than she had.

"I can't promise." He looked so stricken that she squeezed his shoulder. "But I won't tell Davis Lee right now."

"You mean it?" Relief was stark in his shadowed face, his swollen eyes.

"For now. I'll figure out what to do."

Her brother clasped her waist in a tight hug. "That's good."

She rubbed his back as he stepped away. "When are you supposed to leave the food?"

"As soon as I get it."

"You'll have to find a way to pay Mr. Haskell and Mr. Doyle back for the things you took."

"I will."

The thought of her brother being near those outlaws made Catherine queasy. "I'll go with you."

"You can't!"

"You're not going alone."

"I'll be all right. They're never there when I leave the food. Besides, what if the Ranger gets back home before we do?"

"You were listening when he came to the door tonight?"

He nodded.

Andrew was right. If Jericho returned to find Catherine gone so late, he would surely become suspicious.

"I can do it, Catherine."

Her brother wore the same determined look he had the night he'd rushed into her bedroom with the shotgun pointed at Jericho. He was only twelve, but he hadn't been a little boy for a long while now. Not with their mother's illness and death, and now this. Still, Catherine didn't like him going alone.

"You must go as quickly as possible. Take Moe and get home fast."

He nodded. "I will."

"Don't come in through your window. Use the back door and be as quiet as you can."

"I'll be like a mouse. Last time I used the door, the Ranger heard me. He said y'all both heard a noise."

The night she had told Jericho about her attack. She ruffled her brother's hair as they walked behind the livery and started home. "I don't want you to be near those men ever again."

"After tonight we'll figure something out, won't we?" He looked at her with desperate hope.

"Yes."

She longed to confide in Jericho, but Andrew really believed the McDougals would kill her and the Ranger if Andrew didn't do what they wanted. Knowing what she did of the outlaws, having seen the burn they'd inflicted on her brother, she had to believe he was right. If Jericho knew any of this, he would go after the McDougals immediately. There were four of them against only him, and he had yet to regain full use of his gun hand.

The risk was too great. She closed her eyes as fear snaked up her spine. She couldn't let Jericho know what she'd learned.

The next morning, Catherine worked in the garden. Feeling jittery, she looked over her shoulder every few seconds, not sure if she was anxious about seeing Jericho or frightened that one of the McDougals might appear. Andrew had come in very late last night, long after Jericho had knocked on the front door and let her know he was back. Jericho and Davis Lee had been unable to find any identifiable tracks. That bit of news had hitched her panic even higher. She had been out of her mind with worry, fearing that the outlaws had hurt her brother or taken him.

Her concern wasn't unfounded. After Andrew returned, he crept into her room and told her that Angus, the oldest brother and the gang's leader, had been waiting. Relieved to have her brother home safe, she had finally gone to sleep, only to be plagued by dreams of Jericho getting shot again, this time in front of her. Her heart had been beating too fast all morning.

Andrew walked into the garden and came over to kneel beside her.

She took in his wan features, the shadows beneath his blue eyes. "Are you all right this morning?"

He nodded, casting a glance over his shoulder to make sure Jericho wasn't around. "They want you to come today, Catherine. As soon as you can."

"I'll have to make an excuse." Last night Angus McDougal had coerced Andrew into finding them a bed somewhere indoors. They had also demanded that he bring Catherine to check on Ian. "Jericho knows I'm not needed at the fort today."

"I don't want you to go," Andrew said fiercely. "I wish I'd had the shotgun yesterday. I would've killed—"

"Shh." She squeezed his knee. "It's okay. I'll be all right."

He looked doubtful. "I'll be with you."

"No. You can direct me to where Widow Monfrey lived." Andrew had told her he'd taken the outlaws to the empty house of a woman who had died about a year ago.

"Angus said I had to come, too. He's the meanest one. He's the one who burned me."

Along with her other fear was the fact that Andrew had been exposed to tuberculosis. Of course, he hadn't become ill after all those months with their mother. "I guess if you haven't gotten sick by now, he's not contagious."

Dread knotted her throat. What if she couldn't help Ian McDougal? Would the others make good on their threat to do something to Andrew? To her? To Jericho?

"So what do we do?" Andrew whispered.

Catherine stopped pulling weeds and wiped the back of her hand across her damp forehead. "You and I will say we're going to take a pie to Davis Lee. I owe him one, and Jericho won't try to come if he thinks we're only going to town."

"Okay."

"If I knew how sick the man was I could stop and get some supplies at Haskell's. I can't very well walk out of here carrying supplies."

"Angus told me last night that Ian was coughing a lot," Andrew said helpfully. "But I don't know what that means."

"It's lunger's cough." She jerked at more weeds, frustrated and nervous at how she and Andrew had been drawn in by the outlaws.

She did not want to obey Angus McDougal's orders, but she was more afraid not to. Fear scratched at her steadily. Fear for Andrew and herself. Fear for Jericho. She had hardly been able to look at him today because she wanted to fall against the broad shelter of his chest and tell him everything.

"We have to go, Catherine," Andrew whispered urgently. "They'll be mad if we don't go now."

"We can't make Jericho suspicious," she whispered back, her hands cold and trembling as they had been ever since last night. "I'll finish weeding, then wash up. Take these potatoes to the root cellar for me?"

He filled his arms with the vegetables, then turned away. "Uh-oh," he said in a low voice.

Catherine looked over her shoulder, following his gaze. Jericho leaned against a porch column, arms folded across his chest, his hip cocked as he bore his weight on his good leg. He watched them quietly, his gaze piercing and speculative.

Her stomach plummeted and she looked away. "Go on and put up those vegetables. Try and act calm."

"Okay."

As Andrew walked out of the garden to the root cellar, she heard him speak to Jericho. She should probably do the same, but she didn't think her tongue would work at all. As she rose, she could feel his gaze on her, and her body tightened in response. Yesterday she had practically begged him to pay attention to her. Now his quiet scrutiny sawed at her thin control.

She felt as if he could see right through her, as if he could read her mind. She'd better pray he couldn't. His life might depend on it.

Chapter Fourteen

The sky was a perfect blue with a few wispy clouds. Morning sunshine baked her neck, yet she shivered from the apprehension slicing her nerves like a razor. She couldn't forget the intensity of Jericho's gaze before she and Andrew had told him they were going to town to deliver an apple pie to Davis Lee. As she'd expected, he didn't insist on accompanying them, though she could feel him watching as they walked toward Whirlwind.

Andrew carried the dessert, and they delivered it in short order, Catherine's heart pounding harder and harder. She was so nervous that Davis Lee's simply asking what they planned to do today had her nearly blurting out everything. But the pinched look on her brother's face kept her silent.

After they left the jail, she rented a buggy at the livery and drove southwest of town about five miles, as Andrew directed. He told her that Riley's ranch was two miles farther west and two miles south of the widow Monfrey's place. The small unpainted frame house, barn and chicken coops were plopped in the middle of the flat prairie, the only structures visible in any direction.

Unease sliding under her skin, Catherine followed her brother onto the shallow porch. He rapped twice on the front door, then three times in rapid succession. The door swung open and she tightened her grip on his hand.

As they walked in, her gaze skipped around the large front room with a fireplace in the far corner and stove in the middle of the room. Dirt and bits of grass were scattered across the weathered pine floor. Faded calico curtains hung at the windows; dust-covered dishes sat on the simple wall shelves in front of her. A scarred kitchen table was flanked by three straight-back chairs, and a doorway opened to their right. Andrew stuck close as they moved toward the room.

He had told her to expect Ian, the sick one, to be pointing a gun at them when they walked in, but that didn't stop her heart from skipping a beat when she saw the barrel aimed right between her eyes.

"This is my sister," he said, his hand clammy in hers.

Ian, his thin face waxy, lowered his weapon. Andrew had said there were four McDougals, but only two men flanked the sick one in the small bed, which had been stripped of its linens. A tall narrow wardrobe backed into the opposite corner, and nailed into the wall next to it hung a shelf holding a washbasin and pitcher. A thin layer of dust coated everything in here, too.

Andrew pointed to the big-armed man on the right side of the bed. "That's Donald and the other one's Bruce."

The man in front of the room's only window squinted as if he couldn't quite make her out. She said nothing; she didn't want to know them at all. All three brothers had brown eyes and thick brown hair with a healthy tint of red.

The front door slammed behind them and Catherine jumped.

"Well, well." A hard voice came from behind her.

"That's Angus." Her brother scooted out of the doorway, pulling her with him.

The one who had burned Andrew. Catherine's stomach knotted. A man with shoulders and a chest like a bull moved in front of her. None of the McDougals was more than three inches taller than her five foot six. Angus was the most stocky, but Ian was the only one who could be considered slender.

"So this is Catherine." Angus's eyes, brown like his brothers', were shrewd and cold. His gaze slid over her like clammy fingers, and she struggled to keep the repulsion off her face.

His eyes narrowed to slits as he circled her. The smells of sweat, dirt and tobacco rose around him. He reached out and touched her skirt, bumping her hip suggestively.

Reflex had her slapping his hand away, and she sucked in a breath when anger deepened his already ruddy complexion. His fingers tightened on her dress. Beside her, Andrew went still as stone.

One of the brothers laughed. "Can we keep her, Angus?"

He turned and Catherine let out a wobbly breath, edging back slightly. Angus silenced his brother with a glare. "Don't be stupid. Every lawman and bounty hunter in Texas would be after us for sure."

Ian, who looked no older than her, covered his mouth and coughed. It was severe and from deep in his chest, she noted.

"Well, there's plenty of 'em already after us," Donald muttered.

"Yeah, but we know the comings and goings of Lieutenant Blue." Angus shot Andrew a look. "Don't we, boy?"

Foreboding formed a knot under Catherine's ribs. The oldest McDougal reached out and pinched Andrew's cheek hard enough that her brother winced. A red spot bloomed on his face.

Catherine put an arm around his shoulder. "I should probably check your brother now."

Keeping his gun on the bed beside him, Ian coughed several times, watching her from narrowed eyes.

"Yeah." Angus waved her toward his youngest brother, and she noticed that Bruce and Donald moved to flank Andrew.

Dread pricked her. What were they doing?

"Go on." Angus gave her a push and she walked to the head of the bed.

The straw-filled bed tick wasn't too badly soiled. Ian sat propped up against the wall behind him. His shirtless, hairless chest was lightly sheened with sweat, and a couple of blankets covered his lower half, for which she was grateful. At least she wouldn't have to check anything below his waist.

She realized the blankets were probably the ones Jericho told her had been stolen from the Baldwins. She reached out a trembling hand to see if Ian had fever. He did. Another spate of coughing seized him and he turned his head into a balled-up bandanna.

"Has your cough become more frequent lately?"

"Not really. It's my chest that hurts. So bad I can't breathe."

"Have you coughed up any blood?"

"No. Is it gettin' worse, do ya think?"

"I don't know. How long have you known you were ill?"

"About three years."

Still feeling Angus's irate gaze on her, Catherine kept her attention on the McDougal who seemed the least dangerous right now. "And none of your family has come down with it?"

"No."

"That's good." She breathed a little easier, knowing chances were good that neither she nor Andrew were at much risk. "Do you have heavier sweats than this?"

"Not really."

"Any chills?"

"Look, lady, I already answered these questions for a quack

doctor, so why don't you just give me something to help my chest not hurt so bad?"

"I have to ask you these questions so I can determine what you need," she said steadily.

"Well, get on with it."

"At this point the best thing you can do is eat regular meals and rest."

"Is that gonna make him well?" Angus demanded from the foot of the bed.

"No. There's nothing that will."

"That's what a doctor in Galveston told me." Ian leaned back against the wall, coughing again.

"If you can, you should give him milk every three to four hours," she said to Angus. "It's been reported to help some people."

"Yeah, boys, get that milk," Angus said mildly. Then he snarled, "Do you see a damn cow around here, lady?"

She drew back at his vicious tone, lacing her fingers to keep them from trembling. "The other things I suggested are more important."

She had no idea if that was true, but she didn't want to encourage them to steal a milk cow on top of everything else they'd taken.

Another series of coughs shook Ian's chest, and his eyes were bright with pain. "Can't you give me something? It hurts."

"He had some laudanum and that seemed to help," Angus said. "Give him that."

"I don't have any with me."

"Why not?" he snapped, stalking around the bed to stand in front of her. "You knew he was sick."

"I didn't know how sick." Her insides were a mass of nerves. Somehow she managed to keep her voice from shaking. "It's not typical to administer laudanum until you know if there's pain. Besides, I couldn't walk out of the house carrying medicine. Jericho—er, the Ranger—would've really been suspicious about that."

She was hoping Angus hadn't noticed her familiar use of Jericho's name, but she could tell by the cunning speculation in his eyes that he had.

"Go get him some then," the oldest McDougal ordered in a razor-sharp voice.

She rose and turned, but he planted himself in her way, his eyes menacing.

"You should let me go for Dr. Butler," she said. "He'll—"

"No."

"Your brother really needs to see a doctor."

"You're the one who's gonna help him."

"My skills are limited."

His eyes went flat and cold. "You."

She swallowed. "All right. I'll go get something."

"Laudanum."

"Yes, I'll try."

"You have two hours. And we'll keep your brother here until you return."

Alarm shot through her. "No! Please let him come with me."

"You bring back the medicine and he can go with you." Angus paced to the window beside the bed. "And don't take no longer than two hours."

She hesitated. She couldn't just leave Andrew here with these monsters.

"You're losing time," Angus mocked.

There was laudanum at her house—the bottle Jericho had never used—but she couldn't risk going there. Haskell's General Store sold laudanum and the *Dr. Kilmer's Indian Cough Cure Consumption Oil* that Andrew had bought for Ian. But if she went back to town she risked running into Davis Lee or Jericho. One look at her face and they would know something was wrong.

She would have to go to the fort. But how to get the medicine without arousing Dr. Butler's suspicions?

She gave Andrew an anguished look.

"I'll be okay." He looked as pale as she felt.

"Don't hurt him," she said fiercely.

All of them except Ian laughed.

She threw an apologetic look at her brother, who tried to smile. He looked so small and helpless between the two thick-fisted men. "I'll hurry."

Catherine drove the buggy as fast as she dared over the prairie, heading straight north for the fort. Fear and worry pelted her about what the outlaws might do to Andrew, about Jericho becoming suspicious, about what she was going to tell Dr. Butler.

In the end, she told him the truth. That a man passing through town was in the middle stages of tuberculosis and needed some laudanum to ease the pain in his chest.

She couldn't believe the doctor said nothing about her unsteady voice or shaking hands. Her fingers and toes had gone cold with fear. Trying to quell the panic that clawed through her, she thanked him and drove away, forcing herself to think only about getting back to Andrew. She kept the horse at an easy trot until she was out of sight of the fort, then she let the mare have her head.

She reached the widow's house with thirty minutes to spare, stumbling over her skirts as she lunged out of the buggy. Angus opened the front door and she rushed inside, desperate to assure herself that Andrew was okay. He appeared fine. Relief flooded his features when he saw her.

Thank the saints. She handed Ian the bottle of laudanum, holding up her thumb and index finger to show him how much to take. Instead he downed a big swallow.

If he drank it all, he would go into a stupor. Too bad she couldn't get them all to drink it.

She motioned to Andrew. "Let's go."

Angus edged up to her. "In case you're thinking about sic-cin' the Ranger on us, we ain't stayin' here."

"I told you we wouldn't say anything." She hated that her voice was wobbly.

She cried out as Angus grabbed her hair in his fist and yanked, jerking her head back and destroying her chignon.

Andrew lunged. "Let go of her!"

Bruce grabbed her brother's arms and Donald jabbed an elbow into Andrew's ribs, then landed a blow to his stomach.

He moaned and Catherine automatically reached for him, coming up short when Angus yanked again. Her scalp stung and tears burned her eyes. She pressed a protective hand to the roots of her hair. "Don't hurt him! He's just a boy."

"He knows not to get in my way." The outlaw's breath, musty with tobacco, burned her cheek.

She tried to see Andrew; he was bent double, still restrained by Bruce. Anger and fear boiled inside her. "I won't help you if you hurt him again."

Angus chuckled. "Yeah, you will, or your little brother is going to get more than a good thumping. And if the Ranger finds out about us, if you say one word about Ian or any of us, you and I are gonna have ourselves a long talk."

He leaned into her and before she could recoil, he flattened his tongue against her skin and dragged it up the side of her face. Biting back a cry of outrage and disgust, she flinched, immediately wiping away the repulsive feel of him. Nausea churned in her stomach and she thought her heart would pound right out of her chest.

The others laughed as Angus grinned. "You'll be getting some more of that if you don't do like I said."

His words turned her stomach, but she kept silent.

"If that Ranger gets within smellin' distance, I'm coming after you, dumpling."

"He won't."

Finally Angus released her. She faltered as she straightened, reaching for Andrew. When Bruce and Donald released him, her fingers closed unsteadily over his shoulder and the two of them rushed out, the sound of Angus's laughter scorching the air behind them.

Andrew vaulted into the buggy. Catherine's skirts tangled around her legs as she scrambled up in turn, and a whimper of distress escaped her. Before she even sat down, she snapped the reins against the horse's rump, urging the mare faster and faster. Andrew kept turning around to make sure they weren't being followed.

Her skin felt dirty and she thought she might retch. But she wasn't doing it here.

She didn't ease up on the horse until they were nearly a mile away. Shaking uncontrollably, feeling hot tears roll down her cheeks, she reined the buggy to a stop.

"Are you okay?" she and Andrew asked in unison.

He threw his arms around her. "That was scary."

"Yes." She hugged him, pulling away quickly when he winced at her touch. "Let me see."

Grimacing, he pulled up his shirt. The burn was healing, but already she could see a bruise at the top of his rib cage. Pressing gently, she felt for breaks.

Andrew cried out.

"I'm sorry. I had to check. I don't think your ribs are broken, which is good."

She smoothed a hand over his face, tears welling. "I'm so sorry, Andrew."

"I'm sorry about what Angus did to you," he said shakily.

"You're not going back there. Ever."

"What are we going to do?"

She made the decision in a split second. "I'm taking you to Riley and Susannah's. You'll be safe there and you can stay until I figure out what to do. I don't want those men threatening you anymore. I won't let them find you."

"But they'll be able to find *you*, Catherine. You have to stay, too."

"No, Jericho would be too suspicious."

"But—"

"It will be all right." She tried to calm her voice and reassure him, which was difficult when she was a shivering mass of nerves.

"What are you going to do? How long will I have to stay there?"

"I don't know yet." With shaking hands, she took down her hair and smoothed it back into a chignon as best she could.

"But I want to be with you."

"I know." She clucked to the mare and the buggy lurched forward. "This won't be for long."

"Do you think Miz Susannah will mind?"

"No, honey."

And she didn't. When Catherine reined up in front of the two-story, white frame house, the petite blonde met them on the porch with her baby daughter. She had seen them driving up the dusty road and was delighted they had finally come for a visit. But after one look at their faces she knew something was wrong.

Exchanging a glance with Catherine, Susannah asked calmly, "Andrew, would you mind taking Lorelai inside? The sun's a little hot for her."

"Okay." He gave his sister a worried look.

"It's all right. Go on." Her knees still felt watery and she couldn't rid herself of the disgusting feel of Angus's tongue. She lifted a shoulder and rubbed her cheek against it.

When Andrew took the baby inside, Susannah squeezed her hand, concern darkening her eyes. "Has something happened?"

"Yes—" Catherine stopped abruptly. She couldn't tell Susannah about any of this. That would certainly put her and Riley in danger, too. "Maybe I shouldn't have come."

"Of course you should have. What can I do?"

She hesitated, reliving the moment when the McDougal brothers had punched Andrew. "I can't tell you what's going on and I don't mean to sound mysterious, but I need—I wonder if Andrew could stay here for a bit. Just until I have some things under control."

"Absolutely. We would love to have him." Susannah's blue gaze sharpened. "Will you at least tell me if you're in danger?"

"I'm not right now."

Alarm widened the other woman's eyes. "What about Andrew?"

"He'll be safe here. He won't be if he's with me."

Susannah considered her for a long minute, plainly struggling not to ask questions, but finally she asked one. "Does Jericho know about this?"

Angus's threats played through her mind. "No," she said hoarsely.

"Don't you think you should tell him?"

"Yes." But there was no way she could.

Susannah studied her quietly. "Yes, of course, Andrew can stay. I just wish you could tell me what's wrong."

"I can't." Knowing her brother would be safe released some of the tension in her chest. "Not yet."

"It's all right. He'll be fine here, and if you need to stay, you're welcome."

"Thank you." Touched that the woman would take Andrew in so willingly, Catherine squeezed Susannah's hands. "I'll be back for him as soon as I can."

"Please don't worry about it. I'm happy to repay the kindness you've shown to Jericho."

"Thank you." She went inside and told Andrew what she'd said to Susannah. "Don't worry that she or Riley will ask you questions. You'll be safe here."

"I'm worried about you," he said in a low whisper, hitching the baby to his other hip.

"I'm fine. Truly." She kissed the top of his head. "I don't think your ribs need to be wrapped, but if it's painful to breathe, I want you to tell Susannah right away."

"All right." He still looked disturbed.

She hugged him. "I'll be fine. I'll figure something out. You'll see."

As he waved goodbye, Catherine's heart clenched. She had no idea how to thwart the McDougals; all she could do right now was keep them away from Andrew.

By the time she reached Whirlwind, her muscles were locked tight and her hands were freezing. Desperate to rid herself of Angus's touch, she rubbed at her face until her skin burned.

She tried to block thoughts of the outlaws from her mind as she returned the buggy to the livery, tried to keep from screaming as she spoke to people in town on her way home. Feeling as if she might come unhinged at any moment, she hurried up the slope behind the church, moving faster when she saw the house.

Reaching the porch, she called out, but Jericho didn't answer. Good. Working feverishly, moving on raw nerve, she dragged the tin tub over in front of the fireplace and dumped in two buckets of hot water from the kettle, then buckets of

cool from the sink. She stripped off her white bib and gray
day dress, then pulled the pins from her hair.

Shoes and stockings came off next, then her chemise and
drawers. She grabbed the tin of lye soap and sank down into
the lukewarm water as if it were the welcoming arms of her
mother. Still trembling, she ducked her head underwater, then
scrubbed her hair and her face over and over. At last, when
her skin nearly puckered, she felt steady enough to dry off and
get dressed.

The water-filled bathtub was too heavy to move by herself,
so she let it be. She sank down on the edge of her bed and
began combing out her wet hair. Finally the band of fear cutting into her chest eased. Thank goodness Jericho wasn't
here. She had to pull herself together. And stay as far away
from him as possible.

Jericho didn't know what was going on with Catherine and
Andrew, but he meant to find out. He made his way back
through town, still seeing no sign of them. Davis Lee said the
Donnellys had delivered his pie well over two hours ago. So
where were they?

After Catherine and her brother left him, Jericho had spent
an hour with his revolver and rifle until he was satisfied he
could hit a target more than twice in a row. Then he'd let Moe
and Cinco out into the pasture while he cleaned their stalls
and put down fresh hay. Catherine and Andrew still hadn't returned by then, so he washed up at the pump and went into
Whirlwind, looking for them. No one had seen them since
early that morning. After a shave at the barbershop, he made
another slow round, then finally limped out of town.

Brother and sister had been acting strangely since the pre-
vious evening. Catherine had sounded odd last night when
Jericho let her know he had returned from his ride with Davis

Lee. Then, through Andrew's open window, Jericho had heard their hushed voices until well after midnight, though he couldn't distinguish any words. This morning, they had both been as skittish as new colts. He hadn't missed the looks they had exchanged several times at breakfast. Or the way they'd stopped talking in the garden as soon as they noticed him on the porch.

At first he had thought Catherine's avoidance of him was related to their conversation behind the barn, but then he'd noticed the kid staying out of his way, too.

Stepping onto the porch, Jericho heard a sound from inside and leaned over to look through the window. Catherine was at the sink, but there was no sign of Andrew. Where had they been all morning? Jericho limped back down the steps and circled the house, but didn't see or hear the boy anywhere. Well, she could answer his questions as well as her brother.

He knocked on the front door and heard an exclamation from inside, then the sound of something heavy clattering to the floor. He opened the door and saw her kneeling on the other side of the table, her eyes wide with alarm.

"Did I startle you?"

"A little." She appeared visibly relieved when she saw it was him.

She rose, clutching the lid to the Dutch oven in one hand, and pivoted toward the fireplace, swiping the left side of her face with the back of her hand as she settled the lid onto the pot. "Lunch will be ready soon."

"There's no hurry." He stepped inside and closed the door, teased by the scent of fried ham and a faint hint of soap. She was pale as a cloud, her eyes sapphire-blue and huge in the whiteness of her face. "I can help you."

"Oh, no, but thank you." She opened the stove door and

stared blankly inside, as if she couldn't remember what to do. After a moment she scooped in more coal.

His gaze slid over her. The dress she wore was not the one she had worn to town. That one had been gray and white; this one was white with tiny blue flowers and a square-cut neck that bared a creamy patch of skin. The sleeves ended at her elbows, revealing the blue tracery of veins at her wrists, the delicate bones of her forearms. The light fabric swirled around her legs as she moved to the sink. She rubbed again at her face, then picked up a peeled potato and a small knife.

Even from here he could see that her hands shook. He frowned. "How was your trip to town?"

She stiffened, each knob in her spine plainly visible beneath her dress. Being able to see that meant she wasn't wearing a corset. "Fine."

She was already rattled and he hadn't even started with his questions. Hell, she was *tense.* And more than just her change of clothes roused his curiosity. Her not wearing a corset was very unusual. Her hair was different, too. Black as night, it hung straight and thick to the middle of her back. And it was damp. His gaze tracked to the tub full of water in front of the fireplace. Usually when she wore her hair down, she caught it back with a kerchief. He'd never seen her hair loose like this before. Never seen that dress, either.

"I just came from Whirlwind," he said casually. "Must've missed you."

She sent him a look over her shoulder, her smile as tight as the lines he noticed at her eyes. He glimpsed something he swore was fear before she turned away.

What the hell? He stepped up to the table, his fingers closing over the back of a chair. "Where's Andrew?"

"With f-friends."

Was her voice wobbly?

Her hand moved again to the side of her face. "I apologize that the meal is so late."

"You don't have to apologize. I appreciate you feeding me at all."

"I know you're hungry." She picked up another potato and promptly dropped it. Tension radiated from her in short jerky bursts.

This was how she'd been since he'd returned last night, as agitated as if she were face-to-face with a rattler. "What's wrong?"

"Nothing." Clumsily retrieving the vegetable, she began cubing it. Her movements were choppy and abrupt.

"Want me to help you with that? Wouldn't want you to cut yourself."

"No." She brushed again at the left side of her face. "Everything will be ready shortly."

He eased around the table and came up on her right, stopping in front of the cupboard a few feet away. She quivered like a plucked bowstring. "Catherine, what is it?"

She diligently cut potatoes and added them to the skillet, saying thinly, "You said you were going to leave soon, but maybe you should go now."

He frowned. What had brought this on? Her tone was urgent, nearly desperate. Was it because of what had been said between them yesterday? "I'm not ready to leave," he said evenly.

"You're getting around well enough now." She fumbled the small knife she held, catching it by the handle before it fell. "You've been working your hand better than I have."

"I'm not going anywhere until that gang is captured." He admitted now what he had realized as he'd searched for her in town. He couldn't walk away from her. Ever. He didn't know how he would handle his problem with Andrew, but he would find a way. "I won't leave you and Andrew. You'll be safe."

At his words, she looked away, her hand closing on the knife until her knuckles blanched white as bone.

He closed the distance between them but didn't touch her. "What's going on, Catherine? And don't say it's nothing."

He saw her shudder, and lightly cupped her shoulder to turn her toward him. "Did something go on in town— What happened to your face?"

Sliding a finger beneath her chin, he angled her head for a better look. The left side of her face was splotched and red, as though she'd rubbed it raw. "How did you hurt yourself?"

"I'm fine." Her pulse jumped wildly in her throat. "It just itches."

He stared down at her, but she wouldn't meet his gaze. "You're trembling and you're pale as chalk. What's happened?"

"It's nothing I can't handle." Her voice was brittle, lost.

What had her so upset? Slowly, soothingly, he tucked her hair behind her ear. "You can tell me. I'll make it all right."

He would. She knew that without question. How tempting it would be to lean against his strength for just a moment, tell him everything. "I'm fine, really."

"I promise I'll fix it."

His crooked grin sawed at her resolve to keep silent. He was the one man who *could* fix things. She knew deep in her bones that he would lay down his life to protect her. And he might have to. The McDougals had nearly killed him once and they had every intention of trying again. Andrew might be next. Or her. She kept hearing Angus's threats, seeing his brothers hit Andrew.

How was she ever going to find a way out of the trap they'd sprung? Helplessness welled up, spilled over into her fear. It was too much. With a choked sob, she slid her arms around Jericho's waist.

"Hey." He folded her against him and laid his cheek against her hair. "It's going to be all right."

She was scaring the hell out of him. She cried silently against him, her tears dampening his shirt. He stroked a soothing hand up and down her spine. "You can trust me, you know."

Her slender arms tightened around him and he felt the desperation rolling off her. Seeing her like this made his chest constrict.

He cradled her to him, pressing a kiss to her hair, nuzzling her temple. She burrowed into his chest. "Catherine, let me help you," he murmured against her damp cheek.

She turned her face toward him, her head against his chest. "I will, you know. I'll do anything for you."

That only seemed to make her cry harder. He didn't know what to do. "Catherine, please."

He kissed her cheek, then her eyelid, tasting the salt of her tears. A feeling of utter helplessness sliced through him. He brushed kisses on her forehead, her nose, her lips. "Please, darlin'."

She quieted, her fingers curling into the front of his shirt. He felt so good, so solid. All she wanted was to be held by him, touched. Protected. She had no control over anything in her life except for this moment.

"That's good." He nuzzled her temple. "You're going to be okay."

With him, she would. He could chase away the cold dread gnawing at her, right the world that had begun to spin so crazily. Andrew was safe at Riley and Susannah's. Catherine was safe here with Jericho.

When his mouth grazed her cheek again, she turned her head, seeking him as if she were dying of thirst and he was water. Her lips met his.

For one aching second, he froze, and everything in her did, too. Then his mouth settled over hers, his tongue sliding inside as he gathered her against his hard strength.

Chapter Fifteen

⟡⟡⟡⟡⟡⟡

She melted into him, touching her tongue to his. He clasped her head in his hands, his kiss growing impatient, more demanding. Catherine thrilled to it, curling one hand around his nape.

When they finally broke apart, their breathing rasped in the silence of the house. His chest rose and fell as rapidly as hers.

The hungry, tender look in his eyes nearly undid her. He'd looked at her that way yesterday, too. As if she belonged to him. As if she always would. Heat swept her entire body and she shook now from desire, not fear. They came together again, mouths searching, fusing. Her arms went around his neck and she kissed him with everything in her.

"Come closer," he said in a smoky voice.

She laughed softly. "I am close."

"A little closer." His hands curved over her bottom and he pulled her hips to his.

She caught her breath at the delicious jolt of pleasure, and rubbed against him, curious, testing the feel of his arousal. "Like this?"

He made a sound deep in his throat and took her mouth again, his tongue searching deep. He tasted of coffee and her.

He moved his lips to her ear, breathed her name as he tickled the delicate shell with his tongue. She shivered. His mouth softly grazed her cheek, and the memory of what Angus had done evaporated. Heat raced along her nerves. Jericho kissed her neck, her collarbone, his freshly shaved jaw smooth against her skin. Then his mouth came back to hers, insistent and demanding, rousing a dark need inside her.

Her arms curved around his hard shoulders. She stroked the corded strength in his neck, buried her fingers in his hair. She couldn't get close enough, her hands moving over him with an urgency that startled her.

Shaking, she touched the high slash of his cheekbone, ran her fingers over his jaw, held his face in her trembling hands. His tongue stroked the silky underside of hers, his arm pinning her to him. The scents of soap and leather and dusky male filled her.

He shifted her to the crook of his right elbow, his hard biceps cradling her. He kissed her deeply, gentling now. She felt as if she was spinning, with colors wheeling crazily behind her eyes.

His left hand curved over her breast, and the unexpected touch had her moaning, arching into him. Her nipple hardened against his palm. His heat reached through her dress, her chemise, traveled to a spot between her legs. She made a sound and he slid his hand up, splaying his fingers to rest against the swell of her breasts as his thumb stroked the hollow of her throat. All the while his tongue played in her mouth.

She lifted, trying to move his hand back down to her breast. He undid the buttons between them, and a wave of longing rose in her. Her bodice loosened and he tugged at it until the fabric parted, then he reached for the tie on her chemise. The ribbon gave and he slipped his hand inside, his callused fingers closing gently on her flesh. She gasped as a piercing pleasure melted her. Gently he thumbed the peak of her nipple.

Catherine's hands slid down his chest, gripped his hips to steady herself. His arousal pressed strong and hard against her belly.

He dragged his lips from hers, trailing hot teasing kisses from her ear down her neck. His hand moved to her other breast, already aching for him. Wanting to touch him, needing to, she tugged his shirt from his trousers and slipped her hand beneath, finding hot supple flesh. The harsh sound he made encouraged her, and she tentatively ran her fingers across the hard planes of his stomach, teasing the thin line of hair that ran below his navel.

His hand left her breast, and as she protested, he picked her up and took the few steps to her bedroom, murmuring, "I want to make love to you, Catherine."

"Yes, I want that, too." Her lips skimmed the edge of his jaw. She'd never been more certain of anything in her life, and she wanted him to touch her again. Now.

He set her on her feet next to the bed. Sunlight flooded the room and he turned to pull down the oilskin shade. Watching the play of filtered light on his face, she moved into his arms, initiating their kiss this time. He nibbled at her lips, teasing her with the promise of more as he reached between their bodies to release the rest of her buttons.

He nipped her lightly where the slope of her shoulder met her neck. He tickled the spot with his tongue, and she made a little sound in her throat, shifting to give him better access.

Her hands moved on him restlessly, down his arms, across his shoulders. She kissed his neck, tasting the salty heat of him, then grazing her teeth against his flesh, as he'd done to her.

With her dress loose now, he slid the sleeves down her arms and pushed the garment to the floor along with her petticoats so that she stood before him in her chemise and drawers. His large, dark hands bracketed her waist, then slid up over her ribs to the underside of her breasts. He brushed his thumbs across the nipples until they strained against the thin linen.

A sharp pleasure darted from her center to her breasts, and her eyes drifted shut. She'd never felt anything like this. She wanted to touch him. Pushing up his blue shirt, she looked at him.

His chest was broad and deep, burnished brown by the sun. Black hair whorled on his chest, then veed into that thin line arrowing into his trousers. Thin bands of muscle flexed fluidly across his belly. She ran her hands over the tempered strength of his chest, her fingernails grazing his flat brown nipples. He squeezed her waist, then pulled the shirt over his head and dropped it.

She watched her hand slide down his belly to the band of his trousers, saw the evidence of his arousal straining against the denim. She expected some trace of fear, some hesitancy, but she felt only excitement and anticipation. And the calming sense of safety that she always felt with him.

She shivered at the searing promise in his eyes. He tugged at her chemise until it sagged enough to bare the swell of her bosom. His eyes darkened and he lowered his head, nudging the fabric down. As he buried his face in the valley between her breasts, she felt his warm breath flow over her. He kissed her there, his lips soft and drawing gently on her flesh, as if he were drinking her in. A heaviness settled between her legs.

"Hold on to me," he murmured against her skin.

The way his voice curled around her had her legs wobbling. She grasped his hard shoulder as he leisurely licked his way to the place where pale flesh met rosy pink. His tongue circled close to her nipple, not touching, only teasing. And then he took her in his mouth.

She gasped, her hand tightening on him. While he tongued her nipple, his free hand came up to cup her other breast, and she bit her lip to keep from moaning. The sight of his mouth on her, his hand, sharpened the ache between her legs, and her breathing went ragged.

His mouth moved to her other breast and her head fell back, her hand curving behind his neck to steady herself. Tension coiled deep inside. She felt him bunching her chemise in his fist, the material skimming over her hips, her waist. She helped him draw it over her head, shivering as she stood half-naked in front of him.

"You are…" He cupped her breasts, his big hands unsteady.

She dared a look at him. He stared at her tenderly, enrapt as he plucked at her nipples, then brushed his thumbs across them.

His eyes turned a stormy gray. "I can't breathe for looking at you."

From the expression on his face, he didn't seem to mind. He caressed and kissed her breasts until her own breath broke on a ragged moan. Wanting to feel his strength against her, she wrapped her arms around his neck, drawing him to her. His hands drifted to her waist as she sank into his chest. At the touch of her bare breasts against him, they both inhaled sharply.

She trembled at the anticipation coursing through her. His chest hair tickled her breasts and his stomach was hard against her softer one. Lower, she felt his arousal, and she moved her hips against his as he'd done earlier. Her hand slid beneath the waistband of his trousers. His skin was wonderfully hot against her knuckles and she searched for the top button.

Jericho's breathing changed, grew deeper, and he curved his hands around her bottom, pulling her right into his hardness, the touch bold and intimate through her drawers.

His hands moved over her, hot and gentle, and striking sparks under her skin. He pulled the tape on her drawers and pushed them down her hips, leaving her only in shoes and stockings.

"Shoes," she panted, moving on shaking legs to the edge of the bed to take hers off.

She watched as he worked off his boots and socks. When he pushed his trousers and short drawers to the floor, her heart skipped a beat. His broad shoulders tapered in a ripple of muscle to a lean waist. His dark tan faded to paler skin at his hips. How could he seem even larger without clothes?

She marveled at the flat band of muscle across his belly, the lean, powerful flanks. Her gaze followed that line of hair from his navel to the juncture of his thighs. And she blinked. He was large and intimidating. She looked at that most foreign part of him and a wicked pleasure rushed through her. She'd seen naked men before, but in a professional capacity. She was already reaching for him when he pushed her gently back on the bed and came down beside her.

Soft golden light filtered through the oilskin, drifting across those sleek, muscular arms, those taut flanks.

He kissed her long and deep, playing with her breasts, drawing her nipples into aching points until she nearly came off the bed. He lifted his head, his eyes molten silver as he ran his thumb across her bottom lip. "Do you know what's going to happen?"

She nodded, trying to catch her breath.

"You do?" His brow arched, his eyes smiling. "How?"

Her blood hummed as she eyed his nakedness. "Sister Clem told me."

"Oh." A sound suspiciously like choked laughter came from him.

Catherine smiled. "You think because she's a nun, she doesn't know?"

"The thought did occur to me." He grinned.

"She was married before she came to the convent."

"Oh." His grin faded as he ran his fingers through her hair. "Well, I'm glad she told you."

Catherine stroked his back, ran her hands down the hard muscles of his buttocks. "Would you have explained if I hadn't?"

A flush colored his neck, but he nodded. "Yes. I don't want you to be scared."

"I'm not, just nervous."

"I am, too, a little."

"You are?"

"It's been a long time since I've done this."

"I'm not sure, but somehow I don't think it's something you forget," she muttered.

He laughed and her heart swelled. He had a beautiful smile, full and inviting, with a hint of mischief. She reached up to touch his face.

Fierce heat flared in his eyes. His index finger glided gently down the line of her jaw, then across her lower lip before he gave her a deep, languid kiss. The slow teasing strokes of his tongue melted her bones, and she rolled into him.

She skimmed her hands up his back, across his shoulders, marveling at the feel of his hair-dusted chest against the sensitive flesh of her breasts, the taut touch of his belly, the hard lines of his body against the curved softness of hers. She moved her hand lower, watching his face. A vein corded in his neck and she felt his muscles quiver. She quivered, too, as she looked down.

His arousal was hard and thick, pulsing between them. On the inside of his thigh, his scar was a healthy pink, thin and jagged and long. She leaned up and kissed him, using her tongue the way he had as her fingers drifted down over the hot rigid length of him. His hand tightened on her waist, his tongue plunging deep in her mouth as she closed her hand around him. His entire body contracted.

Wanting to see him, she pulled away from the kiss, shivering at the intense need in his face. He felt like silk-sheathed steel, and when she moved her hand to feel more of him, he groaned and rolled onto his back, taking her with him. She could read the pleasure in his narrowed eyes, and knowing he liked her touch made her wet and achy between her thighs.

She shifted so that she lay against him rather than on top, and continued exploring. She kissed his hot neck, touching with her tongue and tasting salt, along with a faint hint of shaving soap. She spread soft kisses across his chest as she stroked him. He pressed into her hand and showed her how he liked to be touched.

As she measured his length, his breath soughed out. He caressed and played with her breasts. The feel of his hands on her while she held him so intimately made her grow wetter. She shuddered. "Kiss me."

He did, until the sleek heat at her core had her sliding one of her legs between his and pressing down on his hot hard thigh to relieve the ache at her center. He murmured sweet words to her, slipping his hand between them and thumbing the knot of nerves at the apex of her thighs. She cried out against his mouth, her hand moving on him faster.

He stayed her wrist. When she protested, he said in a scratchy voice, "Have mercy, Catherine. Let me catch up."

When she looked at him in confusion, he laughed unsteadily. "I don't want this to be over yet, and if you keep touching me like that, it will be."

"Okay," she breathed. "But do something."

He rolled, spreading her beneath him, and watched her face as he slid one finger deep inside her. The sharp jolt of pleasure caused her to buck. She clutched at his arms and moaned, "Jericho."

His finger massaged her in a deep, intimate rhythm, and she closed her eyes, amazed at the way her body softened for him. Another finger slid inside, stretching her. His thumb circled the spot at the top of her cleft, and she cried out, arching off the bed.

He stroked her faster, pulling a thread of tension tighter and tighter inside her until she quaked.

His mouth covered hers, his tongue going deep just the way his fingers were. His arousal lay hotly against the inside of her leg, and the weight of him stoked the pleasure higher.

She felt a rising urgency, and writhed, reaching for something she couldn't name. His strokes slowed, deep and steady and unhurried, until a hard-edged need splintered through her. Something snapped, flinging her into a paroxysm of sensation. She heard sounds come from her throat, heard Jericho murmuring to her as breath after breath shuddered out of her.

"Oh, my," she gasped when she came back to herself.

He stroked her damp hair from her face and she opened her eyes to find him smiling tenderly at her. She wanted him inside her. Now.

"Come closer," she said softly, reaching for him.

He levered himself over her, making a place for himself between her legs. "I don't want to hurt you."

"I know." With trembling hands, she touched his face, loving the way his silver eyes blazed at her. "I know you never will."

"This first time I will, but it can't be helped."

He looked so worried that she smiled, running a finger over his lips. "It will be all right."

She raised up to kiss him and he took her mouth, following her back down. He braced his elbows on either side of her head and settled his weight on her.

"Too heavy?"

"No." She slid her hands up his back, her fingers splaying over warm muscle and tendons. He pressed her into the mattress, sheltering her, gathering her body to his with the same desperate need she felt.

She shifted her legs so that he settled deeper between them, and touched his back, his sides, his flanks. Fire licked at her nerves.

He skimmed his lips over her ear and tickled her with his hot breath before grazing the length of her neck with his teeth. Urged on by the moist ache blooming between her legs, she lifted her hips.

The blunt tip of his arousal replaced his fingers at the entrance of her body, and she melted, throbbing against him.

"Come closer," she breathed, framing his face in her trembling hands. "Now."

His eyes glittered like moonlight as he pushed inside just a bit. She drew in a breath at the invasion, the stretch of her body, the incredible feel of his flesh joining hers.

He swept one hand downward and gently pushed her knees wider. She moved against him, wanting more.

He smoothed her hair away from her face. "Wrap your arms around me."

She did, fighting the urge to arch against him. He was so hot and male and impossibly strong.

His lips covered hers and she shook, anticipating the moment when he would fill her completely. He drew her tongue into his mouth and began to stroke her in deliberate measured motions. Hot, aching need blistered her center and she tightened her arms around him.

He eased himself deeper into her, murmuring sweet words against her neck. She gasped at the fullness of him and involuntarily shrank back from the burning pressure.

He stilled and waited, giving her time to accept him. "Okay?"

She shifted and wriggled, trying to accommodate him.

"Catherine, be still. Let me help you." His voice was labored. Sweat sheened his face and neck; the tendons in his arms strained. "I know it's hard, but try to relax."

Frustrated, she said, "I don't see how you're going to fit."

"Like a glove, sweetheart. I promise." He kissed her forehead. "I'm sorry about this."

Before she could ask about what, he flexed his hips and surged completely inside her. She felt the barrier of her maidenhead give, and bit her lip against a cry as a stinging pain filled her.

He pressed farther inside and she clutched at him tightly. After a moment, he eased back until he almost left her, then moved forward with a long slow glide.

"Oh!" The pain dimmed, and the next time he moved she felt a sharp-edged pleasure. Her knees fell wider apart and her legs hooked over his calves.

Tension bowing his back and arms, he nudged inside her, teasing the knot of nerves his fingers had touched moments ago. Then he began to move in slow deliberate thrusts that pushed her up a ladder of sensation. She panted with him, arching with inexpert eagerness. He grasped one hip, guiding her into his rhythm, and she widened her eyes in wonder as their flesh connected, sliding ever deeper.

He rocked her until she lost all sense of time. She held on to him, fighting for balance against the vortex of sensation battering at her.

His mouth covered hers and his tongue delved inside. The delicious shock of having him within her at the same time sent heat splintering through her.

"I can't hold on, Catherine," he finally groaned.

She wasn't sure what that meant, but she sensed his shattering restraint. His thrusts became shorter, more determined, until he was moving rapidly, breathing harshly.

Overcome with emotion, she kept her gaze locked with his, instinctively lifting her hips to meet each thrust. His breath rasped in her ear. He whispered her name, told her how much he wanted her, how beautiful she was. His hands slid under her bottom and he pumped into her hard and fast, then stilled, resting his head next to hers.

She felt warm and full, her heart bursting. She stroked his back, swept with a protectiveness that surprised her. As she held his body in hers, a realization came upon her slowly and surely, filling her so completely that she didn't question it. She loved him.

With tears burning her eyes, she kissed his shoulder. His hand slipped between them and he rose on one elbow. While he was still inside her, his finger went to the knot of nerves between her legs. "Next time we'll do it together."

"Do what—oh!" His touch splintered a cord of tension buried deep inside. Suddenly her inner muscles clenched around him, pulling him farther into her body. They both groaned and she sank her hands into the taut muscles of his buttocks.

Tiny convulsions started deep inside, rippling with exquisite sensation. In the split second before her mind blanked with pleasure, she understood.

Long moments later she lay trembling beneath him, lazily kissing his neck, his jaw.

He nuzzled her cheek. "Are you okay?"

"Yes. Are you?"

He chuckled, kissing her eyelids and the side of her face. He left her body and rolled to his side, pulling her close. She snuggled into him, her head on his shoulder.

"What do you think about that?" His voice rumbled quietly in her ear.

The tenderness between her legs felt strangely wonderful. "I think it's a good thing I decided not to become a nun."

He laughed, hugging her to him.

Drowsy, her bones feeling as soft as melted wax, she cuddled against him. Her head rested over his heart and her leg twined intimately with his. She stroked his belly and chest, loving the supple feel of him. Her fingers floated down to the smooth skin between his hip and groin. The wound in his thigh had healed nicely, but the scar was still a reminder of how close he'd come to dying.

She stroked the puckered flesh gently, as if by touching him enough she could erase the mark.

His hands stroked her back and her hips as they lay together in a lazy, comfortable silence. He was a good man with a good heart. He made her feel safe and protected. If anyone could find a way out of the mess she and Andrew were in with the McDougals, it was Jericho.

She had trusted him with her body and her heart. Now she had to trust him with her brother.

She propped herself up on her elbow, her gaze meeting his. "I need to tell you something."

Chapter Sixteen

Jericho watched her sit up, draw her knees to her chest and wrap her arms around them. The sheet covered her front, but not the tapering line of her back, the flare of a creamy hip.

Tantalized by her soft scent, he couldn't keep from trailing his finger down the silky flesh of her spine, brushing his thumb over the sweet curve of her shoulder. Her skin gleamed like mother-of-pearl in the soft light. The dark fall of her hair was tousled from his hands, her body still flushed from their love-making, and Jericho felt himself already growing hard again.

She glanced at him. "Last night after you left with Davis Lee, Andrew sneaked out and I followed him."

Jericho's hand stilled. Had Andrew gone to the Mc-Dougals? What had she witnessed? Had they seen her? He didn't want her within a hundred miles of those bastards.

"He went to Haskell's."

The coil in his gut eased somewhat when he heard she hadn't been near the outlaws, but he waited expectantly.

"My brother was stealing food, and it wasn't the first time." She took a deep breath. "He did it for the McDougals."

Jericho slowly pushed himself to a half-sitting position, the wooden headboard rough against his back. The sheet slid low on his hips. Why was she confessing to him? How much did she really know? Did she know about the ambush? About Andrew killing Hayes? "He told you he stole food from Haskell's?"

"Yes."

"For the McDougals?"

"Yes."

"And the rifle cartridges from Jed Doyle?" His voice was clipped.

Her words rushed out. "Yes, but he's going to reimburse Mr. Haskell and Mr. Doyle for all of that. We've already discussed it. He's involved with the McDougals, Jericho, but not because he wants to be."

"What do you mean?"

"I mean, he was willing at first. He ran errands for them and stole supplies and told them things—"

"Told them I was here," he said flatly.

"Yes." She turned toward him, her beautiful blue eyes pleading for understanding. The sheet sagged low on the swell of her creamy breasts. "But he tried to break his ties with them and they wouldn't let him. Last week, Angus burned him, then today—"

"*Today?*" He boomed out the question.

She explained how Andrew had convinced her to let him take the stolen food so the McDougals wouldn't become suspicious that he had told anyone about them. How they had forced him to find them a dry place with a bed. "One of them has tuberculosis."

"Ian." Urgency spooled inside Jericho, but since she trusted him enough to tell him, he reined in his impatience. He knew he wasn't going to like anything she had to say from here on out. "How did they force Andrew?"

"They threatened to kill me." She put a trembling hand on his sheet-covered thigh. "And you. I know they'll do it. They nearly killed you once already."

Tension lashed her entire body, and he swore he smelled fear mixed with her musky womanly scent.

"They wanted me to check Ian and get him some medicine."

With grim certainty, Jericho said, "And you did it."

"Yes," she said hoarsely. "They made Andrew stay with them while I drove to the fort for some laudanum."

He thought his jaw might break clean in two. Anger drove through him like a spike. She could've been hurt, *killed*. His words were rough and wrenched out of him. "Do you have any idea how dangerous that was?"

"Of course I do," she snapped. "I was scared to death, but I was more afraid of what they would do if I didn't go. As it was, they beat up Andrew and—"

"Where is he? How badly hurt is he?"

"His ribs aren't broken, but he's bruised. I took him to Riley and Susannah's."

Good. Someone was keeping an eye on the kid, and he was safe for the moment.

Jericho noticed that Catherine still trembled, and his instincts told him there was something else. He recalled how terrified she'd been when he'd walked into the house. What had happened? Those bastards couldn't have hurt her, could they? Jericho's hands, his mouth had been all over her just minutes ago. He would've known. "Did they touch you?"

Her fingers closed convulsively on his leg, and dread shot through him. "Catherine?"

"Angus. He grabbed me by the hair and—" She swayed, her face pale as she struggled to speak.

A hush came over Jericho's body the same way it had

when he'd watched the life bleed out of Hays. He was going out of his mind. "Cath—"

"He licked me."

She spoke so quietly Jericho had to strain to hear her. His entire body shut down for a heartbeat, maybe two. Then a black fury screamed through him, filled him until there was nothing inside but a molten seething pulse. "He *what?*"

Tears glistened in her eyes. She raised a hand to the left side of her face, the red place he'd noticed earlier. "Here."

His pulse throbbing painfully in his neck, he curved an arm around her and settled her against him, trying to reach past the fury to be gentle with her. He cupped her cheek, finally able to get the words past his clenched teeth, "Anywhere else? Did he touch you anywhere else? *Do* anything else?"

"No."

"And you're all right?"

"Yes." She placed her hand over his where it lay on her cheek.

He crushed her to him as rage shattered every rational thought he possessed. A near-crippling cold slid like needles under his skin as he struggled to control the viciousness welling from some deep hole inside him that he'd never known existed.

He wanted to murder Angus McDougal. He would. The oath he'd taken as a Ranger be damned. No one touched his woman.

Tucking her against him, he held her close until the fury settled into something manageable. "You're sure you're all right?"

"Yes." She lifted her head and skimmed a kiss along his jaw. "It feels good to tell you."

He knew he had to tell her, too. All of it.

She sat up, her eyes dark with knowing. "You're going after them."

"Yes." He brushed his lips across her hair, then slid out of bed and limped around to her side for his pants. He pulled on his trousers, buttoning them with crisp precision.

"But where will you look?" She swung her feet to the floor, wrapping the sheet around her. "Angus told us today that they weren't going to stay at that house."

"I have to talk to Andrew." Jericho forced himself to look at her. He couldn't let her learn the truth only when he returned with her brother in irons.

Soon that trusting look in her soft blue eyes would turn frigid and unforgiving. He steeled himself. "There are things you need to know, Catherine, and there's no easy way to tell you."

"What things?"

He wanted to bolt, but knew he'd run smack into the door to hell. There was no going back. "I came here to arrest Andrew. After he led me to the McDougals."

"Arrest him for what?" She gave a small disbelieving laugh. "Stealing?"

She had no idea the extent of her brother's involvement. Pants only half-buttoned, Jericho sat down beside her and placed a hand on her leg. To steady her or himself, he wasn't sure. He hated the alarm that flared in her eyes. "He was at the ambush."

"The amb— Where your friend was killed and you nearly were, too?"

"Yes."

She stared at him for a long moment, then disbelief, denial, skittered across her face. She stood, jerking the sheet tighter around herself. "No."

"I tracked him here, to your house," he said gently. "Moe's shoes match the prints I followed."

She turned toward the door, then the window and back, as if she were cornered. Her chest rose and fell rapidly. "No."

Jericho curled his good hand against his thigh. "I found one of the rifle cartridges stolen from Jed Doyle in your barn."

"How do you know—"

"Doyle identified it."

"That doesn't mean Andrew took it!"

Jericho didn't say anything.

She sank down onto the bed, staring at him with disbelief. "If he was there, those outlaws probably made him go. And he can't be held accountable for that. He's been trying to get away from them."

This pain chewing at his gut was worse than any damn needle she'd driven through his torn flesh. Feeling queasy, he swiped a hand across the back of his neck. "He's the one who shot Hays. And me."

Horror creased her delicate features. How could she turn even more pale? "That can't be. You're mistaken."

"I'm sorry." He wanted to pull her onto his lap, soothe her, *something,* but didn't know what to do. "I saw him."

"How can you know that?" she demanded shakily, a tear sliding down her cheek. "When you got here, you couldn't even stand up. You'd lost so much blood you didn't regain consciousness for three days!"

"I know what I saw."

"How can you be sure?"

"I wish I weren't."

Looking as if she might shatter at any moment, she wiped at her eyes with unsteady hands. Suddenly she went very still. "So, you've suspected from the night you arrived that Andrew was involved with the McDougals?"

"I've known, yes."

"Why didn't you tell me?" She recoiled from him, color burning high in her cheeks. Her eyes were painfully bright with anger, and tears poured down her cheeks. "Why didn't you say something? We might have prevented Angus from burning him! And those others from beating him up!"

"Sweetheart, I never meant for Andrew to get hurt. I didn't

know anything about what they were doing to him. If he'd told me what was going on, I could've helped."

"Why did you keep secret the reason you were here? Maybe he would've told you then. Why didn't you just arrest him?"

"First, I had to be sure he was the kid I saw at the ambush. Then I had to make sure he was meeting with the outlaws. If I'd tipped my hand, Andrew would've warned them."

"He also wouldn't be hurt!" she cried accusingly.

The anguish in her face carved him deeply. "I had no way of knowing about that. He did know they were dangerous when he became involved with them."

"He's twelve years old!"

Jericho knew boys, good and bad, who had killed when they weren't much older. He didn't say it.

"So," she said slowly, "you've been spying on him."

There really was no other word for it. "Yes."

Her gaze slid to the bed. "And me? Was *that* part of—"

He knew where she was going and it angered him. "Don't think that, Catherine."

"Did you… Did we… Because I threw myself at you?" Pain welled up, smothering her. "Are there no feelings—"

"Stop!" His hands curved over her bare shoulders and he forced her to look into his face. "What happened between you and me was about *us*. No one and nothing else. Don't doubt that, Catherine."

She searched his eyes, her own wary and hurt.

Couldn't she see? "Only about us. Trust me."

"I want to." She chewed at her lip.

"You know it's true." He tucked a silky strand of hair behind her ear, rubbing her lobe. "I love you."

He hadn't meant to tell her like this, but there it was.

Some indefinable emotion flitted across her face and her throat worked. "What are you going to do about Andrew?"

Inwardly he flinched that she had ignored what he said. Hadn't he told himself she would turn away? Probably hate him? That didn't ease the jagged rush of pain through his chest. "First I'm going to talk to him."

"And then?"

Damn it all. "I'll probably have to arrest him."

"You can't," she moaned. She closed her eyes, aching so much her muscles cramped. The numbness that had started through her body when Jericho had first told her all these horrible things had spread to her fingers and toes. "He's only twelve!"

"He rode with them." Angry at himself, at her, Jericho bent to grab one of his boots. "You can't expect me to ignore that."

She understood how deeply he felt his duty. He was in the right to chase the McDougals, bring them to justice, but not Andrew. "Do you mean to see he goes to prison?"

"I need to talk to him first—"

"And if you decide it, then he'll go," she said baldly.

He looked up from pulling on his other boot. "You know what that gang has done, the people they've killed."

How could her brother have been present during that ambush? Could Jericho be wrong? What if he was right? "But Andrew—"

"Was with them. I can't make that go away, but don't jump the gun. Let me talk to him and see what I learn. If he helps me, there might be something I can do for him."

"He won't know where they are! Angus told us this morning that they weren't going to stay at Widow Monfrey's, and Andrew has been at Riley's ever since."

"I still have to talk to him."

"I understand why you came to our house, that you tracked him *here,*" she said, trembling.

Jericho sat up, hope skittering through him.

"I want those outlaws captured, too," she added. "Andrew isn't one of them."

The hollow ache in his gut spread to his heart. "I'll be fair."

"Can you? They killed your friend, nearly killed you. If Andrew *is* responsible, as you say, how can you be objective?"

"I didn't say objective, but I can be fair. Can't you at least trust me that much? His age will be taken into account, Catherine, but he can't be ignored. He *was* with them."

She was so pale, huddled into herself as if he'd punched her in the stomach. Jericho's chest felt as if it were being slowly crushed. He reached for her and she withdrew slightly—only a fraction but it was enough. He dropped his hand, his heart twisting.

"This can't be," she whispered. "I want to be there when you talk to him."

"No. He needs to tell me in his own words." Jericho fought the urge to shake her or kiss her until she understood. Until she *agreed* with him. He scooped his shirt from the floor, pulling it over his head. "This is between him and me."

She rose, the sheet bunched around her slender curves, pressed tight to her breasts. "At least let me go with you to Riley's."

"It's better if you don't. If things work out, Andrew will take me from there to the McDougals. You're not getting anywhere near them again," he said gruffly, his throat closing up at the thought.

"What will you do? Just talk to him?"

"Yes."

"Then take him to jail?" Her voice cracked.

"I don't know."

"If you do, will you bring him here first? I don't want him to be alone."

"I can do that."

She lifted her head, tears swimming in her eyes. "And then what? You leave and take him with you?"

"I'm not leaving, Catherine." He clenched his fist to keep from reaching for her. "Ever. I told you that and I meant it."

He refused to consider that he might have just killed any feelings she had for him.

He took a step toward her, needing to touch her, hold her. Make her understand or at least accept. When she didn't retreat, something hot clutched at his throat. Gently he took her hand and folded it into his.

She didn't pull away. She couldn't. She did believe Jericho wouldn't leave. The raw agony in his eyes told her he hurt as much as she did, that she hadn't imagined his feelings for her. But how would they ever be able to deal with this? If Andrew went to prison, Catherine would never forget that Jericho had sent him there. And what if her brother really had killed Hays Gentry? Injured Jericho so severely that he might never have full use of his hand? Committed murder?

If Andrew had done those things, he should pay for it. But she didn't know if *she* could.

"It'll work out," Jericho said softly.

"You don't know that."

The agony in her blue eyes had him aching clear to his toes. "I want it to. Don't you?"

"I don't want to have to choose," she said with a sob, her hand squeezing his hard.

He stroked a knuckle down her cheek, breathing in her fresh scent and the faint spice of their mingled bodies. "Expecting Andrew to take responsibility for what he's done isn't making you choose."

"I can't go to him without you thinking I'm betraying you. I can't stay with you without making Andrew feel he's been abandoned."

Jericho's eyes closed, regret and frustration jagging through him. There was no sense putting it off any longer. "I have to go," he said quietly.

She winced as if he'd laid a whip to her. He wanted to take her back to bed and love her until the issue went away, but it wouldn't. Despite the protest ripping through him, he released her hand.

Hurt darkened her eyes, but she let him go. He walked out of her bedroom, through the front room.

Close behind him, her voice quivered. "He's all I have left."

"You have me." Jericho turned, his chest aching at the raw vulnerability on her features.

Her face crumpled and her voice was so faint he could barely hear it. "If you take him, I don't know if I can be with you."

He'd half expected the words, but not the crippling hurt in their wake, the brutal slashing of his defenses. "I won't let you go, Catherine. I can't."

Tears welled in her eyes, magnifying the brilliant pain of loss and betrayal in the blue depths. She didn't reply, just stared for a long moment, then looked away.

Jericho forced his feet to move, to carry him outside. He went to the barn for Cinco, shaken to the core to realize that Catherine might not ever be able to accept what he did today. And if it meant he lost her, Jericho wasn't sure he could accept it, either.

Chapter Seventeen

Jericho managed to saddle Cinco and mount up. Clenching his teeth at the painful jarring, he rode hard behind the businesses of Whirlwind and headed west toward Riley's ranch.

Angus McDougal had touched Catherine. Not just with his hands, but also his mouth. Fury raked through Jericho like a jagged blade. His hands shook.

As much as he wanted to lay all that fury on the eldest McDougal, Jericho was the one who had hurt her deeply. He tried to push away the picture of utter helplessness, the devastation on Catherine's face.

Once this was over, they could sort things out. Couldn't they? He wouldn't consider that they were finished before they had even started. A fierce urgency to be done with this business about Andrew and the gang seared him. Locking out further, distracting thoughts of Catherine, Jericho marshaled his anger into calculating a strategy. First, talk to Andrew, then get him to lead the way to the McDougals.

Andrew. Jericho replayed the ambush in his mind. He and Hays had been hard on the gang's trail for two days. They had approached a shallow slope of land and the McDougals had rushed over the slight incline ahead.

Andrew had been in the front, his horse next to Angus's, the three brothers fanned out behind them. Jericho and Hays had been caught completely unaware. They both dived from their horses in a hail of bullets. Sharp pain had burned through Jericho's gun hand, his right thigh. Lying on the ground, his blood soaking the earth, he had watched in a fog as his friend fell. The bullet had come from the boy. The outlaws rode off, no doubt believing they had killed both Rangers.

Dragging his mind back to the present, Jericho cursed. Andrew had been there, and Jericho thought the boy had committed murder but he wasn't certain. He couldn't dismiss it, even for the woman he'd come to love more than life itself.

He was a mile from Whirlwind when he saw a horse coming fast. As the coal-black animal neared, Jericho realized the rider was Riley. He reined up as his cousin's mount danced to a stop beside him.

"I was coming to find you," Riley said.

"I was just coming to your ranch," Jericho said at the same time.

Noting the concern that darkened his cousin's face, Jericho tightened his hand on the reins. "What is it? Susannah? Have the McDougals—"

"It's Andrew. The kid's gone."

Damn his scrawny little hide. "Since when?"

"I'm not sure. Probably an hour or less."

Dread unfurled as Jericho thought about the boy trying to break ties with the outlaws. "Did he leave on his own?"

"I think so. Susannah would've heard if anyone came close to the house. She said he was out in the pen with one of my mares when she went in to give Button a bath, then feed her and put her down for a nap. When she came back outside, she noticed Andrew was gone."

Why couldn't the kid stay put? Now that Jericho knew Andrew had tried to distance himself from the gang, he worried about the boy's safety even more. And if Catherine found out…

"Maybe he's gone home," his cousin suggested.

Jericho had no idea what Andrew would do.

Riley swept off his hat and wiped an arm across his perspiring forehead. "Susannah said something's going on with him and Catherine. Catherine wouldn't give her any details, but she was quite upset when she brought Andrew out to the ranch. I thought you might want to know."

"Thanks." His concern edged into irritation. "He may have gone to the McDougals."

Surprise flashed across the other man's face. "Why would he do that?"

"I'll tell you on the way to town." Jericho swung Cinco around. "Can you help me look for him?"

"Sure."

"The more men, the better," he muttered, kneeing the Appaloosa into motion. "We need to find him fast."

"What's going on?" Riley urged his own horse into a lope and they headed back to Whirlwind. "Is he in danger?"

"Very likely." He told his cousin about Andrew's involvement with the gang and what had transpired that morning at the widow Monfrey's house. Riley's features were hard when they reached the jail and dismounted.

When Jericho got his hands on that kid, he was going to tan his hide. He hoped something hadn't happened to Andrew. And he hoped Catherine didn't learn the boy had skedaddled before Jericho found him.

For long minutes after Jericho left, Catherine stood rooted to the floor, holding the door so her legs wouldn't give out. Her head spun. Jericho loved her. And he meant to arrest her brother.

Hard on the heels of their lovemaking—the most beautiful, meaningful experience of her life—had come the revelation that Jericho had known all along about her brother's involvement with the McDougals. He had come here because of Andrew. He had stayed because of him.

Hurt was the one emotion she could define out of all those crowding through her. She loved Jericho, too, but how could she accept what he meant to do? Logic said she should understand he was doing his job, but logic was buried beneath the stifling extremes of euphoria, devastation, loss.

It was too much. The crush of feelings confused her, flayed her nerves like a newly whetted knife until she went numb. She moved woodenly into her room, staring at the bed, the rumpled sheets where she had given herself to Jericho. She knew he didn't want her with Andrew when he questioned him, and she would respect that. But she wouldn't let her brother face this alone. He'd faced too much alone already.

Maybe if she'd gone against Mother's wishes and come to Whirlwind earlier, Andrew wouldn't have felt the need to keep company with a family of outlaws. She could go to Riley's ranch and let Andrew know she was there, but stay at a distance until Jericho finished. She pulled on her underclothes, then the light dimity dress that he had taken off of her. At the memory of what they had shared, a bittersweet pain stole her breath.

With shaking fingers, she buttoned her dress, then laced up her shoes, and starting to braid her hair as she walked out of her bedroom toward the back of the house, heading for the barn.

When she stepped off the stoop, the door clattered shut behind her. She stopped dead at the sight of Angus Mc-

Dougal reining up ten feet away. Her arms fell limply to her sides as panic choked her. How had he known where they lived?

Fear and anger and a desperate plea for Jericho, for any-one, tangled inside her.

"I figured I might have to come in there and get you."

"What do you want?" She backed up until her heel hit the step.

"More medicine." His lecherous gaze crawled over her.

"He can't have already used that entire bottle!"

"He needs some for travelin'. C'mon now. There isn't much time. I waited until your Ranger left, but I won't be waitin' for him to get back."

Angus had been watching the house? Any attempt at bluff-ing about Jericho being there would be futile. A shiver ran down her spine. She fervently wished he would return right now.

McDougal urged his horse closer and motioned to her sharply. She shook her head, feeling her way onto the stoop. She wasn't going anywhere with him.

"I ain't got all day. You're ridin' with me to that fort for more laudanum."

For a minute Catherine's brain was too frozen by the fact that he was here and she was alone. "No."

His face darkened and he started to dismount.

"No! I mean, going to the fort isn't necessary." She did not want him coming near her or trying to get into her house. "I have some laudanum here."

If she could get inside without him, and slip out the front, she could run for town.

Angus stopped in midmotion, one foot already on the ground. "Get it then and be quick about it."

She backed into the house, not taking her gaze from him. "Stay there. I'll hurry."

A cruel smile twisted his lips.

"Stay there. Please." Once inside, she snatched up her skirts and hurried to the front door, opening it soundlessly and stepping onto the porch.

The unmistakable cock of a gun had her gasping in alarm.

"I figured you might try this." Angus stood at the corner of the house, his pistol leveled at her.

Bless the saints, what was she going to do?

"Now you go in there and get that medicine." He leaped onto the porch quite nimbly for a man with such short legs, and edged along the wall. "Just to be sure you don't try anything stupid, I'll come with you."

She thought about lunging off the porch, but when his gun nudged her ribs, she backed into the front room. She was shaking so hard that her muscles burned. With his weapon trained on her, she wouldn't be able to go for the shotgun behind the door. All she could do was pacify him, get the medicine and pray he would leave.

"All right," she said. "I'm getting it."

"Where is it?"

"In the pantry."

His gaze went over her shoulder to the tall cabinet that held her good dishes. "Go on."

She edged around the table, her gaze riveted on the gun, which she actually preferred to his vicious face. Groping behind her for the latch, she opened the cabinet door, then knelt, giving a quick glance back before her fingers closed on the bottle of medicine Jericho had never used.

The glass container slipped in her sweat-dampened hands, but she grabbed it and rose, offering it to Angus. *Just take it and go,* she willed silently.

"Uh-huh." He waggled the gun at her, gestured toward the door. "You're gonna take it out back for me."

She fought down the rising swell of panic, telling herself to remain calm. *Just do as he says and he'll leave.* Without turning her back on him, she stepped sideways behind the stove and around the wall, inching down the narrow passageway.

He closed the distance between them, forcing her out the door and off the stoop. When he moved around her, Catherine turned, keeping him in her sights. Her hand trembled on the bottle.

Pistol aimed steadily, he mounted without taking his gaze from her. Sliding his gun back into its holster, he gestured for her to give him the medicine.

She had to step forward to do it. When she did, his hand shot out, clamped on her wrist. She cried out, jerking against his grasp as he pried the bottle from her fingers. He kept a firm hold on her as he slid it into the saddlebag.

"Okay, you've got your medicine. Let go!"

Snatching at her upper arms, he hauled her off the ground, his fingers digging in with bone-crushing pressure.

"No! No!" She kicked and struggled, trying to throw him off balance.

He tightened his grip and shoved her facedown over the saddle. Her left sleeve ripped from her dress.

She reared up, screaming. Her head slammed into his chin as she tried to throw herself off. He crammed a dirty kerchief into her mouth. Then he clucked to the horse, which lurched into motion.

Terror iced her veins. No! She struggled, the pommel biting sharply into her hip as she came up off the saddle and clawed at his face. Her nails raked his forehead and one eye.

In the next heartbeat, he punched her. Light burst behind her eyes as her head jerked back. She sagged across the saddle, tasting the salty tang of blood.

Dazed by the blow, she didn't realize what he was about

until he flipped her toward him and raised her into a sitting position as if she weighed no more than that bottle of laudanum. He arranged her so that she rode sidesaddle, and lashed her hands to the pommel. Vaguely she realized the horse had stopped. She struggled sluggishly, her efforts easily thwarted when he kicked the gelding into a gallop.

Jericho! Catherine's stunned mind screamed his name over and over as they bounced along. Grass and dirt flew beneath her. She curled her hands around the saddle horn, the rope biting into her wrists. The overwhelming odors of sweat and tobacco, so strong this morning at the widow's house, nearly choked her.

Angus bit her earlobe and she cried out. "That medicine ain't all I came for. I liked that little taste I had of you this morning. When we get settled, I'm gonna take me a big ol' bite."

She arched as far away from him as she could. Crushed between the saddle horn and his thighs, she felt her composure break, and she sobbed behind the gag.

Where was he taking her? What did he plan to do? How long before someone realized she was gone?

How long before *Jericho* realized it?

Jericho was behind Riley, heading into Davis Lee's office, when he heard someone call his name. Looking toward the end of town, he saw Andrew on Moe, the pair of them flying down the middle of the street.

"Jericho!" The kid's voice was sharp with alarm. The mare pounded past the Whirlwind Hotel, the telegraph office, swerving around a small group of people about to enter the Pearl Restaurant.

"He doesn't look any the worse for wear," Riley muttered beside him.

Something was wrong. Jericho moved to the bottom step.

"He took her!" Andrew reined the mare to a skidding stop, spraying dirt and pebbles. He nearly slid off the horse's bare back.

Jericho reached out a hand to steady him. "What—"

"Angus took Catherine! Just now. I saw him!"

Between one heartbeat and the next, a black haze blurred Jericho's vision, and for a moment he could register only a buzzing in his head. Cursing, he swung back into the saddle, roaring, "What are you talkin' about? And you better tell me the whole truth."

He ignored Riley's surprised look at his harsh tone. By now Davis Lee and Jake Ross had come out of the sheriff's office to join them.

"I couldn't stay with Miz Susannah," Andrew panted, his face flushed. "I didn't want Catherine to be alone, so I went home. I was at the front door when I heard a scream from behind the house. By the time I got back there, Angus had Catherine and he was riding off!"

"Are the McDougals going to start kidnapping our people now?" Davis Lee asked, whipping out his revolver, checking the cylinder for bullets.

"No," Jericho said coldly. "Just Catherine."

"Why?" Davis Lee stepped down to gather his horse's reins before swinging into the saddle. "How the hell did he know where she lived?"

"That's how." He jabbed a finger toward Andrew. Cinco sidestepped nervously, picking up on Jericho's fury. "This is going to be the last thing Angus McDougal ever does."

Riley was mounted and Jake Ross had one foot in the stirrup. Jericho's eyes narrowed on Andrew. The kid was chalk-white and terror dilated the pupils of his blue eyes. Jericho tried hard not to resent the boy for bringing those bastards to his sister's door. "Which way did they go?"

"South." Andrew still breathed hard as he nudged Moe up next to Cinco.

Davis Lee waved him back. "You'd best stay here, Andrew—"

"No, I want to go!"

"He's coming," Jericho said curtly. "In case he's forgotten what these outlaws are capable of doing."

Riley and Jake said nothing. Davis Lee frowned. "Do you think that's a good idea?"

Jericho ignored his cousin, leveling his gaze on the boy. "Maybe you'll understand now why your sister doesn't want you involved with the McDougals."

"I already understand." Andrew rubbed his eyes with his knuckles.

"Involved with the outlaws?" Davis Lee's gaze sliced from Jericho to the boy. "What are you talking about?"

Riley quickly explained to Davis Lee and Jake about Andrew and the gang.

"I never meant for Catherine to get hurt," Andrew said thickly. He was shaking so hard Jericho could hear his teeth click together, but the boy held his gaze.

"We need to ride. *Now.*" Jericho gave Cinco a sharp kick in the flank and the horse bolted into motion. The only reason he didn't throttle Andrew was because he knew the kid blamed himself. It was in his favor that he had acted quickly and smartly when he saw McDougal snatch his sister.

Catherine. Jericho's chest ached. Thundering out of town with the others, he shut down as much emotion as he could. He narrowed his focus to riding and spotting a lone rider in the distance. If he let himself consider what the McDougals might do to Catherine, might already be doing to her, he wouldn't be rational, and that would endanger her.

Cold methodical thinking would help her, but nothing

would help Angus McDougal. Whatever happened to the other McDougals, Angus was a dead man.

After a couple of miles, Angus angled west toward the setting sun. The glare magnified the throb behind Catherine's eyes. The repeated slam of the saddle horn into her hip joined the ache in her swollen jaw. Had Jericho discovered her missing yet? Had anyone?

She and Angus rode across the prairie. A lone mesquite tree, then, minutes later, a stand of pecan trees, marked the passage of miles. Catherine held on, jarred and bruised as she tried to think of a way to escape.

Maybe when they stopped—

Suddenly Angus cursed, kicking the horse into a flat-out run. Catherine pitched forward and gripped the pommel for balance. What had happened? What had Angus seen? She tried to peek over his shoulder but her awkward position prevented it.

She noticed that he kept the horse parallel to a dry creek bed, or maybe an old river channel. They passed through a small copse of oak trees and scrub. Up ahead, under a scarred oak, she spied two men on horseback. Her hope for escape flickered as their faces came into view. Bruce and Donald.

Before she could wonder about Ian, Angus yelled to his brothers, "Riders behind me! Think I saw three!"

Catherine's heart skipped a beat. *Oh, please, let it be Jericho or someone who can help!*

Angus jerked his horse to an abrupt stop, causing Catherine's teeth to snap shut.

"What the hell did you bring her for?" Donald snarled. "Did you get the medicine?"

"Shut up and get her down." Angus motioned both men over with a sharp gesture.

He practically pushed her onto Bruce, and Catherine shrank away from the mean hands grasping for her. Bruce pulled her roughly out of the saddle, heedless of the ropes scraping her flesh.

Angus dismounted, slapping his horse on the rump. "Take cover!"

Catherine didn't see anyplace for them to hide, but her elation over that disappeared when Angus grabbed her by the arm and dragged her down into the creek bed. Wind and weather had eroded a hollow in the dirt bank, providing an awning of sorts—a hiding place where they wouldn't be seen.

Bruce and Donald hurried to join Angus. The oldest Mc-Dougal planted himself on her left and Bruce on her right. "You're in the line of fire, girl, so I'd think twice before trying anything."

Catherine didn't acknowledge him, her mind racing to come up with possibilities for escape.

He tore his attention from her. "Donald, you're on my left. Where's Ian?"

"Waiting in the wagon around the bend," his brother said. "This gully snakes around to the north, so no one can see him from here. He's not doing too good."

In the distance, Catherine heard the pounding of hooves. Beside her, Angus stiffened and lifted up for a peek. The earth vibrated slightly. Someone was coming! Surely they would help her.

When the other two McDougals raised up to see for themselves, Catherine eased backward on her knees. With their attention diverted, this might be her only chance. She spun and scrambled to her feet.

Before she could find her footing, a hand hooked into the shoulder of her dress where her sleeve used to be. "Get back here!"

Angus yanked and she fell hard on her bottom. A ripping sounded as the seam under her arm gave way. Hand fisted in the straining fabric, Angus hauled her up to him and pushed her into the earth wall. "Do that again and I'll do worse than kill you."

The thought of his hands and mouth on her curdled her stomach.

Bruce held up his hand, saying in a hushed voice, "Listen."

The quiet was abrupt. Shattering. No hoofbeats. No rustle of movement through the grass. Straining, Catherine heard only the occasional whisper of wind stirring the grass, the coarse squawk of nearby ravens in the trees. Her breath hitched painfully in her lungs.

Beside her, Bruce tensed, and she looked past his shoulder to see a black horse step tentatively into a far curve of the bed. She didn't recognize the horse, but the rider looked familiar. Riley?

She couldn't be sure, but her breath caught at the hope that it was him. If so, Jericho was surely with him.

Bruce leveled a steady hand and fired. Horrified, Catherine cried out behind the gag. The black horse leaped back out of sight as the man squeezed off several shots. A dull thud sounded over her head and dirt sprinkled down on her. A bullet. Too close.

"I know I saw at least three of 'em back there," Angus repeated in a low voice.

"You think it's the Ranger?" Donald asked from the other side.

"I'd bet money on it."

Catherine tried to think how she could help, let them know she was here and alive. When she saw a chance, she would rip this gag out of her mouth and scream with everything she had.

The air rippled with expectation, and adrenaline stung her

nerves as she huddled into the dirt wall. What was happening? What were they doing? Was Jericho out there?

Suddenly gunfire erupted, loud and close. Bruce swore and fired back blindly over the lip of earth that shaded them. Angus and Donald did the same. The noise swelled in her ears. She burrowed into the dirt, making herself as small as possible. Bullets whizzed past, plowed the ground behind her and the opposite bank.

The two sides exchanged fire for a while, although it was probably only a minute. Sweat pooled between her breasts and terror pulled ragged breaths out of her.

Angus eased up to get a look, shot his gun, then ducked as Donald did the same. Bruce followed his brothers, the three of them repeating the pattern a couple of times. Then Bruce raised up, pulled the trigger, and suddenly fell back against Catherine.

She shrank away, pushing at him with her bound hands. His head bumped her leg and he stared sightlessly up at her. At first she didn't comprehend that blood was trickling from a hole between his eyes. More stained the ground beneath his head, spread onto her skirt. She screamed behind the gag, then mentally crossed herself, terrified that the very men who had come to rescue her might be the ones to kill her.

Chapter Eighteen

$\mathcal{A}$ll sense of time fled. What happened next could've taken seconds or minutes or hours. Hammered by the loud crackle of gunfire, the scent of burned powder in the air, Catherine was too overloaded to feel anything. None of this seemed real.

When Angus saw Bruce was dead, he roared in outrage. "Donald, start backing up. Stay under this shelf of dirt until we reach the creek bend, then we can run for the wagon."

Catherine would not go easily.

Angus jammed his gun into her ribs. "I ain't so hot for you that I won't kill you, so you better move with us."

They began to scoot along the edge of the creek bed. Twigs poked Catherine and tore at her dirty, grass-stained dress.

"You're surrounded, Angus!"

Davis Lee! Catherine stilled, placing his voice somewhere on the opposite bank behind them, even as Donald swung in that direction and fired his gun.

More shots came from over her head and down the creek, where she'd seen Riley earlier. Donald and Angus also fired. Bullets seemed to whiz from every direction, and Catherine huddled against the bank, finally realizing that Davis Lee and

Riley were purposely aiming away from her. Angus finally removed his gun from her ribs so he could join the fray.

Taking the only chance she might have, she pushed Donald as hard as she could. He fell forward, catching himself
with one hand. It provided an opening. The next bullet
dropped him.

Angus wrapped a beefy arm around her neck and rose,
dragging her to her feet. The weight of his arm crushed her
windpipe, and spots danced before her eyes.

"You better lay down your weapons," he yelled. "Or she
gets it."

With her bound hands, she clawed frantically at his arm,
an immovable bar across her throat.

Angus backed away toward the bank and she had to take
quick steps to keep him from strangling her. She worked to
keep her feet under her, desperate to ease his hold, frantic for
air. He moved between two trees.

Across the creek bed, Catherine saw Davis Lee start toward
them. Movement to the left caught her eye. Riley and Jake
Ross. That meant Jericho was here. Overwhelming relief had
her stumbling as Angus continued dragging her past the trees.

"You're outgunned, McDougal." Davis Lee stopped at the
edge of the opposite bank, his rifle leveled at the outlaw.

Angus exerted more pressure on her throat and she rose on
tiptoe to try and combat it. Where was Jericho?

"If you don't let her go right now," Jericho growled behind
her, "I'll part your skull with this bullet."

An ominous click sounded. Angus froze, his body rigid
against her back. "I'll shoot her."

"You won't have time to shoot or breathe or blink. If your
finger so much as twitches on that trigger, you're a dead man
from all sides."

The outlaw didn't move except to push harder against her

windpipe, cutting off her air completely. She felt herself grow-ing faint. Suddenly Angus pivoted to face Jericho, and she lurched around with him.

"I can at least take you with me," Angus snarled.

Fear made Catherine wild. She bucked violently against his hold, startling him, and when his arm loosened, she nearly slipped free.

He caught her around the waist, his gun wavering from Jeri-cho. The Ranger lunged. Catherine hung over Angus's arm and he jabbed the gun into the side of her neck. The hammer clicked.

Mind-blanking terror flooded her. A shot sounded and in a suspended moment, she waited for pain. Then Angus fell. Released suddenly, she stumbled, scrambling away and rip-ping the gag from her mouth to drag in huge lungfuls of air.

Sobbing, she strained at the ropes around her wrists, fran-tic to loosen the knot. Suddenly Jericho was on his knees in front of her, pulling her to him, whispering her name brokenly. She fell against him, sobbing.

"I've got you, sweetheart. I've got you." Her cries tore at him. Already unsteady from her close call, it took him a cou-ple of tries to untie her.

Catherine was shaking so hard he thought he could hear her bones rattle.

"There, got it." He pushed the rope from her wrists and caught her to him when she threw herself against his chest, her arms locking around his neck.

She held tight, tears wetting his shirt. He gathered her to him and buried his face in her neck. Sharp relief ached in his chest. For a long moment Jericho held her, stroking her hair and murmuring soothing words to her until his pulse settled into a semi-regular rhythm.

"Sweetheart, let me look at you." He tried to pry her arms from around his neck. "Are you okay?"

"Y-yes."

She pressed into him as if she wanted to crawl inside his skin. He ran his hands over her and was relieved when she didn't wince or cry out in pain. Her dainty white dress was streaked with dirt and grass stains. And blood.

His heart skipped a beat. "Where are you hurt?" he asked urgently. "Where are you bleeding?"

"It's not mine," she said raggedly.

Dragging in his first full breath, Jericho ran gentle hands over her again. One sleeve of her dress had been ripped off, and he checked the bare slender arm around his neck for bruises, marks. He found none. But when he tipped her chin up, she winced.

"Let me see," he murmured.

She shuddered, lifting her face, and he saw the beginnings of a bruise on her jaw and cheek. Raw fury slashed at him, but he cautioned himself to remain calm.

She turned her face into his neck and his hands went to her waist, discovering the gaping tear under her arm, the soft fabric of her chemise.

Her sobs quieted, and though her hold didn't loosen, some of her tension eased. He feathered kisses against her temple, stroked her back.

The others walked up, all staying a discreet distance away except Andrew.

"Catherine!" Her brother raced to her, dropping to the ground beside Jericho.

She reached for the boy, hugging him tightly.

"I'm so sorry," Andrew said thickly.

"It's all right. I'm fine." She held him to her, and when Jericho would've drawn away to allow her to embrace her brother, she caught his hand at her waist, curling her fingers into his.

He stayed, his heart finally slowing its reckless pace. That had been too damn close.

The other men moved forward and she lifted her head to look at them. "Thank you," she said shakily.

"Glad you're okay, Catherine," Riley said soberly.

Jake murmured his agreement.

Davis Lee gave her a crooked smile. "You scared ten years off my life."

She smiled tremulously, wiping away her tears. "I think my hair has turned completely gray."

"*Mine* has." Jericho helped her to her feet, careful to keep an arm around her to cover the rip in her dress. Andrew stood, too, holding her hand.

Angus lay motionless behind them. Jericho caught Riley's gaze and, with a side glance, silently requested that they take care of the body when he got Catherine away from here. The other man nodded to show he understood.

As Jericho guided Catherine toward his horse, he heard the men behind him making arrangements to carry the Mc-Dougals' bodies back to town.

She slowed and looked up at him, her lashes still spiky from tears, her eyes crystal blue. "Ian. He's in a wagon somewhere around the creek bend, waiting for them."

"Okay." She was so pale, so fragile beneath his hands. Jericho stroked her cheek, calling the information over his shoulder to his cousins and Jake.

Jake and Davis Lee took off on foot up the creek bed, and Riley started toward Jericho and the horses.

Jericho gently lifted Catherine onto the saddle, glad to finally see a hint of color in her cheeks.

She touched his right arm. "You used your gun hand."

"I did it without thinking."

"I hope you didn't set back your recovery."

"If I did, it was worth it." He pressed a soft kiss to her lips. At a tug on his sleeve, Jericho looked down to find Andrew.

The boy tipped his head, indicating that he wanted to step away from his sister. Jericho lightly squeezed her waist. "Will you be okay for a minute?"

"Yes." Her gaze went questioningly to Andrew, but her brother didn't look at her.

As Riley walked past, leading his horse, as well as Davis Lee's and Jake's, Jericho joined Andrew.

"I'm in trouble, aren't I?" the boy asked quietly, so Catherine couldn't hear. "For running with the McDougals?"

Jericho appreciated the kid's effort to shield Catherine, even though she already knew. "I need to ask you some questions."

"About what all I did?"

"Yes, and the ambush."

Guilt flashed across his young face. "All right. What do you want me to do?"

"We'll get your sister home, then you can go with me to the sheriff's office."

"Okay." Fear shimmered in his eyes, but Andrew squared his shoulders. He chewed at his lip, then said, "Please don't be mad at me anymore."

Jericho's heart softened at the agony in the boy's blue eyes, and he laid a hand on Andrew's shoulder. "I'm not mad."

"But in town you said—"

"I was angry," Jericho interrupted. "But I'm not now."

"Good." The lad's eyes were painfully bright and he turned away, choking out, "I'll get Moe."

Jericho gave him a boost onto the mare before returning to Catherine. "Still okay?" he asked quietly, curving a hand over her knee.

She nodded, her gaze shifting to her brother. Regret and disappointment chased across her features, and Jericho didn't know if it was for him or Andrew.

He swung into the saddle behind her, wishing he could

forget the whole thing with her brother. But too much had happened.

As soon as his chest met her shoulder, she melted into him. His body hid the rip down the side of her dress, and she snuggled against him, one arm around his waist. He rested his head on hers, wrapping his right arm around her.

Davis Lee rode up, his even tone at odds with the anger in his eyes. "We'll take care of the McDougals, but you should know Ian is gone. Unhitched the horse from the buckboard and took off."

As sick as the youngest McDougal was, Jericho didn't think he'd get far. "We'll deal with him later."

His cousin nodded, his gaze settling softly on Catherine. "I'm sure glad you're all right."

"Thank you." She smiled, still looking slightly disoriented.

He touched the brim of his hat. "We'll see you in town."

Jericho nodded, urging Cinco into an easy walk. Andrew fell in beside them. Catherine lay against Jericho quietly, and he closed his eyes, inhaling her sweet soothing scent and swallowing against a burn in his throat.

They rode silently toward Whirlwind, the setting sun flowing across the prairie like glittering liquid gold.

She shifted slightly, her voice quiet and sad. "You're taking him in, aren't you?"

Andrew glanced over as if he'd heard, and Jericho's heart clenched. "Yes."

"Just for questions?"

"Yes." Frustration and reluctance stirred. He didn't want to doubt his duty or the justice he owed Hays, but he couldn't ignore the fact that Catherine stood to lose her only living relative.

He wished they could ride on forever, but too soon they reached her house. With a stiff silence between them, he helped her down and steadied her on her feet.

She reached for him. "I—"

"Shh, Catherine. Just let me end this, all right?"

Indecision mixed with the sadness in her eyes. She nodded and went to her brother.

Feeling ancient and exhausted, Jericho curled his hand over the saddle horn and remounted.

"I'll change my dress," she said quietly to Andrew. "Then I'll come to the jail. I don't want you to be alone."

"I'll be okay." Andrew sat up straighter on his horse.

"I know, but I'll be there anyway." She squeezed his hand, then stood back as he nudged Moe into motion.

Jericho met her troubled gaze, an unfamiliar heaviness pressing down on him. He wanted this over and done. He couldn't bear to see more pain in her eyes. It was like drawing a knife through an open wound.

Her eyes begged for mercy, not justice. He hoped he could give it.

Chapter Nineteen

"So you saw Ian in town and bought some medicine for him?"

"Yes." Andrew sat in a chair in the middle of Davis Lee's office, the sinking sun causing shadows to creep across the floor.

Jericho perched on the edge of his cousin's desk, while Davis Lee occupied the chair behind the desk. The boy was pale and watched Jericho warily.

"And when you followed him out of town, you met the others?"

"Yes."

"Didn't it bother you to learn who they were?"

A flush stole up his neck. "I thought it was exciting."

Andrew wouldn't be the first boy to glorify a dangerous outlaw. "What all did you do with them?"

"Played cards, cleaned their guns. One night they asked me to get them some food, so I did."

Jericho rubbed a hand across the rigid muscles of his neck, alert to every time the kid's muscles twitched. "And you stole food for them more than once, didn't you?"

Andrew nodded.

"Did you steal anything else?"

"Rifle cartridges from Mr. Doyle," he said in a small voice.

"What about horses? Blankets?"

"No." The answer, as well as his gaze was direct, guileless. "Nothing else. Just food, some medicine from Haskell's and those cartridges."

Jericho stood, limping over to him. Riding Cinco today had left an ache that went clear to the bone.

Andrew glanced up, crossing his ankles, then uncrossing them. Jericho moved behind the chair. He wanted to judge the kid's reactions up close.

He exchanged a look with Davis Lee, who nodded in understanding.

"Were you there when the McDougals butchered the Baldwins' steer?" Jericho asked.

"No."

"Stole clothes from them?"

"No."

"And you weren't keeping company with the gang last fall?"

"No." Andrew tilted his head to meet Jericho's gaze. "Only since February."

The kid was nervous but not lying. At least not about this. "Did you know Whirlwind's stagecoach driver, Ollie Wilkes?"

"Yes."

"Were you present when he was killed?"

"No."

"But you knew they killed him?" At the boy's nod, Jericho continued, "When you found out they were the ones who killed him, why didn't you say anything?"

Jericho fired the questions at him, not giving the kid time to think of any answer besides the truth.

"They weren't here anymore. I didn't think it would matter and..."

"What?"

Andrew mumbled, "I didn't want my ma to know I'd been with them."

"So you wouldn't get a thrashin'?"

"Partly, but mostly because she would've been hurt real bad."

Any twelve-year-old boy—any *kid*—was going to watch out for his skin, but the thickness in Andrew's voice told Jericho that he really had been concerned about hurting his ailing mother. Why didn't the lad realize his mother could've become a victim of the McDougals the same way Catherine had? Hell, the kid could've met a fate worse than that.

"Have you ever been with the gang when anyone was killed?"

Andrew's gaze dropped to the floor. "Yes," he said hoarsely.

So they had come to it. Swept with a sudden fatigue, Jericho shared a grim look with Davis Lee. They both remained quiet, letting the silence stretch out. It didn't take long for the boy to open up.

He squirmed in his chair, mumbling, "I was there."

"Where?"

"At…where you were."

Jericho waited.

Andrew gulped, looking ashamed. "The ambush. Where you were shot and your friend was killed."

At least the kid admitted it. Jericho wondered if Catherine's hearing these words from her brother might enable her to accept that Jericho had brought him in. "Why, Andrew?"

"I didn't know what they were going to do. They told me we were just riding, and then there you were." His voice rose. "And they started shooting. You started shooting."

"And *you* started shooting," he said sharply.

"No!"

"I was there, boy."

"I know, but I swear I didn't shoot. I was right up front with Angus. Can you remember seeing me in that spot?"

"You had a gun," Jericho said softly. "Aimed at me, at Hays."

"Yes, but I didn't shoot. I swear I didn't!" The kid's gaze sought his earnestly. "You have to recall that. Please. Can't you remember? I know you could see me."

Jericho didn't think the kid was lying. Davis Lee darted him a look that said the same thing.

"If you didn't mean to pull the trigger, you can tell me. You were nervous. Your hands were probably sweating. Your finger just slipped. It was an accident."

"I swear I didn't shoot."

Jericho narrowed his gaze and mentally replayed the ambush. Andrew at Angus's right elbow, the other three Mc-Dougals behind. Guns blazing, including Jericho's, as he'd gone to the ground after the shot to his thigh.

Hays had stepped up, partially obscuring his vision for a half second. Jericho had been dizzy, one hand pressing the wound in his thigh as he tried to stem the blood pouring out of his leg like water. His friend had fallen, and Jericho had squeezed off several rapid shots before dragging himself over to the other man.

Andrew's story could be true. The boy might never have fired a shot. Plenty of bullets had been flying. And Jericho's light-headedness combined with his angle from the ground could've easily played tricks with his eyes.

It was more than possible Angus had killed Hays. Mc-Dougal had certainly wanted to murder both Rangers. Whatever lack of judgment Andrew had shown, the kid was no murderer. Jericho knew that in his gut.

The boy stared at him, his face sheened with sweat. His explanation was plausible. He didn't try to avoid Jericho's gaze or questions. Didn't hesitate over his answers.

Jericho believed him. But was it because he wanted things to work out with Catherine? Because he didn't want to be responsible for taking away the last of her family?

"Sit tight while Sheriff Holt and I talk outside for a minute," he said.

"Okay." Worry pinched Andrew's features.

As soon as they stepped onto the porch and closed the door, Davis Lee said quietly, "I think he's telling the truth."

Jericho nodded, turning things over in his mind.

"Do you? What's wrong?"

"I just want to be sure," Jericho answered slowly. "I don't want to make this decision based on the fact that I love his sister and don't want to take away her only family."

His cousin studied him for a minute. "For what it's worth, I don't think you are. I think you listened to the kid and weighed what he had to say. He doesn't act like someone who's lying."

"I agree."

"Well, then?"

"Well, then…" Jericho listened hard to his instincts again, and they still told him Andrew was in the clear. "I think I have some good news for Catherine."

Davis Lee clapped him on the shoulder, grinning. "And here she comes right now."

Jericho turned to see her hurrying toward them. A soft blue dress molded her slender curves, making her eyes a startling hue. Her hair hung down her back in a gleaming curtain. She had scrubbed the dirt from her face, drawing attention to the beginnings of a bruise where Angus had hit her.

His heart turned over. He was relieved to tell her about Andrew, but there was a part of him that wondered if she would have ever accepted him if her brother had been arrested.

"Oh, I'm glad you're out here." She hurried up the steps

to join them on the landing, her gaze searching his. "I need to talk to you."

Davis Lee opened the door. "I'll be inside with Andrew. See you in a minute."

Jericho's gaze traced her delicate features. She was so beautiful. He wanted to hold her, kiss every inch of her. His heart thudded painfully against his ribs. "Catherine, if you're here to ask me not to—"

"Please let me say this."

"I just thought you might want to know—"

"Please, Jericho." She laid a hand on his chest and looked up at him with earnest, sober eyes.

He nodded, his entire body tightening as he battled the urge to blurt out his decision regarding Andrew. He wanted to tell her she didn't have to make the choice she dreaded, but it might not matter. She may have already decided she couldn't be with him.

Her hand smoothed the place over his heart. "I know you don't take this situation lightly. I know you care about my brother and you don't want to hurt me."

"I don't," he rasped, one hand settling at her waist.

She raised a hand to his face and caressed his jaw, giving a little laugh. "When the two of you left a while ago, I was almost more worried about you than I was about Andrew."

"What?"

Her eyes blazed into his, catching his gaze and holding it. "When I was with Angus, I thought I might never have the chance to tell you that I understand you're doing what you have to. I've witnessed your sense of justice and fairness. Those are two of the things I love most about you." She took a deep breath, her voice dropping. "I don't know how I'll feel about your decision regarding Andrew, but I do know how I feel about you. I thought I might never have the chance to tell you I love you, too. Because I do."

Tears shimmered in her eyes, and Jericho stood speechless. The more she had said, the more still and hushed his body had grown. She had come to him before knowing his decision. She loved him. She wasn't turning him away.

She swallowed hard, her eyes uncertain and tortured. "Please say I haven't hurt you so badly that—oh!"

He covered her mouth with his, his hands coming up to gently frame her face. She responded immediately, her arms sliding around his waist to clutch him to her almost frantically. After a long while, they pulled apart.

His thumb floated over the bruise forming on her cheekbone. "I didn't hurt you, did I?"

"No." She turned her head to press a kiss against his palm. "Can you forgive me?"

"There's nothing to forgive, Catherine. You love your brother."

She brushed a kiss across his lips. "I know you have to question him and I know he has to own up to what he's done. But I also know you'll be fair. Before you decide anything, I want you to know *that*."

"Even if I have to arrest him?"

Regret flared in her eyes, deep and sharp, but her gaze never wavered. "Even then."

His arms tightened around her and he said gruffly, "Do you know that my guts have been tied in knots ever since I left you at the house?"

"Mine, too."

After another soft kiss, he said, "I've finished questioning Andrew."

"You have?"

He caught the note of hope in her voice and grinned, amazed at how much he was going to enjoy telling her. "I was wrong. He wasn't the one who killed Hays."

"Did he shoot you?" she asked breathlessly.

"He didn't shoot anyone that day. Only the McDougals did."

"You're sure?" Tears quivered beneath her words.

"Yes." He knew how much it meant to her that her brother hadn't crossed the line.

"So you're not taking him in?"

"No. Let's go tell him together."

Her eyes glowed as she grasped his face between her hands. "I love you, Jericho. I guess if you hadn't come looking for my brother, I never would've found you."

"I would've found you somehow," he said with quiet confidence.

"And how do you know that?" she asked playfully.

"Because you're the rest of my life," he murmured against her lips. "How could I not?"

* * * * *

*Look for the next Whirlwind,
Texas, book coming from Debra Cowan
and Harlequin Historicals in 2005.*

FALL IN LOVE WITH
THESE HANDSOME HEROES
FROM HARLEQUIN HISTORICALS

If you enjoyed what you just read,
then we've got an offer you can't resist!

Take 2 bestselling
love stories FREE!

Plus get a FREE surprise gift!

Clip this page and mail it to Harlequin Reader Service®

IN U.S.A.
3010 Walden Ave.
P.O. Box 1867
Buffalo, N.Y. 14240-1867

IN CANADA
P.O. Box 609
Fort Erie, Ontario
L2A 5X3

YES! Please send me 2 free Harlequin Historicals® novels and my free surprise gift. After receiving them, if I don't wish to receive anymore, I can return the shipping statement marked cancel. If I don't cancel, I will receive 6 brand-new novels every month, before they're available in stores! In the U.S.A., bill me at the bargain price of $4.69 plus 25¢ shipping and handling per book and applicable sales tax, if any*. In Canada, bill me at the bargain price of $5.24 plus 25¢ shipping and handling per book and applicable taxes**. That's the complete price and a savings of over 10% off the cover prices—what a great deal! I understand that accepting the 2 free books and gift places me under no obligation ever to buy any books. I can always return a shipment and cancel at any time. Even if I never buy another book from Harlequin, the 2 free books and gift are mine to keep forever.

246 HDN DZ7Q
349 HDN DZ7R

Name	(PLEASE PRINT)	
Address	Apt.#	
City	State/Prov.	Zip/Postal Code

Not valid to current Harlequin Historicals® subscribers.

Want to try two free books from another series?
Call 1-800-873-8635 or visit www.morefreebooks.com.

* Terms and prices subject to change without notice. Sales tax applicable in N.Y.
** Canadian residents will be charged applicable provincial taxes and GST.
 All orders subject to approval. Offer limited to one per household.
 ® are registered trademarks owned and used by the trademark owner and or its licensee.

HIST04R   ©2004 Harlequin Enterprises Limited